THE *Royal*
RUNAWAY

THE *Royal* RUNAWAY

LINDSAY EMORY

G

Gallery Books

New York   London   Toronto   Sydney   New Delhi

G

Gallery Books
An Imprint of Simon & Schuster, Inc.
1230 Avenue of the Americas
New York, NY 10020

First Gallery Books trade paperback edition October 2018

For information about special discounts for bulk purchases, please contact Simon & Schuster Special Sales at 1-866-506-1949 or business@simonandschuster.com.

The Simon & Schuster Speakers Bureau can bring authors to your live event. For more information or to book an event, contact the Simon & Schuster Speakers Bureau at 1-866-248-3049 or visit our website at www.simonspeakers.com.

Interior design by Alison Cnockaert

Manufactured in the United States of America

1 3 5 7 9 10 8 6 4 2

Library of Congress Cataloging-in-Publication Data

Names: Emory, Lindsay, 1986– author.
Title: The royal runaway / Lindsay Emory.
Description: First Gallery Books trade paperback edition. | New York : Gallery Books, 2018.
Identifiers: LCCN 2018009743
Subjects: LCSH: Princesses—Fiction. | Spys—Fiction. | Missing persons—Fiction. | Suspense fiction gsafd
Classification: LCC PS3605.M65 R69 2018 | DDC 813/.6—dc23 LC record available at https://lccn.loc.gov/2018009743.

ISBN 978-1-5011-9661-4
ISBN 978-1-5011-9662-1 (ebook)

This book is dedicated to the women who have the power to change the world. That is to say, all of them.

"Well-behaved women seldom make history."
—LAUREL THATCHER ULRICH

THE *Royal* RUNAWAY

one

I T WAS MY WEDDING DAY. I IMAGINED OTHER BRIDES HAD similar days. They, too, softly smoothed their white skirts, brushed a piece of lace with their fingertips, and clutched a handkerchief into a crumple.

Other women felt like princesses on their wedding day. Me? I really *was* a princess. I had the tiara, the palace, the framed certificate, and everything.

They delayed telling me about my missing groom as long as they could, until it became apparent that the schedule would have to change, that we wouldn't leave for the cathedral in the flotilla of white carriages drawn by horses in matching ostrich-feather head-dresses.

Because I, Princess Theodora Isabella Victoria, second in line to the crown of the Kingdom of Drieden, had been stood up.

Left at the altar.

People spoke in hushed tones around me, trading whispers I couldn't make out and didn't really want to hear.

Before I found out the truth, I knew we were behind schedule. I should've been loaded into the carriage by now, waving and smiling at the adoring public lining the streets. I shouldn't still have been sitting here, waiting.

My mother was called out of the room, which should have alerted me that something was up. The palace staff usually did everything they could to avoid talking directly to my mother—she had a way of making their lives difficult.

Then Caroline was called out. Caroline was my emotionally stable middle sibling. My maid of honor. Not because she was older than Sophie, the youngest, but because Caroline could be counted on to think through any unexpected problem that arose—the train, the bouquet, the . . . missing groom.

Caroline returned, her mouth in a sharp line. She knelt at my feet, took my hands, and laid out the problem.

My fiancé was nowhere to be found.

I simply stared at her. An avid amateur historian, I racked my brain for any similar situation in the Driedish history books. What was the proper protocol for a canceled royal wedding? What does a jilted princess do next?

Then the whispers stopped. The atmosphere froze. My grandmother had entered the room. Tall and straight, she held her head as if there were always a crown balanced upon it—the big one with the Jaipur sapphire. She came to me and held out a box of tissues.

Something about that gesture undid me. I could be as regal and disciplined as the next royal princess, but my gran handing me a tissue made it real somehow. I had been humiliated in front of my country, in front of the world.

Five minutes passed and my grandmother lifted my face and blotted my wet cheeks. "There will be no more tears shed for him. His name will never be spoken in this house again."

It was an order from my queen.

My eyes immediately went dry.

two

I T WASN'T A SURPRISE THAT I'D BEEN SENT AWAY. IT WAS
easier for people to manage the fallout if there wasn't a lightning rod
continuing to draw the electric attention of the world.

All of the Queen's advisors agreed that the best place for a jilted princess was a cold island in the middle of the North Sea, a Driedish territory
called Perpetua. Why they couldn't have agreed that jilted princesses
should spend four months in the Maldives, I would never understand.

I'd returned to the palace three days ago, and since then my nights
had rapidly deteriorated into an endless cycle of nightmares, herbal
teas, and television reruns. It was really so boring. I was over Christian
Fraser-Campbell. Completely. The man had left me at the altar. Why I
kept having the same dreams about him, I had no idea.

He would be in a dark tunnel, running away from me. Then I would
run after him (which would never happen in real life—I have my pride).
I'd call his name, praying that he would stop running, that he would
shout something back in his charming Scottish brogue. But he'd always
stay silent; he'd always keep running. And I'd keep chasing. Until the
headlights of an oncoming train would overtake us both.

It was clichéd and predictable.

I disliked being both.

The palace doctor had left the sleeping pill prescription wordlessly on my desk the day of the wedding, after being among the group of ten Big Gran had ushered into my suite to deliver the bad news.

I hadn't taken a single pill yet, and now I was wondering if I should. I had an interview scheduled tomorrow—"PRINCESS THEODORA'S FIRST POST-JILT INTERVIEW"—with Chantal Louis of *The Driedener*. Another lost night of sleep would mean that the dark circles under my eyes could not be concealed by the usual layer of makeup. My makeup artist, Roberto, would have to bust out the hard stuff, which he would moan about, and then I'd apologize for it and there would be a whole uncomfortable balance of power over heavy-duty concealer. #Princesslife #thestruggleisreal

I was over my ex. Really, I was. Which is why I was heading toward my bathroom to fill a glass of water and take a pill. To forget about the bastard. And to prevent under-eye circles.

But instead, something drew me back to the large window that over-looked the city below. The palace stood above the city on a bluff that probably had been quite daunting in the Middle Ages. In the twenty-first century, the city had climbed up to meet the palace, many of the buildings standing at or above the height of the tallest tower of the ancient home of the rulers of Drieden.

I pulled the thick brocade curtains back and stared at the lights of the city, still beaming bright even after midnight.

Sharing the name with the country, Drieden City was a beautiful mix of modern and historical, quaint and contemporary. It had started to crumble into redundancy in the early twentieth century with the decline of the traditional shipping industry that had sustained it for centuries. But then oil was discovered. First, crude oil bubbled out of the marshlands, then it oozed out into the triangle of the dark, cold North Sea that Drieden controlled, and a nation was given its second life.

Growing up royal, every minute detail of Driedish history had been drilled into my head. As the second in line to the throne—after my father, the Crown Prince Albert, God help us all—I took its study seriously and applied myself dutifully to the stories of my homeland. Often I would close my eyes and imagine what the kingdom looked like in 1350, when Olaf the Conqueror first claimed the fertile lowlands. Or in 1650, when King Henry III refused to send colonists to the New World, condemning colonization as a foolish, wasteful enterprise.

I loved those stories. I loved this view and the city lights that seemed to throb inside my veins.

Later, I would look back on this moment and wonder why I hadn't simply popped the sleeping pill and crawled back into my gilded four-poster bed, the same one that my grandmother and great-grandmother had slept in before their ascendancies to the throne.

I'll never know what made me change into street clothes, pull my hair into a bun, and slip on running shoes. But that's exactly what I did.

I knew the covert ways out of the palace like the back of my hand. Part of it was due to a natural gift for observation and investigation; part of it was thanks to my formal education. It had been impressed on me by my tutors, secretaries, and Big Gran herself that a good princess should learn everything about her country.

That included secret ways out of the palace.

This wasn't the first time I'd slipped out undetected. That had been when I was a teenager, a university student. There were things I'd wanted to do, places I'd wanted to go, people I'd wanted to see without my official security detail getting involved. For years, it hadn't been a problem. Drieden is a small country and the monarchy can still be informal if it wishes. My uncle John, the Duke of Falender, works as a banker in the financial district. My brother serves in the armed forces. Until my engagement, I produced documentary films. With a discreet and small security presence, my family has been able to keep up the pretense that we're normal folk who just happen to live in that big old house on the hill.

With my recent notoriety, though, and my resulting cloistering in the palace and assorted hideaways, I hadn't been outside royal boundaries in over three months.

And sometimes a girl just needed a change of scenery.

My feet flew over the carpet, down the southwest stairwell, across the landing, into the upper gallery through a service entrance, then down another set of stairs that led into the herb garden, which was next to the kitchens with their loading dock and abandoned at this time of night.

Just like that, I was outside in a small courtyard. There was a guardhouse at the bottom of the cobblestone drive, but I pulled up the hood of my jacket and hopped into a nearby white Fiat with plates that matched the keys I had snagged from the loading dock bay.

The gates opened swiftly (as they should for an official palace vehicle) and I drove two hundred meters and . . .

I had no idea where I was going.

To the lights?

Why?

Because the lights were pretty?

Was I insane?

Probably. Now I was talking to myself. Just like Prince Karl the Holy when he believed a trout told him to invade France.

My foot pressed the gas pedal, indicating that I was, in fact, insane. Sleep deprivation had sucked all the common sense out of my head.

But I kept driving. Instinct and a memory pulled me forward.

There had been a night, two years ago, right after I had started dating Christian. I had gotten a call from him; he had flown to Drieden to surprise me. "Come see me," he had urged. He had given me the name of a bar where I was to meet him in an hour. And like tonight, I had managed to slip out of the palace completely undetected.

Romantic, right?

Without being aware of my destination, I now suddenly found myself parked outside that same bar. It seemed just as I remembered it. A cocktail lounge in the theater district, its raucous crowd was decidedly different from the posh, upper-crust circle Christian usually ran with. As soon as I walked into the disorienting mix of shadow and neon, I remembered that I hadn't brought any money or identification. Another sign of my deteriorating mental state. Still, I took a seat at a table covered with chipped red paint. After all, the point of this excursion wasn't to drink. If I'd wanted to get drunk, the palace had vast cellars full of very expensive spirits at my disposal. If I'd wanted to lose myself, I would have just taken the damn sleeping pill.

The point of this trip was . . .

I had no idea.

Now I closed my eyes.

I saw Christian, as he was the night I met him here. His longish blond hair curled around his collar. His skin still tan from the ski season. Was this what I wanted? To see Christian again? Was that why I came here?

"Excuse me. Is this seat taken?"

A deep voice. A Scottish accent. *Christian?*

"No," I answered, wondering if I was dreaming. A new part of my nightmare, perhaps? I peeked through my eyelids.

My new tablemate settling into the chair opposite me was not Christian Fraser-Campbell, ninth Duke of Steading. This stranger was the complete opposite of Christian, dark and rough, but not altogether objectionable.

"Hello," I said, automatically being polite and proper even though I desperately wanted him to leave me alone.

"Hallo there. What brings a beauty like you out on a night like tonight?"

At the word *beauty*, the rest of my defenses rose. I was in a dim bar with eyeglasses I'd borrowed from my secretary and a hood still pulled over a messy bun. Any man who thought I was a beauty at the moment was either delirious, drunk, or dead.

I said the first thing that popped into my head. "I'm meeting someone."

"A boyfriend someone?"

I noted that he did not offer to get up. Instead, he leaned back in his seat and crossed his arms, all ears for whatever my answer was.

Rude, I thought.

"No," I informed the ill-mannered Scottish stranger. "A coworker." It was the blandest answer I could imagine. Maybe boredom would make the man go away.

His eyebrows rose. "At this hour? Here? What kind of a job are you working?" His eyes draped over me in a perfect expression of sarcasm and speculation. "You're not . . . picking *up* anyone?"

It took me a moment. "Are you insinuating that I'm a prostitute?"

"Well, if you are, you're a badly dressed one."

"What, are you an expert?"

His mouth slid up on one side, clearly amused. "Not regarding fashion, no."

Ugh. How could I get him to go away?

I imagined the most boring profession ever. "I'm actually a historian." It wasn't too far off from my former job producing documentaries.

"Are you now? How fascinating."

Damn. Now I'd really have to turn on the boring. "I specialize in Driedish rural agrarian history." I made a tenting motion with both hands. "Specifically the congruence between animal husbandry, agricultural economics, and women's health."

There. Dull-level ten. That should do it.

Instead of running away from the madwoman ready to discuss the most obscure, driest subject ever, though, the stranger leaned forward, as if he were eager to hear more.

"Ah." He brightened. "Farming. A noble profession, indeed, although given to long days, uncertain futures, and way too much drink." He waved a hand and caught the attention of a nearby waitress. "Two whiskeys, please."

"I couldn't—"

He interrupted with sparkling eyes. "But my lady, you already have."

three

TWO GLASSES OF WHISKEY WERE SLAPPED DOWN ON the table, droplets of amber liquid splashing out onto the chipped red paint.

I'd had my first sip of whiskey at thirteen, stolen from my father's glass at the Royal Lodge in Kasselta in the Northern Province. If any of the adults had seen me, they'd ignored it. Misbehavior was to be dealt with by a nanny or Big Gran. No one else had dared—or cared—to discipline me.

Tonight I was only misbehaving a little, and I still loved the burn of whiskey. It always reminded me of a roaring winter fire, heat and comfort with an edge of danger.

Like this moment, when someone at a neighboring table was glancing over at me with this stranger: *this* was danger. I ducked my head and lifted the glass to my lips.

"What are you doing?" the man asked me, sounding rather affronted. "It's customary in my country to toast before a drink."

"What would you like to toast to?"

He regarded me thoughtfully for a moment as if considering his options. Then he lifted his glass. "To the Queen's health."

"Which one?"

He drew back. "What do you mean, 'which one'?"

"You've got a queen. So do I. Which one are we toasting to?"

He smiled. "To yours, of course. As a Scot, I've always had a wee problem with Queen Liz."

My toes curled at his reference to Elizabeth II of England, Scotland, and Wales as "Liz"—and not in a good way. I had met Elizabeth only twice, and had no personal relationship with her, but a lifetime of etiquette conditioning couldn't be undone by one unintended late-night drink with a Scot that I was already regretting.

"To Queen Aurelia," he said rather loudly.

"To the Queen," I murmured before taking my sip and then immediately making a face. I'd had much better whiskey.

My drinking partner made a face, too, after tasting his. "Jesus, what is this?"

"Something cheap." I pressed my lips together. Could I sound more like a snob?

But the man laughed instead of being offended, and when he did, I noticed him for the first time.

Really noticed him.

He was not just dark and rough. He had the look of a man who, after being punched in the face a few times, hadn't quite bounced back to his original features. There were marks and scars from a myriad of dubious adventures, no doubt. No, he wasn't Hollywood handsome, but he was something far more interesting.

A survivor.

He was crude, rude, and from tonight's display, clearly socially unacceptable. But for the past four months, I'd been wallowing in self-pity after my public humiliation, and here was someone who probably knew something about how to overcome bad things.

"What's your name?" I asked impulsively.

He rubbed a thumb across his glass before answering. "Nick. Nick Cameron. Yours?"

Damn. I'd walked right into that one. My tendency to ask people questions about themselves was seen by the royal advisors and courtiers as a benefit. I was comfortable with "the people." My questions made them comfortable with me.

But now . . . My stomach tightened. Even though I knew his name and had allowed him to buy me a drink, Nick was still an unknown. He wouldn't be comfortable with Princess Me. And I didn't know if I could trust him.

"Thea," I answered finally, giving him the name that only my family and closest friends use.

He repeated the nickname and the way that he deliberately said it, pressing the tip of his tongue behind his front teeth, was irresistibly attractive. He was a man who did things with purpose. With a plan.

I wished I had a plan.

The hood of my sweatshirt fell off my head as I took another sip of the third-rate whiskey, but the lights were low over our table and I highly doubted anyone would recognize me. And if they did? I could move pretty fast and make it back to the Fiat before more than a few camera phones could be whipped out.

Cameras. The interview tomorrow.

My stomach clenched as I tightened my grip around my glass. The thought of trying to hold it together while a reporter asked me questions about Christian was nearly debilitating.

Nick noticed. "You all right?" His eyes followed my glass as it hit my lips and stayed there for a good gulp or two.

"I have an interview tomorrow," I said. The whiskey was loosening my tongue.

"For a job?"

"No." I said it automatically and wondered why in the world I was telling this man anything close to the truth. "For work," I explained, hoping to stop him from asking any more questions. A man like him should not be interested in a historian's interview.

He cocked his head. "It's a big one, then? You worried about your boss breathing down your neck?"

A strangled giggle escaped me, thinking of my grandmother the Queen as a "boss." It was eerily accurate. Queen Aurelia was the final authority on all things in the palace, from proper punctuation to big events like weddings.

"Yeah, she's a hard-ass."

"Me? I'd skip out. Let someone else take it on."

"Why does that not surprise me?"

I thought of my father then, the heir to the throne, currently ensconced at his country house as he was for 80 percent of the year due to gout and hypoglycemia and cramped toes and whatever other ailment he invented whenever Big Gran asked him to fulfill a royal duty or two.

And my siblings, scattered around the globe, hiding themselves in helicopters, on Turkish yachts and Nepalese mountaintops, in whatever places didn't have cell service in case Big Gran called to ask them to attend a ceremony or ribbon cutting. Nope. There was no one to take the fall for me this time.

"I'm not a highly respected historian, though." Nick's words snapped me back to an alternate reality. The one where I'd told this annoying man I was a dreary academic.

"I'm not that respected," I said sharply. "Hardly anyone listens to me." Another truth, accidentally told.

He leaned over the table and through the haze of cigarette smoke and cheap whiskey, I saw that his eyes were green. Green with flecks of gold. Like those of a feral tomcat.

"I'm sure that's not true. I'd love to listen to you."

When my mouth dropped open, he gave me a quick grin. "Besides, I'm somewhat of an expert on the connection between husbandry and women's . . . health."

Ew.

"Does this work with women, usually? This . . ." I gestured to all of him. "This roguish scoundrel act?"

"You're having a drink with me; you tell me."

I looked at what was left in my glass and debated throwing it in his face. I'd never done such a thing before. What would it feel like? Could I get away with it?

"People would stare," he said in a low voice.

I jerked, confused, and looked back into those green eyes.

"If you threw the drink in my face," he explained. "You don't seem like a woman who wants that kind of attention."

With that, I tossed the rest of the whiskey back instead, discomfited by the fact that he had read my mind.

"Another round?" he drawled.

I was sober enough to consider using my manners. I should have said, "No thank you" immediately. But . . . for some reason I didn't, and Nick waved to the waitress and ordered another round. As I watched him, I had a fresh wave of curiosity about the man who was steady and sober—and plying me with alcohol . . .

"What are you in Drieden for?" I blurted out.

It was a reasonable enough question. He was obviously a foreigner. He should have an interesting reason for being in the country. But he seemed surprised by my question and hesitated before answering. "Family business."

That didn't sound right. A family business? He didn't seem like a man who would inherit his father's factory or law practice. Not like my ex. Not content to simply be a penniless Scottish duke (was there any other kind?), Christian had gotten a job in a respected corporate law firm when he'd moved here. And unlike this Nick, Christian would have gotten the hint and left me alone.

Which he had.

On our wedding day.

"What sort of family business?" I asked, suspicion lacing my voice.

"There was a will. Some property was left to a relation who had em-
igrated here. We're just trying to track him down." He shrugged as if it
were nothing important, but I leaned my elbow on the table and placed
my chin in my hand. Now *this* was fascinating. No one got lost in my
family. There were family trees that detailed every shit some king's bastard took in the woods. And a bequest that someone didn't know about?
My property was traced back to the Vikings, and Parliament wrote laws
distributing it amongst children I didn't even know I would have yet.

"Who is the relative? An uncle? Cousin? Was he working here?
Did he fall in love with a Driedener? Did he get citizenship?" That
question reminded me that I could make one call to the home office
and get the address of Nick's long lost relative, but I couldn't offer. I
wouldn't offer. Not for a sketchy guy in a bar.

"And what's the bequest?" I had to know. What could be so important that Nick would come to Drieden himself to deliver the news?

Nick's expression was bemused. "So many questions. I suppose this
is how you write your history books or papers or whatever you do?"

Right. My mythical historian alter ego. "I'm known as a very dili-
gent researcher."

"Spend all your time with your nose in books, I suppose."

"Oh yes, I'm just so excited to learn about a live person," I said,
sarcasm dripping from my tongue. "It's quite a change from the all the
dead people I usually talk to."

The smile faded. "Dead people are easier to deal with, I suppose."

I lifted my chin from my hand and sat back. I had been too forward,
too cavalier, even with someone who had sat down at my table without
permission and bought me drinks I hadn't known I'd needed. Nick's
concern for his relative seemed real and his family's struggle wasn't for
anyone's entertainment. Even a non-princess should know that.

"I apologize, I didn't mean—"

We were interrupted by the arrival of three denim-clad young
women.

"Oh my God," one breathed.

"It's her!" another squealed in an American accent.

"I'm sorry, we don't want to interrupt, but you look so much like—"

"Are you, like, related to Princess Theodora?"

I froze. They weren't really asking if I was related to Princess Theodora. They were asking if I was . . .

And oh God.

Each had a cell phone in her hand.

Suddenly, my cavalier attitude about being recognized seemed like another insane delusion. Me in a bar, looking like this? After four months away from the public eye? This couldn't be how the country saw me again.

"What, all Driedeners look alike to you?" Nick's question startled me. I wasn't expecting him to jump in, and certainly not in Driedish-accented English. Not when I'd just heard him speaking Scottish-accented Driedish. It was all very confusing under the influence of two glasses of cheap whiskey.

"Oh no . . ." one of the Americans nervously said. "But she looks exactly like her."

Nick scrunched his nose my way. "Her? In those sloppy clothes and that greasy hair? You think our very own princess would be in a dump like this?"

I opened my mouth to protest. I *had* washed my hair that night. But then I realized Nick was doing me a favor. "Americans—they think we're all blond and stone-faced," I sassed. Cheap whiskey made me bolder, apparently.

Must remember to avoid cheap whiskey.

Nick caught my eye as the Americans stammered their denials.

"She's not as beautiful as Her Highness," Nick said, contemplating me. "But I can see a slight resemblance. Maybe you ladies have a point."

The three girls were in their early twenties, with rain jackets and backpacks and high-tech sneakers, probably from California or Florida,

someplace warm, because they were overdressed for a Driedish summer. They shot each other dubious, embarrassed looks, and I felt sorry
for them. Princess Me would always be gracious to visitors.

"Maybe we've got ourselves a new business venture, love: you
could be one of them—whatsitcalled—

"Impersonators!" one of the blond Americans supplied.

"That's it," Nick agreed. The risky sparkle in his eyes was back.
"You could impersonate Princess Theodora for parties and such. We
could make a killing."

"Too bad you don't have a friend who looks like Prince Christian,"
one of them said.

"He wasn't a prince."

"Not yet. He would have been if he hadn't totally skipped out on
her."

"Ohmigod, I am still so mad at him."

"Poor thing . . ."

"Who runs out on a princess?"

"Yeah!" her friend said enthusiastically. "A fucking princess!"

Sounded like the Americans had been served cheap whiskey as well.

Nick rubbed his chin as he followed along with the conversation,
and even though the Americans didn't know it was me, it still irked me.
"Can we stop talking about it?" I snapped. "I'm not going to dress up
like her."

"You could make a lot of money," one of the girls said.

"Just get your hair done . . ."

"And maybe your eyebrows . . ."

"And your nose . . ."

My nose? Really? The light in this bar was *dreadful*.

"How much do you think people would pay in America?" Nick
asked them. "For someone to dress up like Theodora?"

"Like, a hundred?"

"Fifty?"

"Twenty?"

"Really? Twenty euros?" I exclaimed.

"Twenty dollars," an American clarified. With the exchange rate, that was an even lower offer. Great.

Then one of the girls got excited and reached into the purse she had strapped across her chest. "I'll give you twenty euros right now if you pose with me."

"Jenni!" one of her friends squealed. "It's not even Theodora!"

"Oh, come on—everyone back home will shit themselves."

I stood. I didn't really know why.

Nick pushed out of his chair and motioned at me. "So sorry, ladies, I've got to get my friend home. She has a big work event tomorrow and she's had a bit too much fun tonight, if you know what I mean." Since he mimed drinking out of a bottle, I was sure they understood his meaning perfectly.

The woman who was now dangling a twenty-euro bill in the air between us waggled her eyebrows at me. "Come on, one quick pose for my Instagram."

"She doesn't look anything like a princess. You're wasting your money," Nick said.

The American paid him no attention and the crisp bill, fresh from an airport ATM, wiggled in front of me. "My friends back home are going to die. Please?"

"Are all Americans this dumb?" Nick waved at my outfit. "A Driedish princess wouldn't be caught dead in these rags."

"Sure," I said to the girl, ignoring him and stepping forward.

There was no time to reconsider my actions. There was only a lot of squealing and giggling as I pulled up my hood and made a duck face along with a strange blond American girl in the dim light of a dive bar in the theater district.

She laughed, handed me the money, and the group went back to their table as I made my way to the door.

"Not that way." Nick grabbed my elbow and pushed me through a corner door and into the bar's office, where a desk overflowing with papers and receipts blocked our way to a back door. I nearly stepped into a liquor crate when Nick closed the door behind us and laughed, a sexy, dry sound.

It should not have been sexy. I checked the clock on the wall and swore. The interview. Dawn was only a few hours away and I had to get back into the palace before the staff started arriving. "I have to go." I moved toward the back door but Nick stood in front of it, a strange expression on his face.

"So soon, Thea?"

The way he said my name, with that deliberate press of his tongue against his teeth, the contemplation in his eyes, should have given me pause.

But I stood in stubborn disbelief, a kind of rebellion I'd practiced my whole life. "It's late."

"And you have a historian job interview in the morning."

"Yes."

"Driedish agrarian animal husbandry."

"Exactly," I said impatiently.

"Tell me something, Thea." There it was again, the slight emphasis on my nickname.

He knew.

"Tell me something about Driedish agrarian history."

I would never see him again. I could have pushed by him without a word. As a woman, as a princess, I didn't need to answer his question.

But as the old saying goes, once challenged, twice stubborn. I lifted my chin and looked into a stranger's green eyes and said, "In 1732, a Driedener named Halper Malzen invented an H-shaped plow that revolutionized wheat farming in the Demble province, because of the rocky, granite soil there."

Nick didn't blink.

"My paper about the effects of his invention will be in the next *University of Drieden Journal of History*."

"Fascinating."

"It is, isn't?"

"I was talking about you."

I shook my head. How many times had I heard that before? I wasn't fascinating. "I'm just a girl who likes history with a crappy job who drinks too much."

He didn't say another word before stepping out of my way.

I said good night softly, left through the back door leading to the alley, and was almost to my car when I remembered I hadn't wished him luck in his search for his lost relative.

The mystery of that family legacy occupied me all the way back to the palace gates.

four

THE KNOCK AT MY BEDROOM DOOR CAME WAY TOO early the next morning. My head throbbed, my mouth felt like a thick wool scarf had been stuffed in it, and yes, when I checked the mirror in my bathroom, I analyzed the view with a magazine beauty editor's eye. The limp blond hair could be sprayed and teased. An extra coat of mascara could make my blue eyes look more alert. But the under-eye circles were going to be the next national concern.

In fact, I didn't even have to wait for the newspapers to be printed. My secretary, Lucy, tutted as soon as she saw me, muttering something about Roberto and "work cut out for him."

"Coffee," was all I said before we got to work. After all, I couldn't exactly tell Lucy the shadows on my face were thanks to my late-night undercover excursion.

"I can't believe you're doing this," Lucy said for the six hundredth time.

She poured me another much-needed cup of coffee. "There's no need for this. You don't have to do it."

I accepted Lucy's proffered cup and thought of Big Gran. That's what my brother, Henry, has called her since we were little. She had been just plain old Gran, sometimes stern, not particularly cuddly, but still Gran. Then Henry saw a banner of her twenty-foot-high portrait flying from the city hall's walls. Family legend said he pointed his chubby finger and declared, "Big Gran looks scary."

My parents agreed; so did us kids. So did the rest of the palace. Queen Aurelia Victoria of Drieden, aka "Big Gran," was scary. Which is why I was in this predicament.

"She says I must do it," I said evenly, but avoided her direct spaniel-brown eyes. Lucy, who was only a year older than me and who had been my right-hand woman since I'd turned eighteen, knew better than to believe my dutiful statement.

"There must be something we can do." She tutted, pushing her glasses back over her straight coffee-brown hair. "You're grieving. And humiliated. Recovering from shock. You've just come home. Surely, this isn't necessary. Especially four months after the wedding. Who wants to hear about all that nonsense again, really?"

Only Lucy could get away with such talk. Anyone else in the palace would nod obediently and immediately once they learned that HM Aurelia had decreed that something "must" be done. But this was Lucy. My Lucy.

A distant cousin, Lady Lucy Monclere was also a goddaughter to Big Gran and had always been a favorite, along with the whole Monclere family, who were known for their jolly adventures and no-nonsense plain talk. The fact that Lucy's father owned one of the finest hunting grounds in all of Drieden also didn't hurt their status with Big Gran. Basically, Lucy was in a sweet spot between me and Her Majesty.

I briefly considered her stance. She was right. A national interview about the wedding fiasco wasn't necessary, and not just because I was still "recovering" from Christian's disappearance on the day planned for our historic nuptials in Drieden's breathtaking Cathedral of St. Julien. Nobody needed to interview me because the whole world had already dug up every embarrassing, private, scandalous detail. How the

wedding brunch was still served to a half-empty hall after many digni-
taries had simply chosen to return to their hotels. How my mother got
drunk and cursed at the British PM. How my honeymoon bags were
retrieved from the private plane and returned to the palace via police
escort. That last one had been covered live on television. A very lonely
matched set of Louis Vuitton luggage was gripping drama indeed.

Lucy still might be able to get me out of this, even though it was so
last-minute. She had done it before, when I was in university. She had
gone to Big Gran to confide that I was overwhelmed, making myself ill,
and couldn't I take a semester off to refresh and rejuvenate in Argen-
tina, tutoring schoolchildren there?

As a result of Lucy's magic, I spent a spring in the Pampas, volun-
teering at a local school. I also helped my mother kick a nasty pill habit
that Big Gran never seemed to know about, after a divorce from an
Argentine polo player that Big Gran *certainly* knew about.

As if she could read my mind, Lucy reached over and poured
nearly a half liter of cream into my coffee. "You've lost too much
weight. You're frail. Four months away and you're skin and bones.
You'll probably catch pneumonia this winter, and then where will the
monarchy be?"

It was a practice argument for Big Gran. Keep me healthy and happy
and the future of the Driedish royal family will be better off.

As arguments to Big Gran went, it could be a winner.

Last week, however, the Liberal leader had once again invoked the
R word in a speech to Parliament: *republic*.

Big Gran did not care for the R word.

She wasn't anti-democracy or hopelessly old-fashioned. But she
was Queen: the latest monarch in a six-hundred-year rule over a tiny
coastal nation on the bony shoulder of Europe that had rebuffed English, French, Dutch, and German advances. You don't just give that
up because a sliver of the current crop of subjects answered an internet
poll.

Which meant Big Gran was on the offensive *again*. And I, the Princess and second in line to the throne, was her most effective weapon. Being engaged to a handsome (if penniless) Scottish duke and subsequently being left at the altar had helped reignite the nation's enthusiasm for supporting the Crown.

So I had been summoned back to the palace last week. My office had dealt with most of the headaches Christian's abandonment had left us. Sending back hundreds of wedding gifts to VIPs around the world had required a staff of nearly thirty secretaries alone, not to mention all the thousands of other royal wedding details that had to be carefully unstitched under the avid media spotlight. And now Lucy's eagle eyes were watching the coffee grow cold in my hands as I debated whether I should utilize her impressive methods of persuasion in order to skip out of the Chantal Louis interview for Drieden's most-read weekly news magazine.

"It's my job," I finally said, remembering the long hours the palace staff had been putting in to reassemble my routine, my life. I knew this was best. I couldn't stay in hiding forever. My life was a public one and if my Queen said I had to be interviewed in a national magazine . . .

Lucy saw the resignation on my face. "Fine, I'll speak with them before you sit down. Give them our usual list of red topics." She was crisp and efficient, but the press of her lips told me that she would have gladly gone to battle with Big Gran for me.

She sighed, pushed her glasses back down on her nose, and began taking notes with a silver fountain pen in her leather-bound agenda.

"There will be no questions about Caroline, Henry, or Sophie." She scribbled the names down, even though this was standard operating procedure for me. I didn't talk about my siblings in public. There were way too many minefields there.

"Or Felice," she added with an extra underline below the name. It was another long-standing rule, although the national (and international) press loved my mother. After she had divorced my father and run off with her second polo player, her titles had been winnowed down considerably, as had her yearly income, but the tabloids and mainstream journalists still gushed over her scandals, her style, and her incoherent "let them eat cake" ramblings that periodically took over the news for a day or two every year. There were Instagrams devoted to her and her lavish lifestyle. Social media fans were fun to try to explain to Big Gran. Yes, the internet adored my mother. No, it probably was not for the "right" reasons.

"What do you think I should talk about?" I mused, reaching for my lukewarm coffee. "What international kerfuffle could I start this week?"

Lucy looked at me with dismay. "Oh, Thea, don't talk like that."

"You know they're going to ask if I'm seeing anyone. What rumor should I start?"

"The last thing we need is another scandal with you and a man."

I bit my lip, remembering the man I'd met last night and the scandal I could have so easily started with just a couple of glasses of whiskey, a stranger, and a few smartphones.

I'd been reckless, not thinking clearly at all when I'd agreed to that stupid selfie. Lucy was absolutely, 100 percent right. If something had happened in that bar with Nick, if pictures had been taken and posted online . . . let's just say I was thankful the guillotine had never been introduced to Drieden.

Speaking of guillotines . . .

"Do you think I could put a bounty on his head?" I closed my eyes and dreamt happily of a WANTED poster featuring my ex-fiancé's face. "Or would that look petty?"

I didn't need to say Christian's name for Lucy to know exactly whom I was talking about. "It would look bloodthirsty and common," Lucy said calmly.

"Maybe we could do an internet poll. Let the people decide how much Christian's manhood is worth."

"Please don't say those things around *her*. You know she doesn't appreciate your sense of humor."

If only it had been my sense of humor that had gotten me into this mess, then I would probably have handled it better. But no, this was all perpetrated by one man. A man who had betrayed me in the most public way possible.

"You never know—maybe she'd agree with me," I said mulishly.

"Or maybe she'd send you away again because she doesn't know what you might do."

"Most women in Drieden would want to do exactly what I'm proposing."

"Most women in Drieden aren't royal princesses."

Lucy frowned at her notes, which would be verbally communicated to an assistant palace press secretary assigned to my media, someone who deserved a huge bonus this year in the aftermath of the Royal Wedding That Wasn't. The palace and the magazine would arrange the terms and in a few hours, after I had been painted and primped, I would sit down with the reporter in a cozy yet traditional drawing room, filled with art donated by my family and then "borrowed" back from the national museum.

A photographer would capture candid shots of me, with blown-out, perfectly highlighted blond hair, artful makeup, and a conservative navy dress that hadn't cost more than one hundred euros. Something the average Driedener could buy. My dress couldn't be black, but I needed to wear a somber color. I was a sensitive, grieving woman, after all. It was important that the people be reminded of that.

THE INTERVIEW WENT AS WELL AS COULD BE EXPECTED.

Roberto muttered under his breath about the dark smudges under my eyes.

Lucy grumbled about mono and the flu and the Zika virus.

My press secretary clutched a cross hanging from her neck during the whole thing.

I wouldn't say I flubbed it. With all of the training and practice I'd been subjected to over the years, an interview such as this was second nature for me: the reporter carefully selected, the questions vetted, the environment tasteful. I handled myself with poise and dignity, even as Chantal Louis delicately prodded into my abandoned wedding plans and my disappeared fiancé.

When I answered, "I don't know" to the question about Christian's whereabouts, surely it wasn't as sharp and brittle as it sounded in my head. I followed up with, "I hope he is well and has many happy years ahead of him." It was well-meaning and gracious, I thought, but Lucy flinched and I wondered just what they expected of me. What was a woman supposed to say about a fiancé who left her at the altar in front of an entire nation? Was I supposed to declare my everlasting love? Offer to take him back? Compliment his excellent judgment?

Afterward, when Lucy came to talk to me about it, I sent her away. I was tired, I said. Maybe even coming down with something. She made me promise to see my doctor and left me alone to crawl back into my bed to sleep for the rest of the day.

Which of course meant that I was wide awake when night fell and the lights of Drieden sparkled through my window.

The twenty-euro bill that yesterday's selfie had earned was still tucked in the pocket of my sweatshirt that I had folded and placed in a drawer in my closet when I returned the night before. If I left it hanging on the back of a chair or in a pile on the floor, one of the maids would have already washed, ironed, and put it away.

I wandered into the massive closet next to my bedroom. This was just one of three that I had attached to my suite. There was off-site storage of my seasonal and special-occasion clothing, and there were vaults for some of the really important pieces.

Like my wedding dress.

With hand-stitched Driedish lace, thousands of real pearls, and a ten-foot train, it would have been worn for a mere six hours, for the trip to the cathedral, the forty-five-minute ceremony, portraits, the royal viewing, and to greet VIP guests.

In the end, it was worn for thirty-six minutes.

A wedding dress of a jilted princess couldn't be donated to a charity. It wouldn't be displayed in the National Galleries when my grandmother celebrated her fortieth anniversary on the throne next year. The dress would be under lock and key in the royal archives, masses of hand-stitched lace and custom satin, rotting away and completely useless. Not unlike certain royals I knew.

After spending just a few seconds thinking about my former wedding dress, my favorite running sweatshirt was suddenly in my hand. Then it was being pulled over my head. Then I was grabbing Lucy's spare spectacles that she kept in my desk, yanking on a stocking cap with the crest of the national football club, and slipping on my sneakers and sliding out the door.

Tonight I took a different route.

Taking the elevator, I stopped on the first floor and walked down the hall that led to the administrative offices. Here there was a back entrance for the staff, and in a few minutes I was out on the street.

I started to walk, not stopping until I was at the bar from last night.

The front doors were marked with their usual neon lights, and when they opened with a couple of loud, probably drunk patrons stumbling out, I remembered the American tourists. If they had come back tonight to look for the Princess Theodora look-alike, if they saw me again . . .

I turned and headed toward the back door. What I wanted to find—what I wanted to see, to feel—I didn't really know, and in the end, it didn't really matter because before I could get to it, I heard a voice calling my name from the alley.

"Thea. It's been a long time."

five

CHRISTIAN.

For an instant, I thought he'd come back to me. As if he'd been here, waiting for the past four months, instead of escaping like a coward.

But, no. The voice may have been Scottish, but this accent belonged to a very different man. A commoner. A stranger.

A charismatic stranger, I amended as Nick stepped forward and the security light on the building caught his features.

"It's been less than twenty-four hours," I said.

"Did you miss me, then?" He was close enough that I could see that light in his eyes. The light that was dangerous.

And sort of fun.

I reached into my pocket, realizing that my subconscious had wanted this. Had planned this. I slapped the twenty euros against his chest. "This is yours."

"You earned it."

"You bought me a drink. Then you suggested the idea to those girls."

He caught my hand in his and I nearly gasped. His skin was so warm against my cold fingers. It was a trait of mine, cold hands and feet. Christian used to tease me that I had grown up in too many drafty Driedish castles. Little did I know, he was the one with the coldest feet of all.

"Buy me a drink and we'll be even," Nick said with a smirk.

I laughed. "In your dreams."

"What can I say? I've always had a weakness for sharp-tongued harpies."

He squeezed my hand. I ripped it away. The impertinence!

"I'm not drinking with you," I informed him as I started walking back down the alley.

"What are we going to be doing, then?" He was following me, his voice light and teasing.

"*We* aren't doing anything."

"Where are we going?"

That was a good question. I had no idea.

I wasn't really an expert on the bar scene. I knew I should just return to the palace and avoid this Nick person for the rest of my life.

But my feet kept moving.

The alley opened up on the bright lights of Lound, the main thoroughfare heading into the Sterling commercial district, and I felt more confident, even if my security staff would be having a collective coronary right now.

I snuck a glance at the man who was still following me like a good-natured stray dog. His all-black ensemble lent him a piratical air, as did the dark hair sweeping back from his face and his bold, confident stride.

"You don't know where you're going, do you?" Nick asked in my ear. I swatted him away like a nagging fly.

"Go away." I frowned. "Of course I know where I'm going."

"Would you like me to recommend a spot?"

"Just arrived and you're an expert on all the bars in the city. Why am I not surprised?"

He wasn't bothered by my insinuation. He grinned agreeably. "I'm looking for someone. Someone who might go to bars."

Oh, right. His lost relative. My curiosity seized me again. It was fascinating. How did people get lost, anyway?

"How is your search going?" I asked. I couldn't help myself.

He paused, and I presumed it was because a couple was walking past us with their hands in each other's pockets and their tongues in each other's throats, and neither of us could help but stare. But then he picked the conversation back up, rubbing his hand over his chin. "It's a bit sticky, actually."

"How so?"

"The family lost touch awhile back. And I'm here . . ." He made a futile gesture at the city's historic buildings.

"Are the authorities not being cooperative?" I couldn't imagine that a foreign citizen would be treated discourteously by the police. "Or couldn't your foreign office step in?" I searched my brain for the proper channels for this type of investigation. "You should ask them to access their records."

Nick grimaced. "That's the problem. He became a Driedener. Renounced his British citizenship."

So Nick's long lost relative was a subject of . . . well, mine. I stopped in front of a lit door wondering how, or if, I could get involved here when Nick looked over my head and said, "Ah, here we are."

We were in front of a British-style pub, The Crown and Crone. Just the sort of place an expatriate Scottish kinsman would come if he were homesick.

"It looks loud, with all the matches on," he said, and indeed we could see several football matches playing on television screens through the pub's dark windows. "It's probably not your sort of scene."

Here was my chance. I could lose him at the pub. A true Scot wouldn't follow a woman around the city when he had the chance to immerse himself in a few pints and gaze at the pitch.

But the same reckless impulse that had brought me out tonight made me tilt my head so he could see the Drieden emblem on my hat. "I'm sort of a fan. Since birth."

Appreciation and amusement were in Nick's expression as he held open the door for us. "After you."

It was exactly the sort of place Princess Theodora of Drieden would never go, dark and grimy and filled with the stench of fresh beer and old sweat. I seemed to be the only female patron but no one paid me any attention, as their eyes were glued to the various matches broadcast from around Europe.

The tables in the corners were all occupied, which was probably a blessing, as I imagined crusts of filth piled up under the booths. Lucy would have me dunked in disinfectant if she knew I'd been here.

So we took a high table in the middle of the pub. One beer, I told myself. One beer would satisfy this self-destructive urge that had overtaken me tonight. One beer and then I could slip out while Nick's attention was riveted to the television. I would never see him again.

With the twenty-euro note I'd given him earlier, Nick disappeared and returned with two lukewarm ales, and just as I'd expected, his attention was soon commanded by the Bundesliga.

Even though it was smelly and loud and dirty, I told myself to savor it all. This would be my last walk on the wild side.

After this, I would go home and become the princess that everyone wanted me to be, that I was *supposed* to be. The close call last night had made me realize that it was only a matter of time before someone pulled the alarm, inside or outside the palace.

But you didn't let that stop you tonight, Thea.

There were five more minutes left in the match. Five more minutes to enjoy my freedom, I firmly told myself, keeping an eye on the television clock. After that, I'd be sensible again. I would leave.

Nick finished his beer and went to grab another round, leaving me to sip in solitude until yet another burly stranger walked up to the table to take his place. Did this happen to all single women in bars, or did I just have a sign hanging over my head saying, *yes, I want to be accosted in public by annoying drunk men?*

He spoke in sloppy Driedish with a muddled British accent. "Can I buy you a drink?"

"I already have one."

"Come on then, have one with me. I promise I'm more interesting than the loser who just left you alone."

A hand draped over my shoulder. It didn't belong to my new annoying friend. It belonged to my old annoying friend.

"She's with me."

Nick's hand moved up under my hair and he rubbed my neck with his thumb, a clear sign of ownership.

But it wasn't enough for the drunk jerk still weaving in front of me.

"C'mon, darlin'. I can tell you're looking for some real fun tonight, not this lightweight."

"I said, she's with *me*," Nick repeated, a little louder this time.

The drunk leaned over and peered at me with observant if hazy eyes. "She doesn't look like she's with you. Kiss her, then, if you're her man."

Something snapped inside of me.

I slapped Nick's hand off me and slid off my bar stool.

"Ha! See? I knew you were lying," Drunk Idiot said wheezily.

"No, he's not." I glared. Drunk Idiot said something unintelligible behind me as I took Nick's face in my hands and planted one on him.

I suppose I had only meant to give him a quick peck, just long enough to taste his full, dangerous lips and to prove that no man would control me tonight. But, as with most of my impulsive acts, the consequences pulled me into something deeper.

Just a taste turned into a full-on obsession. His lips felt better than they looked, a soft contrast to the rough scrub of his beard against my chin. I hooked my forearm around his neck, and his hands pulled me tight against him.

Distantly, I heard yells and hoots, but . . . *God*.

This kiss was everything.

"Take her someplace private!"

"Get a room!"

Nick's mouth cracked into a smile against mine. "Sounds like a plan," he murmured right before he lifted me up like sack of flour, threw me over his shoulder, and carried me toward the back corner of the pub.

I was stunned. I lifted a fist to pound the man in the back of his skull and then someone shouted, "Smile!" and I saw an all-too-familiar camera flash. "Here's your camera, then."

The body underneath me stopped. "Thanks, mate," Nick said. From my high, upside-down perch, I saw the man slap a small camera into Nick's hand.

The camera that had just taken a picture of me.

On top of Nick.

That camera had just gone into Nick's back pocket.

What the hell?

Nick kicked open the door of the men's room and dumped me on my feet as soon as the door was closed behind us. "There you go, Princess."

Anger, confusion, and thwarted lust rushed through me.

"W-wh-what did you call me?"

Even in the dim light of the washroom, I could see Nick's smirk. He tapped the bridge of my borrowed glasses. "You didn't think a pair of these was an effective disguise, did you, Princess?"

He knew.

No. This wasn't happening. "No one knows it's me."

Nick made a face and patted his rear pocket. "That nice man out there took pictures for me, Theodora."

"Of my ass in the air!"

"It's a very recognizable ass."

"No one will see that photo and see me. They'll just think it's some random girl." I said it as much to convince myself as I did Nick.

"Right. Well. Two nights in a row they've seen you and I have the photographic proof."

I cringed. The American girls.

Nick chuckled. "Those lovely girls were more than happy to text that shot to me. You've now been spotted in two bars, with the same man." He leaned in and whispered in my ear, "And then you kissed him."

An uneasy tremor clenched the back of my neck.

Nick's voice was quiet and even, but it made me as nervous as if he were screaming. "I can see the headlines now: 'Princess Theodora Gets Her Groove Back.'"

"That's not what this was."

"Wasn't it?"

"Not with you," I lied, even with the fresh imprint of his lips still burning on mine.

Nick chuckled softly but didn't say anything as I processed what was happening. "You're a reporter, aren't you?" He didn't answer but he didn't need to. I'd fallen into a trap because I couldn't sleep, and an insomniac princess has very, very bad judgment. "What do you want? You can have an exclusive, if that's what you're looking for."

"But Chantal Louis already interviewed you."

"How did you know that?"

"It's my business to know."

I wrapped my arms around my middle. "What else do you want? Money?" Outright blackmail would be a new experience for me, but after being pulled unwittingly into the scandal of the century four months ago, I knew that Big Gran's tolerance for a new tabloid scandal involving me and a dishonest Scot in a dark pub would be very low. We were talking medieval levels of intolerance here.

Nick regarded me seriously for a long moment, long enough for me to start wondering how much cash I could get my hands on in the next twenty-four hours, but then he said, "I want information."

"Information? What kind of information?"

"Information about Christian Fraser-Campbell."

My ex-fiancé? That didn't make sense. "You said it was your business to know things."

"It is."

"Then what do you need to know about my ex-fiancé?"

"The things no one knows."

It wasn't what I expected. All my life, people had wanted to know the behind-the-scenes details about me. Second in line to the Driedish throne, young, fairly attractive, considerably well-off. This was so odd. I had to make sure. "You don't want to know about me?"

"No."

I had to ask once more. "You want to write an article about Christian? Not me?"

Nick leaned slightly toward me, his lips curved in a slight, mocking smile. "Princess, you're the least interesting person in this room."

I didn't know what to think of that. "So if I tell you about Christian, you won't tell anyone about . . ." I swallowed. "Us?" I finished.

"So predictable," Nick murmured. "Always thinking about yourself."

I took a step back. "You're the one who's taking advantage of people to get a story."

He shrugged and reached inside his coat. "That's my job." He handed me a business card with crumpled corners, blank except for a phone number.

"Call me when you're ready to talk."

I took it automatically and he checked his watch. "Wait here for ten minutes. A taxi will pick you up at the back entrance and take you back to your car."

Then he left without another word, and I wondered what the hell I had gotten myself into.

And how I was going to get out of it.

six

HAD AVOIDED SITUATIONS LIKE THIS MY ENTIRE LIFE.
They didn't occur often, thank goodness, but when they did, they were decidedly uncomfortable.

Me, in a spindly, hard chair covered in a scratchy fabric that made the back of my thighs itch, sitting across from my grandmother in her formal office. She only used this room when she wanted her guests to experience the full grandeur of her majesty, people like that American president she didn't much care for, or my mother, whom she had never quite forgiven for her polo-player-husband-loving ways.

The fact that I was called in today didn't necessarily mean that I was as bad as an American president who used "y'all" to refer to a queen of a sovereign nation, but it also didn't mean she wanted to gossip over a glass of wine and pedicures.

She settled across from me in a matching chair, her spine not touching the stiff back. As a habit, my posture was pretty good, but it did not compare to that of Queen Aurelia right before she was about to lay into someone.

I waited in silence. It would be unwise to speak first.

"I received the photographs from your interview with *The Drie-dener,*" she informed me.

My spine bent automatically in relief. She had called me in to talk about the Chantal Louis interview, not my nightly escapades with Nick the Blackmailing Pond Scum Reporter. "Oh?"

It was a safe choice. There was no way to unintentionally insult her with a vague "Oh?"

I was wrong. Gran's eyes grew cold. "It was unacceptable, Theodora."

She used my full name. Not a great sign.

"I sent you to Perpetua to have a bit of quiet time and recover your health. These photos make you look like you've been drinking yourself into a stupor the last four months." She flicked her fingers as if the photos were right there and she could make them disappear into oblivion with just a snap.

She probably could. The sleep I'd lost by drinking with Nick had apparently shown on my face in the photographs. Roberto was good with concealer, but he wasn't a miracle worker.

I had to say something. Quick. "I apologize, Grandmother." There was no "Gran" now, not in the scratchy, hard chair. "I've been——"

Gran cut me off. "Yes, yes, Lucy keeps telling me how bereft you are from that wedding business." She narrowed her eyes. "It's surprising, considering your feelings for the man."

Surprising? My feelings? I wasn't quite sure what she was referring to—or what Lucy had been telling her. If there was a chance that Lucy had said something to get me out of this situation, I needed to milk that.

"It's kind of Lucy to defend me," I said, carefully picking my words. "But there's no excuse for neglecting my duty."

Gran sniffed. "Your duty. That's exactly what I'm talking about. You were willing to do your duty by marrying that . . ." Her mouth turned downward as she searched for the appropriate word for Christian. "Person," she finished. It was tantamount to an insult, the way she said it, dripping with disdain. "And as I have told Lucy, your duty to the family remains even if *he* did not."

My fingers felt spiderwebby, and I realized I was gripping them tightly in my lap. All this over a bad photo shoot. I was trying to come up with a polite way of telling Gran that I'd wear more concealer next time when she took the conversation into an entirely new direction.

"My fortieth anniversary is next summer. The Ruby Jubilee."

"Yes, I remember." It had been on every calendar in the palace since her thirtieth anniversary of taking the throne.

"The concerts and parades have already been planned. I will expect you to be in full control of yourself by then."

She said that as if I had stripped off my clothes and gone skinny-dipping in the fountain in front of the palace instead of having a few drinks on a weeknight. "I imagine I'll be fine," I said evenly. "As soon as I forget that I'm the laughingstock of the nation."

Gran's eyebrows rose a fraction of an inch. "You are a member of the royal House of Laurent. That *person* does not deserve a thought in your head."

"I don't think about him."

Gran was shrewd. "I know you were still trying to reach him while you were on Perpetua."

I shifted in my chair. "A few phone calls—that was all."

Gran's expression had gone ice cold.

"What do you want me to say?" My voice rose a half octave in defensiveness. "I was going to marry him. He humiliated me and I wanted—"

She cut me off. "It doesn't matter what you want. You are a princess. Duty before desire."

A frustration rose in me, one that was all too familiar. "You've always said that we should put our duty first. I did that with Christian." I had picked the appropriate man, the one who was lovely company, who followed protocol, who knew how to play the game. "But maybe next time I should fall in love with the man first. Like Caroline."

Mentioning my sister's name, especially in this conversation, was like throwing dynamite into the opening of Parliament: destructive, explosive, and treasonous.

But Her Royal Highness Queen Aurelia of Drieden would not be baited, nor would she shock easily. One did not sit on a throne for forty years and get rattled by a purposely provocative granddaughter. "This is *not* Monaco, where princesses may marry circus clowns and unemployed fools," she tutted.

"Stavros is not a circus clown," I said in defense of the Formula One driver my sister had married in an unsanctioned ceremony two months ago.

"And that *girl* is no longer a princess." The reminder that Caroline's royal title had been stripped after her elopement was chilling. And the fact that Gran wouldn't say Caroline's name hurt me, too.

It struck me that this was why I agreed to do my duty most of the time. Because for me? *Duty* was just another word for family. I complied with Gran's expectations, with the traditions, with all the rules, because at the heart of it all, this was my heritage. These were the people I had grown up with, who I knew better than anyone. And if you didn't comply, you were banished. First it was my mother's exile, and then Caroline's. The message was exquisitely clear: do your duty or lose everyone you love.

Which made Christian's abandonment doubly painful. I had been completely willing to marry a man I had no passion for, for the good of my family. My queen.

And what did I get in return?

A multitude of unanswered questions and grief over a few well-deserved whiskeys.

The word was on my lips. My tongue pressed against the back of my teeth, ready to let it fly. I could feel it—a word so solid, so necessary, that it demanded to be let loose.

No.

But what came out of my mouth was, "Yes, Grandmother. I apologize for my appearance in the photos."

Gran nodded her pleasure at my response, then turned her back on me and moved to her writing desk, where she pressed an intercom button. In two minutes, her butler, Harald, would knock softly and our meeting would be over.

Now was the time for me to bring up my illicit midnight runs through the city and the photograph of me slung over Nick's shoulder that could destroy Gran's plans for a neat and tidy Ruby Jubilee next summer. Now, while she was reminding me about appropriate behavior and fulfilling one's duty to the Crown.

But the thought of Nick Cameron, of his disrespectful manhandling and his smart mouth on mine, made my nerves rattle in my lower belly, and in order to distract myself from my entirely un-princess-like thoughts, I fiddled with my watch and brushed my fingers across the scratchy, upholstered chair o' torture.

Harald would be here in one minute.

Gran was looking at the newspaper on her desk. Many of the monarchs in Europe relied upon aides or secretaries to filter the headlines, if they cared to read them at all, but for as long as I could remember, Gran was a voracious consumer of news both domestic and international. She might be only a figurehead in a modern Driedish government, but she cared deeply about the issues and could wield considerable influence behind the scenes.

It wasn't the top headline, but I was sure I knew what Gran was contemplating. The head of the Liberal party, Pierre Anders, had recently made some sort of budget proposal to Parliament, and it was all the papers could talk about as of late. Liberal budgets were only slightly more acceptable than mentioning the word *republic*.

"Will you be speaking to Parliament this fall?" I asked her. It was an event that took place at the Queen's discretion, often when there were contentious issues threatening the usual procedures.

Gran lifted her eyes above the newspaper. "It makes one long for the days when the Crown could exert its true authority."

"And one could just toss Liberal ministers into the dungeons?"

I thought I was making a joke, but Gran replied, without a hint of a smile in sight, "Exactly."

There was a soft knock at the door, which opened a moment later. Gran sniffed, and without looking up from her paper again, said, "Harald will see you out."

I left the Queen's presence with a renewed sense of purpose. Gran had called me in to remind me what I had been raised to do, what I had always done. Princess Theodora of Drieden was polite, respectful, and compliant. She put the Crown and its priorities first. Even if it meant acquiescing to the blackmail of a dangerously cocky reporter.

seven

CALLED THE NUMBER ON THE CARD.

I had to be sneaky about it.

Leaving Gran's apartments, I went to the press offices three stories down, to Jerome's office.

Officially Jerome was attached to my father's staff, but when my father was at his country house, poor Jerome ended up "working from home" with no official tasks to do, which meant his palace office—and his secure landline—was generally available to princesses who needed to make calls with no one listening in.

Nick picked up on the second ring. "Yes, Princess?"

"How do you know who this is?" My hand hovered over the buttons on Jerome's phone. It wasn't supposed to be traceable, but after my meeting with Gran, I was on edge.

"I don't share this number with just anyone."

"Just don't say that . . . word."

"Of course, Princess. Whatever you say."

If Nick had been in front of me, I would have kicked him.

"What do you want from me?" I hissed.

When he told me, I felt like Gran's heaviest ceremonial robes had been dropped onto my chest. "You can't be serious," I said.

The sound of the dial tone was my answer.

Lucy wasn't thrilled when I told her that I needed to attend a football match in the royal box at the National Stadium. She reminded me that I hadn't yet seen a doctor, that she didn't think I was eating well, and that sporting events were a breeding ground for "international diseases." Whatever those were.

My reassuring smile felt brittle and harsh. "I need to get out of here. Do something fun. And besides," I added with some bitterness, "Gran wants me to start getting back to work."

Three hours later, Tamar and Hugh, my two security guards, escorted me up the elevator to the royal box at National Stadium, which overlooked the pitch where Drieden's team was about to face the Scottish team in a friendly game of football.

I called Tamar over after I had finished greeting the people working the box. "There's a man waiting at the ticket booth downstairs." I described Nick and the Scottish scarf he told me he'd be wearing. "He's a friend of Christian's and I invited him to see this match. Please let him up."

She nodded quickly, but from her tight-lipped expression, I knew she wished she could argue with me. Tamar didn't like when I made changes to the plans, but that was what made her good at her job—she protected me from my ill-considered impulses. Except for, of course, right now.

In his team colors like 99 percent of the football fans in the stadium, Nick Cameron walked into the royal box, still seeming like the biggest, baddest wolf that had ever stalked a well-meaning if slightly impulsive woman like myself. The blue-and-white Scottish football scarf draped around his neck seemed to accentuate that his shoulders were too big. His posture too alert. His attitude a little too lethal.

Let's just say, I was glad Tamar and Hugh's bodies were bracketing the door.

I said a nervous "good evening" to him in English. He repeated the sentiment in Driedish, and then it was time for me to do my one official duty of the evening.

When the royal box was occupied, the announcer told the crowd that the national anthem would be sung in the direction of the Queen's representative.

Who was me.

I stepped onto the balcony so I could be seen under the spotlights. While my smart bottle-green leather jacket and dark blue pants were appropriate for a friendly international football match, they were all wrong—too warm, too tight—for my first public appearance since my wedding fiasco.

As nearly a hundred thousand people turned my way, I saw my face on the giant television screens, the same lacquered and plastered tight smile that had been lacquered and plastered on thousands of key chains and tea towels and coffee mugs.

They see what they want to see.

The crowd cheered.

They don't see my flaws.

I thanked God for that.

The familiar canned music started and the crowd sang along to every word.

Our fair native land, one people here we stand, in service to God and Queen.

Out of the corner of my eye, I saw Nick still lounging in the chair. He was out of view from anyone in the crowd, but his refusal to stand during the national anthem was obscenely disrespectful. The song ended, I waved to the cheers of my people, and then I retired out of view, ostensibly to enjoy the match.

But really I wanted to tear Nick Cameron a new one.

"Leave us," I ordered Tamar and Hugh. "We have a lot of catching up to do."

Nick had the audacity to look amused at the turn of phrase. When the door closed, I spun on him. "How dare you!? You are a guest of the Crown and the least you can do is stand during our anthem."

"Or what? You'll throw me in the dungeon?"

My fists balled. "I would if I could."

He made a face. "Duly noted. I won't get on your bad side." He waved his hand at me. "Speaking of sides, will you move over a bit? I can't see the game."

The game? Was he being serious?

"And how does a man get a drink around here? Is there a button to call a serving wench or—"

"A drink!?" I saw red. "You brought me here to drink and *watch a soccer match*!?"

Nick blinked a few times and then shrugged. "Yeah."

I was fuming. "You're blackmailing me."

"So?"

"So get on with it," I said between clenched teeth.

"I have to say, Princess, most women ask me a bit nicer than that."

"Oh!" I exclaimed, throwing up my hands and walking a half circle around the box, staying clear of the line where the lights would touch me. He was the most infuriating man I had ever known. The crowd roared and Nick jumped up, his eyes focused on the field. I couldn't believe this. Only a man would prolong his blackmail so he could squeeze in a free soccer match first. Even for scoundrels, sports came first!

"Christian didn't watch soccer," I spat.

"Really," Nick said distractedly.

"He liked documentaries."

Nick didn't respond. He was following the ball on the field.

"Historical dramas."

Still not even a flicker of interest. Totally concentrated on the game.

"Pornography."

Nick lifted an eyebrow.

"So *that* gets your attention," I muttered as I crossed my arms and gave up trying to talk to him while the men on the field were kicking the ball around. Clearly, the man could only focus on two subjects at a time: soccer and sex, which left me at something of a disadvantage, as I had no desire to kick a ball, and as to the other . . . well, *surely* I could manage the situation using my brain and not my body. I was no Queen Marie-Therese, after all. She didn't get the nickname "The Whore Queen" for nothing. Until I figured out how to convince him that he didn't want to release photographs of me kissing him, I had to manage this situation some other way. Preferably without resorting to watching pornography with the man.

I called for food and drink to keep up appearances that this meeting was simply a reunion of two old friends, and trays of chilled mugs and hot dishes were rolled in. Nick didn't even say thank you—he simply cheered in between huge bites when Scotland scored the first goal and scowled when Drieden soon matched it and earned another one after a penalty kick.

Around the hour mark, when it became clear that Scotland's offense was total shit, Nick threw up his hands. "Do you know where Christian is?"

I took a sip of the champagne I'd been angrily gripping for the past hour. "Now you want to talk?"

"Yes, now that your guard dogs will leave us alone."

I glanced quickly at the door that had stayed closed since the traditional Driedish roasted chicken and buttered noodles had been served. "Where is Christian?"

"I don't know and I don't care."

"You don't care? You were going to marry him."

"I was. Now I'm not. Therefore, I don't care."

He nodded sagely. "Got it. He was just a boy toy, then."

I sputtered at the insult. "Princesses don't marry boy toys."

"So that's why it didn't work out. He was beneath you."

The man was incorrigible. I crossed my arms. The truth was, Christian was a duke in the United Kingdom. And as I was a royal princess of a kingdom, he *was* beneath me, if one wanted to get technical about it. If I pointed out either of those facts, however, I was sure this boor would still mock me. Therefore, I would ignore him until he asked a reasonable question.

"Who called it off?"

I couldn't help but laugh. Loudly. Incredulously. Which, strangely, seemed to confound the crack reporter in front of me. "That's funny?" Nick asked.

"I was in my wedding dress when I was told that my fiancé was nowhere to be found. I think it's safe to say he called it off."

Nick's eyes narrowed. "Who told you this information?"

There was something about that question. Maybe in his inflection, the demand in it. The turn of phrase. The plain sterility of it.

A still, small voice told me to tread lightly.

"Why does that matter to your readers?"

"Personal interest."

"And then what? Will they want to know how long I cried? The months I went without reading a newspaper or watching a television? The hours of sleep I've lost?"

We stared at each other for a long moment. I could have been wrong, but I thought I saw a slight softening in his expression.

"I agreed to talk about Christian," I finally said. "I didn't agree to open up a vein and drain my soul for you."

"Even if I release those photographs of us?" His voice was soft and low. Which was almost sexy, if one ignored the threatening words. "What will you do to stop that?"

I thought of my overworked press secretary and the palace staff that had worked tirelessly to orchestrate a royal wedding and then dismantle it, piece by piece. I thought of the stacks of tea towels and souvenir mugs that had mysteriously disappeared from gift shops around Drieden. The effort to maintain the illusion of my life was monumental and never-ending.

Letting Nick publicize those photographs could bring it all crashing down. Another scandal on the heels of my disastrous wedding would not be forgiven—by Big Gran or the country.

Maybe I wasn't sure how to fulfill my duty to the Crown after I'd failed so spectacularly at the whole royal wedding thing, but I wasn't ready to burn the whole monarchy down. I wouldn't submit to an unscrupulous reporter's blackmail. But I would make him a deal.

"I'll answer fifteen questions. About Christian only," I warned him. "After that, you'll delete your photographs and we'll never speak again."

Nick pulled back and crossed his arms, looking at me as if I'd spoken in Chinese.

"Perhaps you haven't noticed, you're in no position to bargain with me," he said pointedly.

I looked out over the crowd in the stadium, knowing that with just a few bells and trumpets, I could probably make them shout my name. One day, that anthem that they sang would be about me. Their queen.

Nick Cameron was in no position to bargain with *me*.

I turned and fixed him with my fiercest Princess Theodora stare. "That's my offer. There won't be a better one." I swept toward the door. "I'll call tomorrow at nine to arrange the details. You may stay until the match is over."

I couldn't resist a last peek over my shoulder before I left, only to see Nick staring at me with a strange, sad smile on his face.

My curious streak was dying to know what that was all about.

eight

NICK HAD INSISTED ON SOMEPLACE PUBLIC FOR OUR interview: The Drieden National Galleries. I had been nervous, but the museum was unexpectedly crowded on a Tuesday morning, and I realized that worked to my advantage. Everyone was too preoccupied with hustling bodies and jockeying for space to look at a plain, normal Driedener with glasses and a cap on.

Somehow, the crowds seemed to melt around Nick. No one stepped on his toes or jumped in front of him in the Renaissance wing. Of course, if I had dropped my disguise and announced my presence, I could have had the entire place cleared out in fifteen minutes and Nick and I could have enjoyed a private guided tour.

Other women looked at him when we walked by, which I appreciated. It meant they weren't looking at me, and that they were focused only on the rugged, well-built, green-eyed Scottish bastard next to me.

I turned left, trying to avoid the ever-popular Impressionist hall, and led Nick up a staircase to enter the much less popular portrait gallery.

"It will be quieter up here," I told him when he gave me a skeptical glance.

"Pictures of dead people?"

"*Important* dead people," I informed him. "Do you have the list or not? I don't have all day."

I had agreed to answer fifteen questions—no more, no less—and I had demanded that he provide me a list of everything he planned to ask. I had dealt with reporters like him before. They always tried to sneak extra queries in. Nick took a folded piece of paper out of his jacket pocket and handed it to me, sending a shock of static electricity through my fingers when his hand brushed mine. I ignored the sizzle and unfolded the paper.

He had listed exactly fifteen questions in a tight black hand, just like I had required. But the jackass had written them in English.

"Can't you read it?" he asked, feigning concern.

I hoped my annoyed glance was answer enough. He seemed to be quite fluent in Driedish when he wanted to be.

"Number one. Names of Christian's security guards." I bit my lip. This seemed very real, all of a sudden. "Do you want their birth dates and registry numbers, too?"

"No." Nick stopped in front of a painting and waited for me.

"What if something is classified?" I asked, gesturing with the paper. "I won't answer that."

"I'll substitute another question," Nick allowed. Well, wasn't he generous.

"Aren't you going to write this down?"

"I have an extremely accurate memory."

That seemed unlikely. I held out my hand. "Are you recording me? Give me your phone." It was another one of the points we had negotiated. I refused to speak over the phone, lest I be recorded. He refused to meet in private. Hence, our current argument in front of seventeenth-century paintings.

Nick didn't move a muscle. "You'll just have to trust me, Princess." Then he pointed at a painting of a very somber black-haired man with a pointed beard and a crow sitting in a window. "He doesn't look very important."

Which was annoying on so many levels. "That was Olivier Ekkleson."

"Who?"

I sighed. "Olivier Ekkleson, eighteenth-century philosopher, scientist, and entrepreneur."

Nick still didn't look impressed.

"He was the father of the Driedish printing press."

"Which differs from the printing press that Gutenberg invented?"

"Of course. It was the first that printed exclusively in our native language."

Nick raised an eyebrow and I sighed again. This was going to be a very long trip to the museum if we kept this up. "Fine," I said, and then I rattled off the names of the two guards who had been assigned to Christian during our engagement.

I looked back at the paper. The next few questions regarded the address of Christian's apartment in the city, his business office, and his gym. Nick walked to the next portrait and I followed, beginning to feel frustrated. "You couldn't research all this?" I asked.

He nodded at the next painting. "And this fine woman? Did she invent the first Driedish pot that cooked Driedish food?"

The woman in question was bewigged and beribboned, captured with a coquettish smile on her lips and two intertwined roses on her lap. "Of course not. She was Elsa of Ganvine; at that time she was the mistress of Leopold the Fourth."

"A mistress next to a philosopher? What an open-minded lot you Drieveners are."

"Some might say there are a lot of similarities between the two," I said.

"They both do their best work in bed?"

"They tell people what they want to hear."

"No one's mother ever wanted them to grow up to be either." Nick grinned at me. "Next question, Princess."

In resignation, I gave him the answers to the next three questions on his list. "Tomas Claytere was his closest associate at work, his cousin was the person he spoke with on the phone the most, and never."

Nick clearly didn't believe me. "Never?"

"No."

"You *never* slept with him. Like, ever?"

"No!"

"You never spent the night at his apartment?"

"I don't have to explain this to you."

"You promised to answer my questions."

"And I have."

"But now I have so many more," he said with a sly smile. "A beautiful engaged woman who doesn't spend the night at her fiancé's house? Was it a common hygiene problem or something harder to treat?"

I made a sound of frustration and skipped over the rest of the Renaissance portraits, feeling more and more annoyed at each echoing footstep behind me. Then my aggravation got the best of me. I spun and practically ran into Nick's chest, which ended up being convenient because I already had the impulse to jam my finger in his sternum. "Perhaps Christian and I didn't have the usual type of romantic relationship, but that doesn't mean I'm an idiot, and it doesn't mean that I don't want to kick him in the balls for what he did to me."

"Is this normal behavior for a princess?" Nick asked, his Scottish burr more obvious now that he was amused.

"Oh, shut up!" I couldn't take his sarcasm anymore. "Why do you want to know all this? What possible angle could you have to write an article about something that's old news?"

"It's very much *not* old news."

"It happened four months ago!"

"And no one has seen Christian Fraser-Campbell in those very same four months."

"Probably because he doesn't want to be kicked in the balls!"

Nick put his hands on my upper arms and turned me gently toward a large portrait of the Council of Kinervale during the reign of Otto the Pretender, and I realized too late that a group of tourists was walking and talking by us. "Now tell me who these very proper men were," he said, his lips close to my ear, his voice the only one I could hear.

His left hand drifted to my waist, curling intimately there. I knew he probably was only pretending to be an attentive boyfriend, to distract any curious visitors. But his hand lingered, and my silly heart raced. It had been too long since anyone had held me this close. After taking a moment to collect myself, I managed to tell Nick, "It's the first Driedener rock band."

"And their name?"

"Hell Hath No Fury Like a Woman Scorned."

He chuckled softly. "When was the last time you saw Christian?"

I hung my head low, remembering the night. "At my father's house. There was a ball two nights before the wedding."

"And where have *you* been the past four months?"

I turned and walked past the next three portraits, my eyes not really seeing the historical figures I knew so well. Instead I thought of the long days and nights since my wedding day, of how Christian's desertion meant I'd had to go into isolation, even though I had done nothing wrong.

We stopped in front of a more modern painting. "My great-great-grandmother," I said before Nick could prompt me. "Lucretia of Luxembourg."

He looked between me and Lucretia with that dubious expression I was beginning to know so well. "I don't see the resemblance."

Perhaps there wasn't one, not on the outside. Lucretia had been a big-boned woman, with raven hair pulled tightly away from her face. But I knew that Lucretia's blood was running true within my veins today. "She was the first princess to ask for a divorce."

"Did she get one?"

I shook my head. "No. It was unheard of. But they sent her to Perpetua to live out the rest of her days as a compromise."

"Perpetua?" he echoed.

"It's an island that was transferred to my family from the Holy Roman Empire about four hundred years ago."

"I've never heard of it."

I shrugged. "That's not surprising. It was first home to a convent that was then fortified in the seventeenth century. It's now just used as a retreat for the family, but back then it was where they used to send the women who couldn't be controlled."

"Like Lucretia." It wasn't a question, so I didn't answer it. Even Nick's non-questions were irritating.

We had reached the end of the hall and I saw a children's station nearby, with cups of crayons for mini DrieLdeners to doodle their art to hang on the wall. I palmed the stub of a green crayon and stood for a minute, scribbling down more of my answers for Nick. To hell with it. He would get these words from me and nothing more.

How long had you known Christian before the wedding?
Two years.

Which bank is he with?
Royal Bank of Drieden.

What car does he drive?
Land Rover.

Why did he leave?
I don't know.

How can I contact him?
I don't know.

Where is he now?

I don't know.

I refolded the paper and handed it back to Nick. We walked silently down the next hall of the portrait gallery, even though I could have told him a thousand more facts about each of the notable Driedeners hanging on the museum walls. Especially because here, at the end? These were people I knew. My aunt Beatrice. My father, the Crown Prince. A whole section of Aurelia portraits, in oil and ink and film.

At the very end of the hall, right before the exit, there was a freshly painted rectangle where a frame had been recently removed. Off to the side was a smaller spot, where a plaque had hung, telling the world that the blank space had once held the official portrait of Princess Theodora of Drieden and her betrothed, the ninth Duke of Steading, Christian Fraser-Campbell.

Maybe Nick knew what had been here. As a reporter, maybe he'd come to the museum when it was on display, or interviewed the museum employees who had taken it down. Or maybe he was a mind reader when he stood at my elbow and said in a low, husky voice, "You spent the last four months on Perpetua."

It wasn't a question. I didn't respond.

"The place they send women who can't be controlled," Nick continued, with the slightest hint of a question. Like he wanted me to confirm whatever he suspected.

I took a deep breath and imagined setting all these portraits on fire. "Have a nice life, Mr. Cameron."

He didn't follow when I left.

nine

I T WASN'T UNHEARD OF FOR MY SECURITY DETAIL TO request to speak with me. There had been times that Tamar and Hugh had wanted to update me on new safety procedures or introduce me to a new guard. Sometimes their supervisor, Corporal Mortogne, attended to review plans for public events like a parade or a wedding.

Even though I was perfectly capable of walking down to their administrative offices in the basement, the calendar said they were to meet me in my drawing room, and at half past ten exactly, there was a firm knock on my door.

Hugh walked in first, with Tamar following as she usually did. Officially, they were of equal rank, but I had noticed that the thick-necked, crooked-nosed, muscular man would charge in, while the lighter and more agile Tamar would follow several steps behind him.

They greeted me and I invited them to sit and get on with it.

"What do we need to talk about today?" I asked bluntly. These two had been with me for years. There was no need for ceremony.

Hugh spoke first. "We wished to go over a routine background check we ran, ma'am."

"It wasn't actually routine," Tamar interrupted.

She looked irritated. Whether it was with me, Hugh, or this background check I wasn't sure, but something about the look on her face made my stomach clench nervously. "Yes?" I asked, as vaguely as I could.

"It's about this man." Hugh opened a file to reveal a picture of Nick, which was clipped on top of approximately twenty more photos.

I swallowed hard. I should have known this would happen. Nothing stayed secret in the palace, not even my annoying blackmailer.

But I was still a princess of the Kingdom of Drieden. A monarch in training, my authority was in my blood, so I summoned all of the strength I could and kept my face as inscrutable as possible. "Yes?" I repeated.

Yes.

That was the best I could come up with. I'm a very intimidating princess.

Hugh's square jaw twitched. "Do you know who this man is?"

"Nick Cameron," I said. Then I remembered what I had told Tamar at the football match. "He's a friend of Christian's."

The two exchanged a look. That probably alarmed me more than anything. This pair could spend hours at my side and never acknowledge each other's presence. It was almost a professional requirement, an immense concentration and ability to ignore all superficial bits of activity and noise that would distract from doing the job of guarding my life.

They looked at each other now, communicating something silently. There was a threat in that file. I reached for it, snatching it neatly out of Hugh's leathery hands.

What I saw made my head swim. I leaned back into my chair, one hand going to my throat, as if that would turn on the air flow that had suddenly stopped making it to my lungs.

"It's ... not ... true ..." I finally stuttered. "This is a joke, right?" I looked up at Tamar for confirmation that this file was a total fabrication.

But when she asked, "How did you meet him?" that didn't make me feel any better or assure me that someone was playing a cruel, completely nonsensical joke.

"How did you get this?" I shook the file, ignoring her question. I most definitely did *not* want to disclose my nightly un-secure jaunts to my security staff.

"Like I said, routine background check," Hugh said.

"Not routine," Tamar said through gritted teeth. "We don't regularly conduct background checks on every person who enters your presence."

"But you did on . . . him." I couldn't say his name. "After the football match. *Why?*" I needed to know. What had they picked up on that I hadn't?

Hugh looked at Tamar now, letting her answer. So this had been her idea. Interesting.

"It was his Driedish." Tamar had stopped spinning her red pen between her fingers. Now she was holding it, probably unconsciously, like a dagger. "It was perfect. Too perfect for a Scot."

The irony is, the file confirmed that Nick was, indeed, Scottish. And so much more.

I flipped a page and reread the information that had startled me. Nick's birth name. His place of birth. His family, all dead except for a younger brother.

Christian Fraser-Campbell.

My ex-fiancé.

"Christian told me his brother was dead. That he died in Afghanistan," I murmured, my eyes rereading the page, two, three, four times.

No matter how many times I read it, the information didn't change. Christian's brother was alive. Roaming the streets of Drieden City. Drinking with me. Kissing me.

Had Christian known this? Had he lied to me? Or had Nick been miraculously resurrected somehow?

Hugh flipped open the second file he had. "Nicholas Fraser-

Campbell was a Royal Marine deployed to Helmand province, Afghanistan, eight years ago. According to this, he was caught in an ambush during the siege at Musa Qala and was killed in action six years ago, at the age of—"

My sharp inhale made Hugh stop in the middle of his sentence. I was staring at a photograph of Nick in a newspaper article from Edinburgh. The Duke of Steading's eldest son. Killed in action. A hero.

I'm not sure I would have identified my blackmailer as the man in this picture. Taken in a dress uniform, this photograph showed a clean, sharp handsomeness. He had not yet been punched, scarred, broken.

Another photograph was behind it, showing a group of men in fatigues in a desert, all with wiry beards. Nick was on the far right. A machine gun in his hand, he stared stonily into the camera. For some reason, I would have recognized this picture of him, even though his eyes were hidden behind wraparound sunglasses and a hat was low on his brow. This was the cocky bastard who would blackmail a princess.

The blackmail.

I *could* tell Tamar and Hugh about that part at least. They would deal with this not-dead man who would have been my not-dead brother-in-law.

"Where has he been?" I asked while still staring at the stone-faced jerk in the photo who, unfortunately, was not here to answer my many questions. "Why didn't he let his brother know he was alive? Does Christian know? Has he seen him? And why . . ."

My voice trailed off. I had so many questions myself. The problem was, *I* wanted to ask *him*. I wanted Nick to look me in the face and tell me exactly why he hadn't told me his true identity. Why he'd come after me at all, when his brother had left me humiliated in front of my country.

"Her Majesty was quite clear," I said, summoning all the royal haughtiness I could. "We will not mention the name of the man I was to marry in this house. And that includes talking to or about his family."

"But, Your Highness——"

I held up a hand and Hugh went quiet. Sometimes this princess act really worked. "Obviously, there are some issues that these men need to work out. However, it's their private family business, and this palace will have no further dealings with them. Myself included."

Hugh's face fell. I was sure he was looking forward to implementing his favorite interrogation techniques. Tamar, on the other hand, looked satisfied.

"We understand, Your Highness."

"No one contacts Nick Fraser-Campbell," I ordered them one more time before they left the room.

No one except me.

ten

NICK WAS WAITING FOR ME, AS WE'D AGREED earlier after a phone call from Jerome's office, at the bottom of the National Galleries' grand staircase. I'd come to confront him. To make him answer *my* questions for a change, but my breath caught when I saw him. He had a profile that was meant to be carved in stone for eternity. His lips went up in a small smile when he saw me, and a confusing mix of anger and feminine desire swept through me. He was unnervingly handsome—that much was true—but how could he think he could get away with his lie? He wasn't dead. At least not until I was done with him.

As soon as I reached him, his smile disappeared. His eyes focused on something beyond my left shoulder and his expression suddenly morphed into something serious and all business. "Walk with me." Without asking, he took my hand and threaded it through his arm, and then he was practically dragging me toward the Ancient History wing.

Nick's eyes scanned the crowd, but his body language was that of a concerned boyfriend doting on his girlfriend. *Girlfriend*. That confusing emotional stew stirred again. *He was Christian's brother.*

And I had kissed him.

"Let go of me," I growled.

"Not yet," he replied, sidestepping us both around a group of Japanese tourists all wearing their guided tour headphones. "We had an agreement."

"I didn't agree to be manhandled."

"You did agree to coming without guards."

"And I did," I said defensively.

"You were followed." As if he knew what I was about to do, he scowled. "Don't look."

He was making this up. He was a liar. I knew how to sneak out of the palace undetected and I had made sure no one followed me. I wasn't going to be distracted from the reason I'd arranged this meeting in the first place.

"I know who you really are."

Maybe that startled him, because he gripped my hand so tightly I thought my circulation was cut off. "You're pretty strong for a dead man."

He ignored me, so I went in for the kill. "Does Christian know you're alive?"

With that, he suddenly spun me into a side corridor that led to the restrooms. He picked up his pace, and I struggled to keep up with his long, fast stride.

"Where are we going?"

Nick kept me glued to him as we moved past the men's room. He peeked past the next door and, finding a staff break room, pulled us both in.

"Does Christian know you're alive?" I repeated.

My demand for an answer seemed to piss him off even more, so of course I had to keep pushing. "He doesn't, does he? You're sick. You come after me, *blackmail* me, when your own brother is still grieving you!?"

He leaned down, his face inches from mine. "You don't know what the hell you're talking about."

"I know a liar when I see one."

He huffed, clearly uninterested in my accusations. So I decided to say what I had come there to say. "You're Nick Fraser-Campbell. And Christian needs to know that you're alive!"

"He can't!" Nick's eyes went feral.

"You're telling him or I will!"

From somewhere up above us, there was a loud bang.

"I'm getting out of here."

"Why?" I demanded. This wasn't what I had imagined when confronting him about his true identity. My imagination had included a tearful, repentant Nick, standing below the portrait of King Wilhelm the Executioner for added effect.

Just then, a fire alarm went off, a high-pitched shriek echoing off the marble floors.

"*That's* why." He pushed me against a wall, then reached over and locked the door we'd just come through, which didn't make sense at all.

"Why are you locking the door?" I half-shouted over the screeching alarm. "There's a fire somewhere in the building!"

"We're not leaving that way." Nick nodded at the door. Considering we were in a dark, empty room with a flashing red exit sign hanging above our heads, I wasn't quite getting what he was saying.

A voice came over the intercom. "Please evacuate the museum. Emergency services are entering the museum."

"We need to go," I insisted.

"I won't go out that door."

"Why?"

"I don't feel like getting shot today."

"No one's shooting at you."

A boom sounded down the hall outside the door. I jumped and Nick grabbed me by the shoulders. "The ones who followed you in. The ones from the football match—the big guy and the little woman. And now they're coming for me."

"Why?"

"I'm sure it has something to do with the people who kidnapped Christian."

I smelled something rotten and sharp and looked down, where tendrils of white fog were climbing into the room under the door. Kidnapped Christian? What? I had come for answers and now there were more questions. And smoke bombs. Why?

"Thea." Nick took my chin in his hand and made me look at him. "You may be beautiful, but I'm not dying for you today."

A shot rang out. Two. Three. Four. There was no time. I couldn't think. I could only look into Nick's eyes, where I saw something indefinable that compelled me to say, "How do we get out of here?"

"You're not coming with me."

"You can't stop me."

Well, he probably could have. But he pushed me along the wall until we hit a piece of paneling that Nick slid open, revealing an interior box about three feet wide. He swore when I jumped in first, and then he climbed in before sliding the door closed again. "Hold tight," he said. The box jerked. And then we were falling. Instinct made me clutch at him. Fear made me close my eyes and bite my tongue until I tasted blood.

The box had to be an elevator of some sort with no controls and no brake, because we stopped hard and suddenly. Nick's hand clamped over my mouth, which didn't stop me from screaming an obscenity. In our fall, I had ended up in Nick's lap, my back against his front. I felt his breath over my ear. "Shh . . ."

Surely someone could hear the mad throbbing of my pulse, the rush of blood through my head, but all was quiet until Nick whispered, "Jump."

The door opened, Nick shoved my spine, and I . . . jumped. Sort of. Mostly, it was gravity doing all the work as I tumbled into the blackness below and was enveloped in a foul, sticky Dumpster filled with black plastic trash bags.

Nick landed next to me and even in the darkness outside, I could see he'd jumped with far more finesse than me. But I didn't have time to admire his technique. Before I knew it, he'd grabbed my hand again, and we were climbing out of the Dumpster and running.

Nick seemed quite confident that he knew where he was going, and who was I to stop him? I didn't even know what was going on. Or where he was taking me.

I looked up and realized where we were; after all, I knew this city like the back of my hand. On the back side of the museum, looking down on the wide expanse of the dark murk of the Comtesse River that would let us sneak away undetected—from both whoever was after Nick *and* the police.

A good, compliant princess would run toward the police, back to safety, back to the palace, but there was no way Nick would come with me. And I needed to go with him. He had something I had wanted very badly for the past four months. Something I hadn't even realized I needed.

Answers.

Plus, for some inexplicable reason, I felt safe with him. Like he actually *would* take a shot for me, despite his declaring the opposite only minutes ago.

Nick dropped down to his knees, lifting a manhole cover half a block away from the museum.

Our eyes met, his holding a question for me—run back to my predictable, royal world or trust that he'd keep me safe today. I answered it by putting my foot on the top rung of the ladder.

I climbed down and then saw the lazy passage of the Comtesse below. "What now?" I shouted up to him.

"Jump!"

I let go of the ladder and the frigid water engulfed me a second later.

I'd never dropped twenty feet into any body of water before, much less a murky, cold, salty river running through one of the oldest European capitals, but there was a first time for everything. The cold stunned me, my eyes seeing nothing, but before I could panic, Nick hauled me out of the water and into a small, inflatable rubber boat that had been tied up on the riverbank.

I lay on the floor as he started the motor and got us out of there, going over in my mind all that had been said. I could no longer see the buildings of Drieden looming over the river.

Which meant we were north of the city.

Close to my father's house. Which was the last place I had seen Christian, at the ball celebrating our wedding two nights before we were supposed to say "I do."

eleven

"STRIP."

"Excuse me?"

Nick reached for my still-sodden sweater. "Take it off or I'll take it off for you."

My hurried step backward took me out of his reach, but could not protect me from his order. He was looking at me like he meant his threat. "Do you have any chips, trackers, anything like that on you?"

I shook my head and noticed my hands were trembling with cold as I lifted my sweater. Even though it was late summer, the Comtesse had been freezing and Drieden was too far north for the sun to have completely dried me off as we'd puttered up the river. Nick looked critically at the sweater I'd just handed him, and then he tossed it into the fire he'd lit as soon as we'd arrived at this house.

"Hey!" I cried out, but my favorite blue cashmere sweater was already in flames.

Nick curled his fingers up at me. "Come on, off with the rest. The water would have probably fried any trackers, but we can't be sure."

"How could I possibly have any trackers on me? And just what am I supposed to wear?" I was shivering in my jeans and undershirt, with goose bumps covering my bare arms, but I was certain that being in the nude, roaring fire aside, would result in me being even colder.

"And whose house is this?" I demanded as Nick disappeared into a nearby closet and clothes flew back at me: a black T-shirt, men's large. Black ski pants, also men's large.

"For Christ's sake." Nick stalked back to me and reached for the belt loop on my jeans. "Can't you do as you're told?"

The absurdity of that question stunned me into mute immobility, but when he unbuttoned my jeans I snapped back into reality. "I'll take it from here," I informed him as I worked the wet denim over my hips.

"The woman will freeze to death for the sake of her pride," he muttered to himself.

"Pride?" I choked, hopping on one foot, then the other as I tried to pull the pants off my ankles. This was the least proud moment of my life. "How about you're a *stranger* and you've just demanded that I undress in front of you?"

"To keep you alive, Princess." He nodded at my white undershirt, so thin and damp he must have been able to see that no trackers were sewn into the seams.

"No," I said, using my hands to cover my chest. "I don't have anything on me." I slid one of my hands to cover my bikini briefs. "And why am I the only one who has to strip? Why are my clothes in the fire and you get to keep yours?"

One of his eyebrows rose. "You'd like me to strip?"

"Yes. I mean, no."

This caused the slightest of smirks to appear on his stern face. Right before he reached for my arm, pulling it toward him and running a practiced finger over my skin.

"Are you serious? You think I have some . . . implant under my skin?"

"They do it to dogs. They could do it to princesses." He dropped my arm then, but when he reached for the other one, I clasped his broad forearm with my hand.

The man was checking for devices under my skin. He was most definitely not a reporter.

"Who are you, really?" I demanded.

He dropped my arm. "Get dressed."

I looked at my clothes in the fire, already nothing more than a charred pile of fibers. Oh how I wished I could rebel against that command, but even with the fire, I was still thoroughly chilled. I scooped up the men's clothing Nick had tossed at me, and since it seemed clean enough, I quickly pulled the black shirt over my head.

"You will answer me." My voice had a more imperious tone than a shivering woman shimmying into borrowed pants should be able to muster, but I'd had a lifetime of practice at imperial behavior.

Once I was thoroughly drowning in a very unflattering ensemble of clothing that was five times too big for me, we faced each other.

"Forgive me," he started. "I failed to introduce myself properly at our first meeting. I am Nicholas Fraser-Campbell."

I shivered. Maybe I was still cold. Maybe it was the thrill of hearing his true name with all that cool, calm, deadly authority.

"And who do you work for?" I asked.

His chin lifted slowly and he watched me with keen eyes.

"Who do you work for?" I repeated. "I know you're not a reporter. You're much too thorough in escaping from museums for that."

He hesitated for a half second. "I work for the British government."

"But not in an official capacity, surely."

"Official enough."

"But you have a death certificate!"

His mouth turned up slightly. "My agency considered that a recruiting bonus." He paused. "I'm an intelligence officer."

"You're a spy," I concluded, part annoyed, part in awe. "Like James Bond."

Nick made a face that clearly communicated what he thought of tuxedo-wearing martini aficionados.

The truth of this situation settled in and I had to laugh. My life was seriously fucked up. I was left at the altar by my fiancé, only for his brother—a British-freaking-spy, no less—to take his place. "So the British government sent you here to find out why my fiancé left me." I threw my hands up in the air. "Why not? I couldn't figure it out, so why not ask some foreign spies to look into it?" I started to laugh hysterically. I couldn't help it. This had to be a joke.

Nick's brows drew together. Perhaps it was because of my crazy cackling. Maybe I was finally, irrefutably, losing my mind.

"This operation is not about your wedding."

He was so serious. And so was the word *operation*.

And then I remembered another serious word that Nick had used back at the museum: *kidnapping*.

My stomach clenched as things started to hit home. "Where is Christian?"

Nick shot me a warning look and went to peer out the windows before shuttering them.

If he wasn't going to talk, I was. "You said he was kidnapped. So he's not at his estate in Scotland?" The day after the wedding, Big Gran's secretary had told me that Christian had gone home. The media had reported that he was ensconced behind the gates of Brisbane Castle, the family seat, and had been publicly shamed into hiding after his cowardly escape from Drieden.

"Of course not—that's the first place you'd look," I responded to my own inquiry in a matter-of-fact way. "So was he kidnapped before or after the wedding march? Or is this all just a story Christian has concocted to save face?"

He threw his hands up in the air in frustration. "You ask so many questions you're going to drive me insane."

He thought he was going to go insane? I gripped the back of the nearest chair as I felt my heart race. Four months had gone by and I still had no answers as to why I had been the unwilling victim in the largest royal scandal in centuries. "Please tell me something," I finally said, my voice hoarse. "What has happened? Why are you here?"

Nick's expression softened. "After the . . ." He faltered. "The wedding day, there were inquiries made by the Driedish government as to the whereabouts of your fiancé. When it was determined that he had not reentered the United Kingdom, there was a review."

Inquiries. Reviews. It all sounded so sterile. So institutional. So mundane.

"And what did the review say?" I had never hoped so hard for a mundane answer.

Nick's eyebrows jerked together. "Around the same time, there was a separate inquiry into some secret financial records that had wound up at Christian's law firm. Papers that some British analysts believed implicated the Crown in some way."

My head swam. "Why would Christian's law firm have documents regarding the British monarchy?"

His expression turned careful again. "Not the British monarchy. The Driedish monarchy."

I DECIDED NOW WOULD BE A GOOD TIME TO SIT. MY BRAIN worked better when it wasn't trying so hard not to faint.

Finally, I found my voice again. "I have more questions."

Nick had gone back to looking out the window, but he glanced over his shoulder. "No doubt."

"Whose house is this?"

"John Lock, the lockmaster."

"You're making fun of me."

"I would never."

"Whose clothes are these?"

"A colleague of mine uses this house sometimes. They look like they're his size."

"Another James Bond?"

Nick's jaw worked. "His name is Cornelius. Max Cornelius."

"Does your agency believe that there's a connection between Christian's disappearance and the Driedish Crown?" I asked quickly, hoping to catch Nick off guard. It worked for a moment before he collected his cool.

"That's what I'm here to find out."

My eyes felt hot; my cheeks flushed. I had woken up this morning ready to confront Nick over his true identity. But this had become something I wasn't sure I could handle.

"You can leave, you know." Nick's statement broke the silence.

"Excuse me?"

"You're free to go back. I'm not stopping you. I expect it will take ten hours for Driedish police and royal security to find this house. You're welcome to stay until they surround it with a few dozen men pointing SG 540s at the door in case a bad guy pokes his head out first."

"Was it Tamar and Hugh shooting at us?" I asked.

He continued as if I hadn't spoken. "Your other option is to walk out that door, find a telephone, and call whatever secret number the royal security office gave you. You'll be picked up in ten minutes."

The fact that he knew all these details about Driedish police and royal security procedures was interesting, and it added even more questions to the ones I already had about the kind of man I was dealing with. "You'd let me walk out of here?"

"I wouldn't hold you against your will."

"Let me rephrase the question." I stood again. I was feeling stronger. "Is it safe for me to go back after Tamar and Hugh shot at us at the museum? After they know that you're Christian's brother?"

Nick fell into a nearby chair and rubbed a hand over his face, like it was a burden to explain perfectly obvious things to me. It was rude. And impolite. I was a member of the royal family, and I deserved some answers. Which is what I said.

"No."

"No what?" It wasn't clear which question he was refusing to answer.

His fists clenched and unclenched, as if he were fighting—and losing—some kind of inner battle. "I'm trying to answer. But I don't know. On the one hand, you're their princess. The likelihood of your security guards shooting at you again should be low."

"But they've already done it once."

"To be fair, perhaps they were only shooting at me."

"Well, which was it?"

He pushed out of his chair like he was frustrated by something and said with a snarl, "When someone has a gun pointed at me, I don't stop and ask them for a cup of tea to discuss their motivation." The space between our bodies seemed to shrink. "I do what I was trained to do. I react according to the situation. Attack when necessary. Protect the asset."

There was my answer. In the intensity of his gaze, in his frustrated words.

He had protected me. Because I was in danger. From my own guards, from whatever forces had stopped Christian from showing up to the altar at the cathedral.

"I'm not going back to the palace," I informed him.

"Think long and hard about that."

"I don't know if I can trust the people who are supposed to protect me, but you did."

He let out a sigh. "You're more trouble than getting shot at, you know that?"

"You're the one who brought me here," I slung back.

"And I'm wishing to God I hadn't."

I allowed myself the faintest of smiles as he stalked out of the room. Finally, someone who didn't kiss my asset.

twelve

N THE EIGHTEENTH CENTURY, MY ANCESTOR KING Leopold III funded the building of a system of canals throughout the lowlands of Drieden to further the reach of the capital's shipbuilding industry and nautical trade.

Today the canals are mostly used for domestic tourism. It's a tradition for Driedish families to rent houseboats and share them with friends and neighbors to cruise up and down the canals, enjoying the slim window of summer our little country enjoys.

The house that Nick had brought us to was a narrow chimney of stone, about one room wide and three stories high. Situated at the first canal lock, it had probably been built for the lockmaster to collect tolls and supervise the lock machinery. At some point, someone had modernized the bathroom and windows and added an extra room along the shoreline, but other than that, it was as much the same as it had been in the seventeenth century, with wide oak-plank floors and a smoky coal haze that had never quite filtered out of the rooms.

It was also a very strategic house, I realized, as I watched the early morning activity around the lock. Perched three stories above the riverbank, I could see the boats arriving, full of Driedish families, sleepy mothers clutching their coffees and trying to keep anxious children away from the rails of the deck.

I heard Nick's entrance into the room. Three-hundred-year-old floors did not keep secrets quietly. "You didn't sleep," he said.

"No," I said simply, not offering that I hadn't slept much since Christian left. Or that I couldn't sleep, worried as I was about Nick slipping out into the night.

"There's breakfast on the table." I gestured toward what I had found in the cupboards in the tiny kitchen. Nick opened the paper wrapping of the traditional dried sausage. "You can have the rest. I've had enough."

"Last chance to leave."

I had thought about my situation a lot during the night. Of course I had. What was the best option for me? For Christian?

Beyond a general statement that had been released to the media, no one had reported hearing or seeing my former fiancé since he'd left me at the altar.

The narrative had been easy enough to believe. Christian Fraser-Campbell was publicly ashamed, driven to hide his face because he had been the fucktard to jilt the storybook princess, thereby depriving the world of their fairy-tale romance. I had believed it, too. The tale had been a healing balm for my red-hot humiliation.

But in the silence of the night in this funny little house in my too-big borrowed clothes, alternative narratives had begun to take shape and substance.

Christian had not been seen for four months. Although I had no evidence that he had been kidnapped, as Nick alleged, I also had no evidence that he was free.

I didn't know where Christian was, but I had to find out. Duty had been instilled in me from the time I was old enough to put my hand on my heart during the national anthem. Duty required that I assure his general safety, at the very least, before I kicked him in the balls.

"As I said last night, I'll be going with you," I answered Nick politely.

He exhaled roughly. "Wrong answer."

"You know a lot of things. About my city, about escape routes out of the museum, about the capabilities of palace security forces. But one thing you don't know right now is where Christian is, and you'll never be able to piece together his last weeks in Drieden without me or the people who work for me. Which is why I will be accompanying you as you search for clues to his disappearance." I smirked at his horrified expression. "After all, who better than me to tell you everything you want to know about Christian's life here in Drieden?"

His scowl deepened. Probably because I had just laid out a perfect case.

"And one more thing. I am a royal princess of Drieden and you are on my soil, conducting this investigation *only* because I am allowing it. You will tell me any new information you come up with, and you will consult with me in all things. Are we clear?"

Nick answered me with a raised eyebrow. Good enough.

As he grumpily helped himself to the rest of the sausage, I couldn't help but wonder about the questions that I had *not* been able to answer in the middle of the night. What had happened to Nicholas Fraser-Campbell? Why had he not returned to his family after serving in Afghanistan? And why show up now? Just to find Christian?

And perhaps the most important question of all: Did I trust Nick Fraser-Campbell?

Inexplicably, the answer was yes. Mostly.

He had blackmailed me, tricked me, and taunted me. I realized now that it wasn't because of me. It was because of the brother whom he had come back to find.

And he had never hurt me. Not really. There had been threats, and a few glares, but I had the distinct impression that I meant something to him. My heart tugged a little. There was a strange attraction between us, and so far, I hadn't felt unsafe with him. Now that I knew he was a British agent of some sort, I felt more confident having him on my side. After all, Queen Victoria had ensured her children married into every European royal family, so I had some important connections in London.

But I was also realistic. He was a man with a death certificate already filled out. He might have nothing to lose. Or everything to lose.

God help me, I wanted to find out which it was.

He was magnetic and mysterious, quite possibly dangerous, but even trundling after him in clothes that didn't fit, I felt more alive than I had in months. Maybe years.

When it was time to leave, I followed him down into the cellar of the house, where we had entered the evening before, that led to the river. We passed the short dock where the night before, Nick had set loose the inflatable boat we'd used during our escape, and walked along the dirt path that flanked the canal, under the low-limbed trees heavy with late summer leaves. There were no security cameras under here and no one to report our passage, as the neighbors at this early hour were either sleeping or on a boat, ready to sail up the canal.

A few hundred meters away from the lock house, Nick hopped off the trail and onto a dock where a typical Driedish canal boat was moored. We were above the lock, so there were no other ships nearby— most people were heading into the countryside, away from the hustle of the city.

"Whose yacht is this?" I asked in a low voice when Nick stepped onto the deck, clearly intending to take control of the vessel.

"My friend's," was his easy reply.

"Max Cornelius? Or John Lock?"

"Yes."

I shook my head. "I deserve an answer before I steal a boat."

Nick gave me a scornful look. "You're not stealing it; I am."

"I thought you said your friend owned it."

"Didn't say he knew about me using it."

"Are there ladies' clothes on board?" I asked as I pitched forward, tripping on the hem of the overly long pants yet again.

"Go below and find out. And *stay* below."

"Don't order me around."

"Yes, Your Majesty."

"Don't . . ." Frustration welled. "Don't call me that."

"Why?"

"Because I'm not a queen."

Nick's smiled turned sardonic. "That's right. Let's stick to protocol, then. *Your Highness*."

"That's not what I meant. I'm just . . . Thea," I finished lamely, wishing I could communicate more clearly this morning. But I hadn't slept properly in weeks, I was possibly on the run from my own rogue security forces, and this man, with his cool, capable confidence, threw me off my stride.

Nick nodded toward the stairs leading below deck. "See what you can find. But when I say hide, please do, Your Highness. Unless you'd like to be shot today?"

I didn't bother replying to that.

Below deck, I opened some cabinets and found smaller-sized men's clothes, which I quickly changed into. I took the opportunity to wash up in the cabin and almost fell into the toilet when the boat lurched and motors whirred somewhere to my right.

I climbed the stairs back up and peeked over the deck, quickly seeing that Nick, once again, had orchestrated the perfect escape.

The canal lock had opened and we were now in the middle of a large flotilla of sailboats, houseboats, fishing boats, and more.

And as we crept up the narrowing canal, I heard police sirens in the distance, from the direction of the city.

Nick glanced that way as well, in a disinterested fashion, before turning his attention to the difficulties of steering a boat slowly in a crowded, narrow sea.

His confidence was supremely magnetic. In my mind, he was Batman and Jason Bourne and John Wayne knit together in a dark and attractive package. And I had no idea where we were going, or why, but I knew I had never felt like this before.

And I liked it.

thirteen

WE'D DOCKED FOR THE NIGHT. WHILE NICK HAD spent the day gathering supplies in the nearby village, I'd spent most of it thinking up some questions . . . and some answers.

"I need you to explain a few things to me."

Nick put down his newspaper. "The earth moves around the sun. Those funny little pieces of paper with your grandmother's face on them are called money, and no, you can't get pregnant that way."

"Are you trying to annoy me?"

"Well, it is my second favorite thing to do with you."

The reference to our kiss flustered me. Now all I could think about was kissing him again. I gave him a look because I would not be distracted.

"What happened to Christian?" I paused slightly, then decided to go for it. "I command you to tell me everything."

He smiled slightly. "You're so sexy when you get medieval."

Sexy? Me? Well . . .

No!

I lifted my chin, giving him my best Big Gran impersonation. He folded his newspaper. My imperiousness had clearly worked.

"The last time you saw Christian was two nights before the wedding, correct?" he asked.

"Yes. It's Driedish tradition for a royal bride to spend the day before her wedding in contemplation."

"Like a nun?"

I lifted my hands. "Last chance, I guess." Now it was my turn to ask a question. "When was the last time *you* saw Christian?" Once again, I wondered whether Christian had known his brother was alive before he'd disappeared.

Nick's smile faded. "That's not important."

Maybe it wasn't. I moved on and explained what I had been told after Christian disappeared, that he'd left the royal apartments sometime the night before our wedding and returned to Scotland without a word.

"And didn't you think that was strange?" Nick asked. "That Christian didn't leave you a message?"

"Of course it was strange. A princess being left at the altar is very strange indeed," I snapped.

A pregnant pause grew between us. Finally, Nick spoke, gruffly. "I've never been in his position, but it seems I'd want to talk to the woman I was supposed to spend the rest of my life with before I decided to run off."

"Maybe he knew he wasn't going to spend the rest of his life with me."

"What do you mean?"

"Maybe it was all a scam from the beginning." I hadn't allowed myself to speak those words aloud until now, but the possibility of it had percolated in my brain during those long nights on Perpetua.

Nick looked skeptical. "What would Christian have gained from such a stunt?"

"Fame. Money." I made a useless gesture. "He's the most infamous man in the world right now."

"Except he hasn't been seen in four months."

"And he's not at Brisbane Castle?" I asked. Again.

He shook his head in a single decisive slice.

"What evidence do you have that he's been kidnapped?"

"He's off the grid. No one knows anything."

"Well. That makes me feel a bit better."

Nick's brows furrowed. "How so?"

"Because I've spent the past four months not knowing anything, either," I replied before moving on to inspect the shopping bags he'd brought back to the boat.

All I'd asked for were some personal supplies: a toothbrush, a comb, and some clean underwear. When I saw what he'd bought, I groaned. "Really?" I said, digging into the bag and coming up with a half dozen black lace thongs dangling from my finger. "*These* are what you bought me?"

A mischievous glint sparked in his eyes. "I know you said I must consult with you in all things, but in this you failed to specify your preference, Princess."

Sometimes this man was so infuriating I wanted to knock him overboard. "Fine," I huffed, and shoved them back in the bag.

"Are you sure you don't want to discuss it further? It would be no problem at all for us to weigh the pros and cons of your knickers."

I flipped him the royal bird. Once again, I was going to have to direct this conversation away from Nick's dirty mind. "The last place I saw Christian was my father's house."

His eyes dropped over me, apparently still enjoying his imaginary thong debate, before he answered with a frown. "What's the name of it, Cello House?"

"Ceillis House. It's quite near here. Oh! I wonder if Christian could have left a note there. Or maybe some sort of indication about why he had to leave?"

Nick was now serious. "I'll have to break into the estate."

"We."

"Excuse me?"

"*We're* going to Ceillis House," I told him. "And we're not breaking in."

fourteen

KNEW ALL OF THE WOODS AROUND MY FATHER'S HOUSE. After docking the river yacht at the small pier at the neighboring property, I led Nick through the trees to the stream that would bring us directly behind Ceillis House. But first we ran into someone, as I had suspected we might.

The fisherman was of medium height, his middle age signified by a curved belly and a full array of costly and intricate fly-fishing tools tucked into the many pockets of his oilcloth vest. Pale strawberry-blond hair glinted in the morning sun as he turned and saw me.

"Thea, how lovely to see you."

"Hello, Father."

We did not embrace. We never had. Our relationship was cordial and warm as the current Drieden summer day, which is to say, warmish.

As Father was also Albert, the Crown Prince of Drieden, the Duke of Ceillis and Montaget, and currently the next in line to the throne, I didn't introduce Nick. It wasn't appropriate and frankly, my father didn't care. He barely noticed *me*, never mind the presence of what he'd assume was a bodyguard in black.

My father was obsessed with fly-fishing. A man with all manner of luxury at his fingertips, with enough power and influence to shape public opinion, even history, and the heir to the Driedish throne, chose to spend as many days as he could throwing tiny pieces of string and feather onto the surfaces of streams in the hope that a stray fish would decide it was time for lunch at exactly that moment. Gran had fought my father's nature for years, and had forced him to take part in day-to-day royal life. But after the divorce, everyone slowly started giving up in that endeavor. Whether it was because Father was unpopular or because he often put his foot in his mouth when he did participate in royal appearances, Gran now allowed him to live quietly at Ceillis House and away from palace life—unless she needed him for an important event in Drieden City.

A therapist could spend years unpacking my father's issues. Then again, the fact that I, a royal princess, was currently running away from her own security forces and sneaking around her own country would probably provide content for an entire encyclopedia of psychological analysis as well.

"I've come to pick up a few things from my rooms," I told my father. As we'd all learned, sometimes it was better to tell Father what needed doing than to ask him.

Asking him was frustrating for all involved, as my mother had learned when she asked him first for love, then affection, then a divorce. All of those requests had taken at least fifteen years to be processed by the distant, preoccupied mind of the Crown Prince of Drieden.

"Yes, of course." Father nodded. "You know the way in."

I caught Nick's wry expression. Father was a security guard's nightmare and our best friend today. He didn't ask questions, didn't get alarmed, and didn't care much about what went on around him.

"How's the fishing?" When I could, I tried to connect with the man. After all, we were in the same family business, and we'd have to work together, if nothing else, for the rest of his life.

Father grimaced at the sun. "It's not warm enough. The flies haven't begun to lay their eggs."

I nodded encouragingly. "They'll be out soon."

"I suppose," he said, but he seemed dubious as he frowned at the icy stream lapping about his ankles.

We left the Crown Prince of Drieden on the side of the stream, and I led Nick up the well-worn path to Father's country house.

Ceillis House was where my parents had lived when Henry, Sophie, Caroline, and I were young, before the divorce, when we'd had a relatively normal childhood for being heirs to the throne and all. Occasionally we were called to Big Gran's side for state functions. A few times a year we were dressed in stiff silks and stifling wools to shake hands and salute sharply. For the rest of our childhood we played in the large nursery, rode horses under the sharp eye of Mother's stable master, and attended school at the village academy.

In short, we were raised as typical, if privileged, Driedish children. Even though it was no longer my home, I still could appreciate the handsome symmetry and impressive size of Ceillis House.

Nick had walked behind me as my pretend bodyguard while we were still in my father's sight, but once we were beyond the woods that traced the stream, he was by my side, alert and in charge. "There are no security guards?" he asked for the twentieth time as I opened the doors to the back terrace.

"At the gate," I explained for the twenty-first time. "That's it. No one bothers to come out here." There were acres and acres of farmland and woods surrounding the house, and the paparazzi had stopped hounding Father when my parents' divorce was finalized ten years ago. No one was interested in photos of my father fly-fishing. Or reading. Or drinking coffee. That was as exciting as life got at Ceillis House.

Which was why my father's offer to host the traditional pre-wedding ball had been so surprising. I'd suspected Big Gran might have had something to do with the invitation, but I had been too distracted by the wedding plans to really look into it. I was told that Father wanted the ball at Ceillis House, and I'd agreed with no questions asked.

Now, walking upstairs and into the bedroom that I used on my visits, I encountered memories of that night, of Christian, of endless wedding talk and the nonstop nerves that had flipped my stomach upside down and inside out for months.

"Are you sure no one will report this?" Nick couldn't resist one more look down the hall before quietly shutting the bedroom door.

"Father keeps a minimal staff. They're trained to keep to themselves." If my father hadn't raised a fuss, no one else would question my presence. At least, not until I was long gone.

"What are you looking for?" Nick asked when I immediately went toward the wardrobe and started rifling through it.

"Clothes," I snapped. "I'm not wearing your friend's pants anymore." I pulled out jeans, sweaters, and my own preferred brand of underwear, and then went to find a suitcase in the closet. As both a perk and necessity of being a princess, I had a wardrobe in several houses and palaces around the country, just in case.

When I came back into the bedroom with a suitcase with handy wheels, I found Nick putting my clothes back into the wardrobe.

"What do you think you're doing?" I demanded.

"You can change. But we can't carry out a suitcase."

"No one has to carry it. It has wheels." I reached into the wardrobe to get my clothes back out and he put his arm across the opening.

"If you want all your clothes, you can stay here."

I stared at him.

"Your father might not have any security on this floor, but this is still the house of the heir to the throne. Someone will notice if you're hauling out a suitcase."

"I'm Princess Theodora. I'm allowed to carry whatever I want, wherever I want."

We were at a standstill. He was doing that cold tough-guy act. I was doing my haughty princess thing.

"Shouldn't you be looking for clues about Christian?" I asked, with a challenge in my voice.

I got him there. He looked at my suitcase with wheels, shook his head, then said, "One backpack. Then you can show me Christian's room."

"Fine," I said through gritted teeth. He dropped his arm and let me pull out one change of clothes to wear, one to carry. After a brief internal debate, I decided to change right there in front of him. If the Scot was a prude, he could choose to walk out of the room.

He didn't.

I shed the clothes that presumably belonged to Max Cornelius and began donning the clothes that belonged to another invented persona—Princess Theodora of Drieden.

After I pulled a sweater over my head, I saw Nick watching me, his green eyes aflame like the fire he'd built in the lock house. While it was true that Driedeners were comfortable with nudity, I was not prepared for the heat that licked down my spine under his intense gaze, so I attempted to distract us both with yet another question.

"So what will we look for in Christian's room?"

That did the trick. Nick squinted out the window, which was simply draped with white sheer curtains. "This was the last place he was seen."

Which wasn't an answer at all, really. Was I going to have to do all the work myself? I zipped up the backpack I had found in a bottom drawer and pulled on an old pair of riding boots. With the amount of scrambling through weeds and brush we'd done this morning, the boots seemed a better choice than any of the other options in a princess's spare closet.

"This way," I said.

Christian had stayed in the guest wing on the third floor. We didn't pass anyone on our trip across the house, which was normal. Because

Father used only his own apartment of rooms, there was no reason for maids or other servants to wander the halls of the guest wing at ten a.m. on a Thursday.

Nick stayed alert and eagle-eyed even as we walked in solitude and shut the door behind us. The room was neat and I saw no evidence that anyone had ever stayed here, much less a guest four months ago. There was no half-packed suitcase on the floor, no rumpled bedsheets or a cap left off the toothpaste. But then again, there wouldn't have been even when Christian was here. When guests stayed at Ceillis House, servants unpacked for them, ironed their shirts, laid out warm towels before their bath, and turned the bedside lights on low so that when a bridegroom returned from his wedding ball, his chamber would be cozy and comfortable.

Nick slowly circled the room as I told him all this, helpfully describing the typical hospitality practices of my father's house and how nothing unusual had happened that night.

"We said good night at about two in the morning and then he came up here."

Something about that made Nick react with a sardonic lift of his eyebrow.

"What?" I demanded. "That's what happened."

"He was fucking hopeless, wasn't he?"

"At what?"

"At being your boy toy." Nick made a clicking sound. "Two nights before your wedding, you sleep apart from your fiancé? Hopeless."

I didn't want to hear this again. "Look, I know it's hard for someone like you to believe that two people would act with appropriate decorum in the Crown Prince's house. Not everyone has to strip off their clothes and . . ."

Nick held up a finger to his lips and I stopped abruptly. Obviously, he wasn't interested in my relationship with his brother. He just wanted to push my buttons, and I needed to stop reacting when he did.

The guest room had a simple bed, a small writing desk, a wardrobe, and two chairs flanking the fireplace. Nick had his other forearm resting on the mantel and then, with a flick of that wrist, he pulled a small black disc with a short wire from behind a painting of a bucolic hunting scene that hung above the mantel.

A heavy lead slug dropped into my stomach at the sight of the bug. Before I could ask who'd planted it, Nick lifted a very serious eyebrow. "We need to leave." His voice was low, barely audible.

"Why?"

He wiggled the black disc. "People with guns are looking for us, remember? We can't take the risk that they're not listening in and pinpointing our location right now."

The memory of the museum flashed in my head. Would that happen again? Here? Where I had grown up? Bullet holes shattering the pastoral quiet? Shredding Nick's body?

I swallowed the nausea that rose in my throat as I flung open the wardrobe doors, tore the curtains away from the wall, and toppled the careful row of linen-covered pillows on the bed in search of anything Christian might have left behind.

With shaking hands, I opened a desk drawer and in the next moment, Nick gripped my upper arm.

"How long?" I mouthed.

"How fast can you run?"

Not fast enough, I reckoned. There were no secret trash chutes that would shoot us out of harm's way this time. And there was a wide expanse of lawn around the house where we would be instantly exposed—and slow—as we headed back to the river. So I thought of something better.

Two minutes later, we were on the brick path to the stables. Three minutes after that, I had one of my father's stoutest polo ponies saddled up. There were others that were faster, but this one, named Hercules, would take the both of us.

I swung up on the saddle and offered my hand to Nick, who looked doubtful for a half second before grabbing my hand and landing behind me. He pulled me back into his lap, his arm tight around my middle, and thirty seconds later I was directing Hercules down the tree-lined lane behind the paddock. It wasn't used much anymore. A hundred years ago it was a back entrance for service carts and servants. My siblings and I had raced down here on foot and on our ponies as children, hiding from instructors and nannies, and today, I spurred Hercules as fast as he could go.

Five minutes later we were at the spot where the gate used to be before security had gotten tighter in the seventies. Now there was a large iron fence with ivy and weeds growing tall around it.

"What now?" Nick asked just before we heard the whirring sounds of a helicopter flying over our heads. Through the thick green tree cover, we saw that the helicopter was flying toward Ceillis House, which gave us just enough time to get away, through the woods and back to the neighbor's pier.

I threw my leg over and jumped off Hercules. Nick followed me as I burrowed through the weeds and showed him where two loose poles could be wiggled apart, just wide enough for a certain polo instructor to meet a princess (and mother of four) for an illicit love affair.

I'd seen Marco scrambling through one day while I was playing hide-and-seek with my sisters. Even then it had seemed very amateurish, but now I appreciated that simple was often best.

Thirty minutes later, once we were back at the canal, a single black helicopter shot across the sky above our heads. There was no way it could have identified me, a tiny speck below, but I ducked my head all the same.

fifteen

T HE NEXT MORNING, ON OUR YACHT IN THE MIDDLE
of the river, Nick dumped a stack of newspapers and weekly
magazines on the table and pointed to the one on the top of the
pile. "You've been missed."

My heart stilled. I never thought the palace would have told the media about my disappearance. Turned out they hadn't—maybe my luck
was holding. The headline read, "Theodora in Hiding."

I had missed a scheduled event at the St. Ignatius Children's Hospital the day before and the palace had made excuses for me. "Apparently,
I have a touch of the flu," I said to Nick's back as he made himself a
coffee.

"You look well enough to me," he grumbled.

"But insider sources say that I'm really recovering from a fresh bout
of heartbreak," I said, paraphrasing the article. "They say I'll never
be the same and that large crowds and open spaces make me ill now."
I chuckled at the reporting. It was far from accurate, but stories about
me seldom were.

But in the sports section, I found a more likely story, with an accompanying photo that showed my sister Caroline standing behind her

husband, Stavros DiBernardo, at the Hungarian Grand Prix. Her arm was wrapped around his shoulder, and she was laughing at something he'd said.

She looked good.

Healthy.

Even though my formerly responsible sister had run off and eloped while I'd been exiled on Perpetua, I was happy for her—really I was.

She deserved to choose her life.

One of us deserved that.

"Why did you buy so many?" I turned the pages, leaving my sister behind and looking for something more interesting than how my flu-like symptoms were caused by my grief over my ex-fiancé. It was as if Lucy had written the headlines, what with the obsession about all my imaginary symptoms.

"I like information."

"What kind of information?" I paused on a political report on the second page of *The Driedener*. The Liberal party leader had made another incendiary call for republicanism.

Nick slid into the banquette across from me and selected four of the papers for himself. "Helpful information."

"I have lots of helpful information. Have you thought of that?"

"I did. But when I gave you a list of questions, you were less than helpful."

I sniffed. "To be fair, you were blackmailing me and I thought you were a reporter. Perhaps I wasn't inclined to share openly."

Nick looked over the top of a newspaper. "Perhaps."

I continued as if he hadn't spoken. "At some point, you're going to have to tell me what you're looking for. I can't help you if you don't trust me."

Nick scanned the back page of *The Times*, then put it aside. "Of course I trust you," he said in what was a very placating tone as he pulled *Le Monde* across the table, pausing on a story before absently creasing the upper corner of the page.

"Then why won't you answer my questions?"

"Because you don't need to know the answers." It was as if he'd reached over and patted the top of my head. I hated being patronized.

"This is a need-to-know situation?" I watched as he set *Le Monde* on top of *The Times* and selected *The Wall Street Journal*.

"Yes." He opened the *Journal* and scanned until he stopped at the fifth page, where there seemed to be a full-page advertisement. He took a moment to thoroughly review the page and once again folded the top corner with his thumb as he read.

"Looking for something special?" I asked.

He went alert and still. "Excuse me?"

I tilted my chin at the large advertisement for lingerie that just had captured his full attention. Predictably. "For yourself or someone you care about?"

"For you, in fact. Might as well make this trip a little more interesting."

I held out the copy of *The Driedener* across the table. "Would you like to look at this one?"

"Why, are they discussing your lingerie sizes?"

"Because I want you to be incredibly thorough in whatever research you're doing."

"Sure," he said as he accepted the newspaper just as cool as could be.

"Are you trying to find out information on whether the police are looking for me?" I asked offhandedly.

"Of course they're looking for you, Princess. You're the second in line to the throne."

"I could be the first," I said, relishing his reaction. It was exactly what I had hoped for. He froze, and those green eyes got very serious as they rose from *The Driedener* and settled on me.

"First."

"Yes." I shrugged, second-guessing myself. "Well, maybe."

"First in line. Skipping over your father."

"It would seem so."

Even though I was enjoying finally being able to surprise Nick, he surprised me with his next question.

"Did Christian know?"

I hesitated before answering. What was the point of that question? "Yes," I finally answered.

"When did he learn this?"

"At the ball before our wedding. Big Gran pulled us aside to tell us her decision. It was to be announced on our wedding day that the succession was going straight to me."

"Did your father know?"

"Of course. Driedish law allows for the monarch to change the line of succession, as long as it's someone within two degrees of consanguinity. He and Big Gran have discussed it for years because really, he's horribly suited for it and he doesn't want it. But she was quite opposed to the idea until this year."

"Until Christian came along."

That threw me. "No. Well, I don't think . . ." I paused. "Why would it have anything to do with Christian?"

Nick stood and started pacing the small galley.

"How did Christian react when your grandmother shared this news with you?"

"He was shocked, of course. He seemed a bit overcome and said he would do his best to serve the country."

I remembered the moment well, because I had been a bit shocked and emotional. Preparing to take wedding vows in front of the country had been one thing. Knowing that I then would be taking coronation vows shortly afterward was life-changing, to put it mildly.

Nick stopped pacing and focused on me. "You said *maybe*."

"Well, nothing was final." I twisted my fingers together. No one had talked to me about it in the last few months. "It's all up to Gran, and it probably all had to be scrapped thanks to your brother."

"So you wanted the succession change?"

"*Want* has nothing to do with it."

"Doesn't it? You're gaining a crown."

I rolled my eyes. "It changed nothing but the timeline. It's not like I discovered I was a secret princess with—surprise!—an ancient hereditary claim to the throne. It's what I've been raised to do, sooner or later. It just so happened to be sooner, that's all."

Nick seemed unsatisfied with that answer, so I gestured toward the newspapers again, where the Liberal leader, Pierre Anders, was in a photo shaking his fist and grousing about democracy and the privileges of the 1 percent. "And I'm certainly not pleased to have to deal with this idiot."

Nick leaned over and saw what I was referring to. "You shouldn't speak like that of your government."

"I'm just saying it to you. And I don't have a problem with republicanism, as it goes, but—"

"You're a princess." Nick inserted. "Of course you'd have a problem abolishing yourself."

"No," I corrected him with a sharpness reminiscent of Big Gran. "I was going to say I don't believe the debate over republicanism should divide the country. We're all Driedeners. We should be able to discuss our government civilly."

"'The Driedish elites are sucking from the teat of our motherland,'" Nick read, citing the Liberal minister's quote from the article. "If that's not civil, I shudder to imagine what you think of me."

I assumed the sharp look I gave him was answer enough, and he let the matter drop and left the galley in a sober mood. Silently, I counted to fifty and then collected the newspapers that Nick had looked at. Following a hunch, I opened each one and checked the pages where he had distractedly dog-eared the corners.

Page 11, *The Times of London*. "Cayman Papers Move MPs Toward Reform."

Page 9, *Le Monde*. "The Cayman Islands: World's Wealth Capital."

Page 5, *The Wall Street Journal*. "Opinion: Wall Street–Cayman Connections Must Be Transparent."

Nick had found these articles with laser focus. Clearly the man was interested in something regarding the Cayman Islands.

But why?

My eyes dropped to the rest of the newspapers. I pulled *The Driedener* toward me, ignoring the lurid headlines about my still-conflicted feelings about my fiancé. "SHE WANTS HIM BACK!" the cover screamed.

I did want Christian back. But only so I could scream at him in person.

Maybe all these news articles were just a coincidence, like when a woman's morning toast just happens to burn in the figure of Christ. A believer would see the hand of God. A skeptic would recommend a new toaster.

The kind of military precision that Nick displayed reminded me of my brother, Henry. If he were here . . . I shook off that thought. Henry would have killed Nick by now, and thrown me off the boat along with Nick's body. The ultimate military man, Prince Henry of Drieden had no patience for illicit adventures like the one I was on right now.

Or the one I *wasn't* on right now, as I realized that the boat was no longer moving and the engine had been turned off.

I poked my head outside and saw that once again, we were waiting for a lock to open. Since it was still daylight, I threw on a pair of sunglasses before I went to find Nick, who was staring intently at the satellite navigation system.

"What's going on?" I asked.

"There's a mechanical problem with the lock. We'll be here for a few hours." He peered at the large wraparound sunglasses that I had found in a cabinet downstairs. "That's a good disguise."

He might have been sarcastic, but my sunglasses were a decent cover. No one was expecting to see Princess Theodora on the deck of a houseboat in a Driedish canal.

"A few hours?" I repeated. "Good. That will give you enough time to explain what's going on in the Cayman Islands."

sixteen

THE SMALL BLACK DISC THAT NICK HAD PULLED OUT from behind the painting in Christian's room at Ceillis House lay in pieces on the table inside our houseboat.

"Who do you think put the bug there?"

"Given that it's practically antiquated technology, maybe a private party. Or the Driedish government," Nick added.

"Excuse me?" His assertion made absolutely no sense. "The Driedish government would not spy on guests in the Crown Prince's home. And neither would it use antiquated technology."

Nick lifted a shoulder. "You're just not known for being the best spies."

"Drieddeners are good at everything," I insisted.

"You're not."

"Says the man whose football team was destroyed the other night," I muttered under my breath, for which I received a dark glare.

"Our striker had the flu."

"Of course he did."

"He caught it in Drieden."

"Because it's the best, most powerful flu in the world." I flicked a piece of black plastic on the table. "Drieden does *not* use antiquated technology." It seemed unpatriotic to give in on this point.

"Pardon, Princess, but how much do you know about surveillance engineering?"

I shut my mouth after that and resolved that if one day I ever returned to the palace and resumed my duties, I would get weekly briefings from the intelligence community just so I could successfully argue with Nick Fraser-Campbell.

"Can you get the recordings off it?"

"No." Nick shunted the pieces into his hand and slid them into a plastic bag. "They're transmitted via antenna."

"So we can't tell who put it there, why, when, or what they may have heard? Fantastic use of our time."

Nick didn't answer, but I saw an expression flicker over his face.

"Tell me," I demanded. "Remember our deal?"

"I prefer red silk."

I crossed my arms, mostly so I didn't reach out and throttle him. "Not that deal. The one where you tell me everything. Now what does this bug have to do with the Cayman Islands?"

After a moment, Nick looked resigned. "I can tell you we found two other devices like this—one at Christian's apartment in the city, the other in his law office."

"So this wasn't something left over from my parents' divorce? When they were fighting over my mother's villa on the French Riviera?"

"Um, no."

I sighed. What could I say? There had been lots of nasty shenanigans in my family during that time, and Mother had a fondness for extravagant real estate.

I wanted to get him back on track. He wasn't distracting me from this. "But neither Christian's apartment nor his office is in the Caymans," I said. "What's the connection?"

Nick tilted his head and took a moment before saying, "About six months ago, a large cache of documents from a Cayman law firm was leaked online."

Even though I had been in the middle of royal wedding craziness, I remembered the news stories, which had mainly focused on the revelations that Russian and Central Asian oligarchs apparently were much wealthier, with much greater influence in Western economies and democracies, than anyone had previously speculated.

"Most of the documents were released in the news. But certain intelligence agencies determined that not all the documents were made public."

As fascinating as the inner workings of the international spy organization were . . . "What does that have to do with Christian?" I asked.

Nick tapped a newspaper on the table. "Christian's firm, Boson Chapelle, had some of the papers that were not made public."

"What?" I shook my head. "How do you know? Why?"

"They're not sure."

"Who is 'they'?" Er. "Them?" I shook my head. "Who are we talking about here?"

"My side."

"Your side. The British? How would they know?" That didn't make sense. "If the papers weren't public, then how would British intelligence know what papers Boson Chapelle had, or whether Christian . . ." My voice faded as I realized the only way they would know was if . . . "The British were *spying* on my fiancé *before* he disappeared?"

Nick didn't look happy, either with my piecing it together or with the cold, hard truth: the British government had been spying on one of its own.

Except . . . Christian had surrendered his British passport right after our engagement and applied for Driedish citizenship. Which made this even worse. "You were spying on one of *my* citizens?"

He shrugged. "Currently, my country is negotiating several important treaties with the European Union."

I snorted. That was putting it lightly.

"And Drieden will be accepting the presidency of the EU next year."

"But what does that have to do with Christian?" I asked for the third time.

"You'll have to forgive British intelligence for presuming that a man might retain an . . . interest in the affairs of his former country. Perhaps he'd want to be involved in high-level trade negotiations, that sort of thing."

I stared at Nick. "Did you think he'd spy for you?"

Nick shook his head ruefully. "Me? No. Christian would have made a terrible spy. He only cared for one thing: himself."

I couldn't argue with that.

"But a man of his status? It's reasonable that people would want to know what he intended to do with his influence."

I bit my lip. Once again, I hated my naiveté. My cluelessness. I had been concerned with dress fittings and wedding invitations to heads of state. All the while, there were classified international debates about where my future husband's loyalties lay.

And I hated that I didn't know which way he would've gone.

But I could start trying to figure it out. Clearly, there was a connection between the bugs at Christian's law firm, his apartment, and his room at Ceillis House. But these secret papers being somehow connected to Christian? That seemed like a stretch.

I said as much to Nick. "What about the other people in his office? We should start narrowing down who had access to these papers and whether that had anything to do with Christian being under surveillance."

"I was unexpectedly called out of the city before I could find one to talk to," Nick said drily.

Boson Chapelle, Christian's law firm, was a prestigious boutique corporate law practice—and it relished publicity, so naturally I'd been invited there to meet the partners and the board. I flipped through a mental notebook before I remembered . . . "Tomas Claytere."

"Who?"

"One of the partners. He has a summer home about an hour from here. We could go interview him there, but we'll need to drive. It's miles from the river."

Nick's gaze sharpened on me. "How good are you at stealing cars?"

WITH NICK, SOMETIMES IT WAS HARD TO TELL IF HE WAS joking. When he'd asked me if I could steal a car, I'd assumed it was a joke. I mean, a British spy should be able to get his hands on some tricked-out Jaguar at a moment's notice, right? But the nearest village had no car rental shops, and after a call to Max Cornelius, Nick was informed that no James Bond–style sports cars—or regular normal-people cars, for that matter—were available this far out in the country. Therefore, we ended up driving the first tragic, scraped-up sedan he could find.

He fiddled with the wires and in just a few minutes we were off, driving into the countryside to Tomas Claytere's summer home. I remembered the location fairly well. Christian and I had spent a weekend at a nearby resort the previous year, and Claytere had invited us out for the day.

The discovery that someone had been bugging Christian's apartment and offices worried me. My own rooms were regularly scanned. At least, I believed that they were. That was something else for me to educate myself about when I returned to the palace. *If* I ever returned to the palace.

Why weren't Christian's rooms also scanned for devices? And who would want to listen in on Christian's conversations, anyway? According to Nick, the bug wasn't British government property, so it couldn't have been them listening in. It wasn't the press—if it had been the media, they would have already broadcast whatever tiny morsels had been obtained from such things.

It was definitely a mystery that I had all but given up solving until we arrived at Tomas Claytere's charming cottage that was nestled in a cozy crevice between picturesque crags.

I started to get out of the car, but Nick put his hand out.

"I didn't drive all this way to . . ."

Nick drew a weapon from under his jacket.

"Are you kidding me?" I hissed. "This is a corporate lawyer's summer home. No one is going to come out guns blazing!"

"You're right." Nick nodded quickly. I was gratified that he agreed with me. "No one shot at us in the National Galleries, either."

I was unable to counter that sarcasm.

"You'll stay until I tell you to come in," he said with the inarguable authority of a battlefield commander.

I decided to give him some space.

A tall yew tree blocked my view, and when Nick disappeared into the house I told myself I would hide behind it and take a peek through the branches. Then I scurried to a window to catch a glimpse between the curtains.

A hand wrapped around my arm. I screamed. A Scottish accent purred in my ear, "You don't take directions well for a princess."

"Nick!" I shook off his hand. "You scared the life out of me!"

"You can come in, if you don't mind blood."

Figuring it was a scare tactic, I followed him defiantly because he was absolutely right: I had discovered that I really didn't like taking directions. Not anymore.

But two steps into the house, I had the ghastly realization that Nick had not been joking or trying to employ advanced reverse psychology.

Inside Tomas Claytere's summer house, there was blood everywhere.

Trails of it, to and fro, here a puddle, there a splatter.

"Oh my God." I held up a palm to my mouth, anticipating a sickening stench signifying a pile of lifeless bodies. But my nose detected only the scent of grass from the meadow and a certain stale dirt odor.

"Hmph" was all Nick came up with as he surveyed the scene.

I saw a new side of him for the first time. An intimidating, larger-than-life, all-business intelligence officer. His hand still on his gun, he carefully walked through the rooms with me close at his heels until we came to a stop. There was an office that looked like someone had picked it up, kicked it, turned it upside down, and shaken it until all the pieces had come loose.

Nick holstered his weapon and started sifting through the papers. He looked at me. "Make yourself useful, Princess."

Automatically, I picked up a handful of paper, but I had to ask, "What am I looking for?"

"Anything interesting."

Boson Chapelle specialized in international corporate law. Now, I spoke four languages: Driedish, Spanish, French, and English. However, I did not speak accounting-ese, which was what most of the papers in my hands seemed to be drafted in.

Nick found the important pages about four seconds before I did.

"Ah!" he exclaimed.

"You can understand these?" I asked, with a hint of dismay in my voice. The guy really *was* too good at his job. How was anyone supposed to compete with that?

"Enough to get the idea."

"Are those the secret Cayman papers?" He nodded even as he kept rifling through what he held.

"So, Tomas had some of the Cayman papers," I reasoned aloud. "He obviously got them from his own law firm, or from his own clients. They were probably legitimate business deals that he and Christian were involved with." It was ridiculous that British intelligence was trying to make a big deal out of some papers that were probably covered by attorney-client privilege.

Nick nodded again, a serious expression on his face as he looked at the exploded contents of Tomas Claytere's summer office. "You're right."

"See!" I exclaimed, for no real reason other than that I wanted desperately for there to be an easy explanation for all of this. Something rational, something simple.

"Sure. Normal, legitimate clients break into their lawyer's home, ravage it, and leave a trail of blood a mile wide."

"They . . ." My voice trailed off when I realized he was being sarcastic. I could see where he was going with this.

Then Nick stomped over to the oil painting across from the window, ran his fingers just along the frame, and I knew what he'd produce before he did so: a matte-black disc with a wire.

"Grab whatever you can. We have to go."

"Again?" I hissed, snatching a pile of papers to my chest, but Nick was already heading out the door.

seventeen

"YOU'RE KIDDING ME," I SAID AS WE PULLED UP TO the small cottage outside of Demiel, a small town about fifteen kilometers from Claytere's house. "*This* is the safe house?"

Nick had given me that much information on the ride from Claytere's, probably because I was trying not to hyperventilate during yet another quick exit under stressful circumstances and he was trying to calm me down. But he took my question the wrong way. "Why, it's not grand enough for you?"

I just shook my head. He'd know the reason for my astonishment soon enough. The side door to the cottage opened and we were met with its owner, a slim, dark-haired woman.

"This is . . ." Nick fumbled. "Someone who works with us."

I crossed my arms and gave the woman what I hoped was a disapproving glare.

"Hello, Sybil," I said.

"You two know each other?" Nick's mouth settled into a grim line.

"Oh, quite well," Sybil chirped.

"Not really," I muttered.

"Can we go in, please?" Nick asked with a quick look at the sky.

"They're not going to find us," I assured him as I brushed by Sybil and entered her house. "Not here. No one comes here anymore."

Sybil snorted behind me. I heard the door close and my eyes adjusted to the dim light inside. It had been at least ten years since I'd last visited, but nothing much had changed. The walls were painted the same dark emerald and ruby; silk scarves were still draped across every possible surface. Bookshelves were crammed with dusty, leather-bound classics and crumbling 1960s spy novels. It was exactly the sort of place you'd imagine a psychic and an astrologer to inhabit.

The owner of the house hadn't changed much, either—she was as elegantly slim as ever, with a chic black bob. I had always thought of Sybil as being an older woman, so either she practiced some cosmetic voodoo to limit wrinkles or she really wasn't much more than twenty years older than me.

"I just got the message that you'd be coming," she said to Nick with a fond smile. She put a hand on his upper arm and I felt my lip curl. "I didn't have time to prepare for your arrival. Would you like a drink?" Sybil walked by me and headed toward the kitchen, leaving a cloud of musty rose and sandalwood perfume behind her that made me want to sneeze.

Nick declined, and although I wanted to, I suddenly realized that I was both parched and famished. "Yes, please. Tea. And some ginger biscuits."

Nick gave me a look at my imperious tone. I shrugged. Sybil always had tea and ginger biscuits. Besides, she owed me that much.

He lowered his head toward me and asked, "And how do you know each other?"

I smirked at him. "The great spy doesn't know everything, then." He tilted his head and gave me his very best enigmatic smile, but I knew I had the upper hand. He didn't like not having all the information. But no one had ever accused me of not being generous.

"Sybil was the unofficial court astrologer," I said brightly, making sure my voice would carry into the kitchen. "She's advised many members of my family on their life decisions."

"As did my mother before me, and her mother before her." Sybil smiled gamely when she returned to the room with a bamboo tray, holding a plate of ginger biscuits, a pot of jasmine tea, and several mismatched cups.

It was all part of the performance. As someone neared the bottom of their cup, she would offer to read the leaves. The tray was hand-painted with arcane symbols that she would artfully direct attention toward. This one was for marriage, that one for luck. It would prompt more questions, for which Sybil always had the answers.

The tradition of a court astrologer was long-standing in many of the royal families in Europe and Asia. Astrology had that nice sheen of science that could make it acceptable even for the religious-minded. My mother, a member of a very old aristocratic family, had known Sybil's mother since she was a teenager, as had my aunt Beatrice and my aunt Carlotta, and they'd passed the tradition down to their daughters. Mother had had charts made up for me and my siblings at our births and we'd come to visit Sybil at least once a year.

Sometimes, Mother let us sit with her as Sybil read tarot cards and explained the trajectory of our stars across the skies. Other times, Mother and Sybil disappeared into a locked study while my sisters and I snacked on cookies and played with the various trinkets and boxes that dotted the shelves and tables.

We stopped coming when one of the tabloids reported details of the astrological chart of Mother's new boyfriend—something that had been drawn right in this house—while she was still married to Father.

And now, as I sat on Sybil's wine-colored velvet chaise and helped myself to a cup of tea and three biscuits, all those visits made sense to me.

"And Nick, how long have you and Sybil been working together?" Nick's jaw clicked and his eyes shifted uncomfortably toward his asset.

"Just a few years."

"How fascinating. Did you always intend to betray my family by working for foreign governments?" I asked Sybil innocently.

I noticed that Nick stilled, his hand frozen over the teapot. But Sybil? She laughed, a light sound in the midst of the gloomy, mystical set design.

"Betrayal? Really, Thea. You were never the dramatic one. That was always Sophie."

"You sold my mother out to the press. It's not dramatic to assume you've also sold us all out to the British, the Americans, and the Chinese."

"It was meant to be."

"Which part—the treason or the betrayal of my family?" Now I laughed lightly, an echo of her. "But that's silly. They're one and the same, aren't they?"

Nick shifted in his seat, but Sybil stayed annoyingly composed. "I've provided Nick and his compatriots what I always provided your family. Information. People hire me to uncover secrets—past, present, or future. It's no betrayal to take multiple clients. A woman has to earn a living."

I tilted my head toward Nick and my blood got hotter as I thought of all the things that Sybil could have told his fellow agents over the years. Things about my family, my country. Private things. Secrets. She had been trusted, and now . . . ? "How many other countries are you serving?"

Her smile faded. "I may sell information to other nations, but I am loyal to Drieden."

"The fact that a British spy is using your home as a safe house says otherwise."

"And what does it say about *you*, dear Thea, that you are here with a British spy?"

Ouch. That hit really close to home. But my training ran true, so I simply said, "You have not been given leave to use that name," and lifted my cup of jasmine tea to my lips.

"I have. You gave it to me the first time you came to see me alone."

"Things change. Like my parents' charts. You told my mother the stars were aligned for their union." I'd heard that story for years before my mother stopped believing it.

Sybil lifted a blasé shoulder. "They were. Things changed."

"Don't mock me." Her blithe echo of my words was impertinent and she knew it.

A thick pause filled the room. "My apologies, Your Highness."

I would not accept her apology. If it hadn't been for her, my parents' divorce could have been civilized, not the public shit show it had turned into. And now I had evidence that she'd sold secrets to the tabloids— all those private details she'd collected over the years from her Drie- dish clients were a gold mine of information. I could have her arrested, prosecuted, and sent to prison. Once I stopped being on the run with a sketchy British spy, that is.

For the time being, I would be the bigger person and bite my lip. I reached out, poured another cup of tea, and handed the blue-and-white chipped porcelain to Nick.

"Drink," I told him. Maybe he was thirsty or maybe he was finally starting to listen to me, because he knocked that tea back.

After he put his cup back on the tray, he said to Sybil, "The car might be a problem."

She waved a hand. "If anyone notices, I'll say a hooligan left it in my drive and ran off down the street."

The ease with which Sybil came up with that lie thoroughly un- nerved me. Memories of all those predictions, those confident reassur- ances that my future would be bright and shiny, came rushing back. As if she knew what I was thinking (which she couldn't, I was sure, being the cynic that I now was), she glanced over at me.

"Your mother asked for a chart for your wedding, as well."

Despite the warm cup of tea I held, my hands went to ice. "I hope you gave her her money back," I said. "It's useless if the wedding never took place."

"I did one for Caroline." Sybil shrugged. "But that was just for my curiosity, after the fact."

The thought of Sybil inserting herself into my sister's scandal was infuriating. She kept poking.

"I did one for your fiancé, too."

I turned my head sharply, not wanting to see what was in her eyes, whether it was a lie or not. "There you go, Nick. I'm sure Sybil can simply consult her cards and crystal ball and whatever voodoo altar she's built for the solstice and point you in the direction of Christian." I stood and carefully settled my mismatched china on a nearby table. "Now if you'll excuse me."

The cottage was small enough that I could have located the bathroom easily, even if I hadn't remembered the way. I took the opportunity to splash water on my wrists and neck, and patted my face with a towel. My nerves stayed elevated, though, and I realized that as much as I trusted Nick at this point, we could not trust Sybil at all. I wanted to leave, and as soon as possible.

When I returned to the sitting room, Nick was gone and Sybil was sitting quietly, staring into the cup Nick had used. A swirl of foreboding whisked around my stomach. That was what the ginger cookies were for, I realized. To help relieve the nausea of hearing the worst about one's future.

Even though every instinct was telling me to open the door and make a run for it, I couldn't help myself. "What does it say?" I asked softly. *The tea leaves tell a story*, she would say, back when I was innocent and trusting. A tiny part of me still believed. Still wanted to know the secrets.

Sybil's eyes met mine and she spoke in a shadowy, smoky voice. "There's danger. And the truth will be revealed."

The nausea solidified into an icy brick that inner Thea picked up and threw at my metaphysical head. I woke up. "Truly insightful. And specific. Danger and truth. Thank you very much for that helpful prediction."

Nick came back into the room. "The police are here."

Sybil stood and slapped the cup onto the table and the dregs of tea sloshed out. "You'll need to make yourself scarce."

I couldn't help myself. "Strange how the tea leaves couldn't tell us they were coming."

The old bat ignored me and turned to Nick. "On the stairs, at the landing. Second panel, there's a switch on the cherub."

"A cherub?" I asked in disbelief. What was happening right now? But apparently I was the only one who thought this was thoroughly ridiculous. "No," I said, yanking my arm out of Nick's grasp. "We need to leave." I didn't trust Sybil farther than I could throw her, and learning that there were secret hiding spaces was not making me feel safer.

There was a sharp rap at the door. Sybil's eyes went wide. "Go!"

And then Nick's hand clamped around my arm and I was dragged up the stairs. I swear, if I had known this man was so bossy, I wouldn't have gone down the chute with him at the museum in the first place.

Sure enough, there were carved panels along the stairwell and on the landing, including one that I was pretty sure depicted the birth of Christ—odd for a woman who consulted with ancient spirits to tell fortunes. Nick's long fingers traced the profile of a cherub on the second panel and there was a soft click. He slid open the door to reveal a cedar-lined closet, the type that people a hundred years ago might have used to store their linens or wools. It was barely more than two feet wide, but I soon learned that yes, two people could fit tightly in there.

Then Nick slid the door closed and we were in the dark. Alone. And trapped.

"SHH . . ." IT WAS BARELY MORE THAN A BREATH IN MY EAR. Nick pulled me closer to him, his fingers taking a sure hold of my hips, his hands wide and capable.

The rustle and bumps seemed to come from above and below and beside us. The insanity of what I was doing hit me. I was a princess of this country. I could step out and order the people searching Sybil's house to immediately stop their pursuit. I was due some respect; they would at least pause. Reconsider their actions.

"Thea, no." Nick's arm curved protectively around my waist, in a strong yet gentle hold. His strength told me I was safe with him. His protection reminded me of what could happen if I threw open the door and revealed my presence.

Not even Nick's strength could stop a bullet aimed at his head.

The bumps and thuds of the search below receded. The only sound I could hear was Nick's breath, now heavy on my neck. A sigh from me. The soft swish of fabric as we shifted in the tight space and Nick's leg moved in between mine.

He squeezed my sides and I felt him nuzzle under my ear. He inhaled deeply. My skin was unperfumed, my hair was untamed, but I had never felt more desirable.

"Oh, what the hell," he muttered under his breath just before he kissed me.

Soul-searing.

Earth-stopping.

Panty-melting.

Lots of clichés didn't quite capture the way Nick's mouth dominated mine. He kissed the way he spoke Driedish—like he'd been born doing it.

I wanted more. It was the wrong time, the wrong place, and quite possibly the wrong man. But there in the dark, in desperation and danger, there were no rules. No restrictions, no responsibilities. There was only one true, strong thing: desire.

He clutched me tighter and I leaned into him, taking fistfuls of his sweater in my needy hands. It wasn't enough, but my fevered brain wasn't quite sure what I was looking for until Nick's palms found my breasts, roughly, even clumsily, pressed as tightly in the cupboard as we were. But still I went weak, as he stroked and teased and tested me.

In the course of mere minutes, I craved a multitude of touches, kisses, caresses. My fingers went to his lips, my tongue tasted his neck, his hands brushed my thighs. One hand reached around my knee and pulled it up, wrapping my leg around his waist snugly. He was hard against me, pushing me against the wall, and we swallowed every whimper and growl with deepening kisses.

I didn't notice when the policemen's footsteps thudded away, but the sound of Sybil's voice rang out through the thick door.

"You two! You can come out now! It's safe. Those bastards are gone."

Neither of us moved. Or said a word. Our heavy breathing and thudding hearts were reminiscent of the aftereffects of a car crash.

Finally, I let my leg slip down, trailing Nick's as it did. One last brush of his thumb against my neck before he said, "Maybe you should go out first."

I exited, smoothing my clothes and hair and distracting Sybil with questions while Nick tarried a moment—I presumed to compose himself and readjust his pants.

Sybil described the invasion of the jackbooted thugs who had questioned her with great fervor, using colorful vulgarities regarding their intellects, their mothers, and their likely afterlife destinations. But her story had worked. They were gone.

"You'll have to stay the night. I didn't trust the older one. He might keep an eye on the place."

"Too many stolen cars in your driveway?" Nick asked.

She shrugged. "I can't help the delinquents who keep leaving them here."

Looking at Nick with his mussed-up hair and piratical air, I thought "delinquent" was an excellent description.

eighteen

NICK CHECKED HIS WATCH. "RIGHT. SINCE WE'VE got the night, you can do your thing and help me with some information."

I still didn't trust Sybil but it seemed that she had Nick's confidence, which allayed my concerns slightly as he went over the Claytere situation.

She pulled out a laptop from a nearby bookshelf and Nick moved to look over her shoulder as she searched. "All these names worked at Christian's firm," Nick confirmed. "Several deaths in four months."

Sybil tapped the screen. "This was the first." Her eyes flicked up at me. "He died two days before your wedding."

"What are you looking at, anyway?" I asked. "A countrywide database?"

She avoided my eyes, which was all I needed to know. "Now the truth behind all the psychic pretension is revealed. What do you do, check that thing before clients come over? You hack into their bank accounts and social media profiles to get your phony psychic predictions, right?"

Sybil ignored me and said something I couldn't catch to Nick.

"What was that?"

"The first death that occurred before your wedding," Sybil said, giving me a look. "Christian would have known about it."

"I wish you would stop calling it a wedding. It never happened. It was a colossal waste of money and time. Why didn't your charts show any of us that there wouldn't be a groom for the event?"

"Three dead. Two missing."

"Two?" I asked.

"Christian and Claytere," Nick replied.

Sybil relayed the causes of death: one hunting accident, one car crash, and one undiscovered shellfish allergy.

Such a wide array of events probably seemed like a gruesome coincidence of bad luck over four months to anyone else. But step back and the pattern became clear: several of those whom Christian had worked with had met with a premature end in the last few months.

Or, in the case of Tomas Claytere—and Christian himself—they'd simply disappeared into thin air.

As I sat on the threadbare velvet sofa to take all of this in, I realized just how serious a situation this was.

The power of suggestion is strong, and my reality for the past four months had been that Christian Fraser-Campbell had slunk out of the country in the middle of the night, unable to face a lifetime of being with me.

Even when Nick had said Christian could be dead, I hadn't really believed him. Christian was dead to *me*. But he hadn't stopped living. He was too handsome, too ambitious, too canny to actually die.

But now it looked like the employees of Boson Chapelle had been systematically removed.

One of them had been removed right under the nose of the Driedish Crown.

What type of entity could do that?

How powerful was it?

If something—or someone—could do this to Christian . . . what else could they do? To what lengths would they go?

I found it hard to believe international law was this dangerous, but the blood and the Cayman papers in Tomas Claytere's house said otherwise. If what Nick had said was correct, those mysterious papers were the link between the missing employees of Boson Chapelle.

As I went upstairs to the guest room Sybil had said we could use, the carved wooden cherub on the stair landing seemed to give me a knowing smile. As if he knew Nick had kissed me. And I had kissed Nick back. Again.

It had been amazing.

It had been a colossal mistake.

I'd rather deal with the lists of figures we'd taken from Claytere's house.

I knocked lightly on the bedroom door. When Nick answered, I opened it to find him lying propped up on the narrow bed, Claytere's files spread around him.

We'd had the same idea, then.

I picked up a stack and settled on the floor, my back against the long curtains that framed the small window.

We didn't speak for hours, both of us analyzing and inspecting the financial records that Nick seemed to think were connected to Christian's disappearance.

Finally, I couldn't see straight. I was woozy and dizzy from my lack of sleep and roller coaster of emotions. "You said there are more of the papers online?"

"Not the ones that matter. Other firms have those and managed to retain a full staff." Nick leaned his head against the wall and closed his eyes, and I tried to not stare at the shape of his neck when he did.

"Do you think they took them?" I knew that my question wasn't clear, so I tried again. "The people who tore apart Claytere's office. Do you think they found what they were looking for?"

"Maybe." With the back of his arm, he brushed his hair back from his face and then looked at me. "You should get some sleep."

"I'll sleep when you do. I mean . . ." Embarrassingly, I felt a blush on my exhausted face. "You know what I mean." Several nights on the houseboat together and I'd heard him creeping along the deck at night. "You don't sleep much."

"Neither do you."

I shook my head and threaded my fingers through the ancient scraggly fringe on the bottom of the draperies. "They gave me pills for it after the wedding, but I never took them . . ."

"Do you really miss him that much?" The question was sudden and surprising—not just in its topic, but in Nick's offhand delivery.

"No." I was firm. "That sounds awful now, but . . ." I searched for the right words. "You know how you can be driving along and then you get a flat tire and your day is all thrown off, and you can't stop obsessing about all the things you had to do that won't get done now? It's just a flat tire, but—"

"Your day is ruined," Nick said flatly.

"Not even that. The day could be fine, but your expectations are ruined. And it just takes time to adjust to a new reality." I ducked my head. "I know it sounds ridiculous."

"You compared my brother's disappearance to a flat tire."

"I thought he ran off. *That* was the flat tire."

"What is he now?" Another one of Nick's carefully phrased questions, filled with subtext, but I was too exhausted to parse my words to please him.

"He's a closed highway. One way or another, I have to find a new route to take."

"You Driedeners are a prosaic lot."

"And the Scots are so poetic."

A smile touched his lips. "We're romantics at heart."

Romance. Not a word I'd associate with Nick, or my former fiancé, either, for that matter. "Have you noticed that you tend to kiss me under dangerous conditions?"

The quirk of a dark eyebrow was my answer.

"Toss me a pillow," I demanded, finally ready to curl up on Sybil's floor and pass out.

He rolled off the bed and extended a hand to help me up. "Her Highness should get the bed." I clasped my frigid hand into his warm, wide palm and he pulled me up against his lean, hard body.

"There's enough room for two."

He leaned down and said in a rough burr, "A wee bit too dangerous for me, lass."

THE NEXT MORNING THE KITCHEN SMELLED LIKE FRESH bread and greasy eggs, and my stomach rumbled. Sybil stood at the stove, somehow perfectly chic in a caftan with strings of meditation beads wrapped around her wrists and a pentacle at her throat.

"Good morning, Your Highness." She wasn't cheerful, which I couldn't have borne that morning, but she was quietly reassuring in some way, which I found strangely comforting. The old Thea, the one who believed, popped her head up again. I supposed I needed to hear some version of good, even if it was just a "good morning."

"Where's Nick?" I asked, to keep the optimistic Thea at bay for a moment. After he'd given me the bed last night he'd left the guest room, and I was too much of a coward to go searching for him.

"He's in the study. There's coffee."

As always, coffee was needed more than spiritual reassurance, and I did not hesitate getting myself a mug.

As I sipped, I watched Sybil fry sausages under the dancing light of a web of crystals that hung across a high window. Blue, pink, lavender, and rainbow streaks crisscrossed down, over, and through the warm, cozy space.

"The crystals used to be in the sitting room," I remarked, remembering the times I would stare, fascinated by the designs that could be created on the walls by light, minerals, and energy.

Sybil glanced up before turning her attention back to the smoking sausages. "The house feng shui changed."

I didn't even know what that was. I only knew that the crystals and their refracting lights reminded me of the cathedral windows at St. Julien's. The windows under which I was supposed to be married.

"What did Christian's chart say?"

I don't know which of us was more surprised by my question. I couldn't believe it had come out of my mouth. Sybil seemed frozen. She took several long moments before answering, deliberately sliding the sausages onto a waiting plate, then wiping her hands on a nearby tea towel.

"Come," she finally said.

For the first time in my life, I followed her into her study and was so absorbed by my surroundings that I didn't realize for a minute or so that Nick wasn't in there like she had said he was. Sybil did not seem surprised by this, but went straight to a set of wide wooden drawers and opened the top one. She selected a large notebook and set it on the curiously bare antique desk. It was curious because every other surface in her house seemed to be covered with fabric or paper or assorted clutter.

Her fingers flipped it open, and I saw the same designs my mother would pore over whenever she was here. The concentric circles, the arrows bisecting the personal universe of whomever the chart was drawn for.

Sybil traced the words as she said them aloud, like an incantation: "Christian David Jameson Fraser-Campbell, Leo." She read his birth date and place of birth, and I felt this emptiness grow inside me. Before this, I had never felt like he was truly gone from my life. Something about hearing this wise (or crazy) woman recite his given name distanced me from the man who had once upon a time held me in his arms.

She tapped the symbols, one at a time. "Of course he is a Leo, which wouldn't be all bad. But here. Scorpio in Mars." She drew breath quickly through her teeth. "And in the twelfth house. He was born both to be the center of attention and to keep very dark secrets."

Sounded about right.

Then she flipped the page. "Nicholas Robert Jameson Fraser-Campbell. I didn't have time to draw his full chart."

"Sybil, no," I breathed when I saw what was taped to the empty page.

"Well, I'll do it at some point. But in the meantime, I drew these."

"No one asked you . . ." My words faded when she traced the tarot cards affixed into the book with crooked slivers of tape.

Death.

The Magician.

The Lovers.

She tapped the enrobed skeleton on the Death card. "He was re-born." Her index finger lightly drew a circle over the Magician, with his outstretched hands encompassing globes of fire. "You must trust him." Then her fingernail clicked decisively on male and female nudes drawn in a passionate embrace. "Past, present, and future."

"When did you pull these?" I asked, trying to stay calm.

"Yesterday." She said it as if it were so normal. I rubbed my eyes with the back of my hand. There was every chance that Sybil was making this up, that she chose these cards on purpose, to manipulate me, to influence me to do . . . something. I couldn't think what Sybil had to gain from this, but I knew now that she rarely did anything without a reason.

Which is what I was pondering when she flipped through the journal again and tore out a page. She folded it into a small square and stuffed it into an envelope. Then she scribbled something on the outside and handed it to me. It read, "Open on your 30th birthday."

The believer in me clutched the paper tightly. The woman I'd become itched to throw it away in the nearest garbage bin.

I folded the envelope into my pocket and followed Sybil back into the kitchen, where Nick was pouring coffee. I didn't ask him where he'd been, mostly because I didn't want to explain what I'd seen in the study.

Death. Magic. And Love. Only the first seemed a plausible outcome today.

nineteen

THE DRIEDISH STAYED UP UNTIL MIDNIGHT ON THIS late-summer day every year to celebrate the Queen's birthday. There was a joyous atmosphere on the decks of the crafts around us. Music blared, children laughed, and whiffs of grilled sausages and marijuana surrounded us.

After breakfast, Sybil had driven us back to the village where we'd left the houseboat docked. Now we were back on the river just in time for a national holiday. Even though the last rays of the summer sun skittered across the sky in hazy pink streaks, the night had turned cold enough for me to wrap up in a woolen blanket I had found below deck. Footsteps signaled Nick's approach. I recognized them now, living in these close quarters. Secure, yet soft. He slid down to take a seat next to me and his heat was welcome in the midnight dusk.

I reached out of my blanket cocoon and poured him a glass of the red wine I had already begun to enjoy. "Here. You must drink on the Queen's birthday."

"To Queen Aurelia," he said before drinking.

I couldn't help but laugh. "It's not Aurelia's birthday."

He frowned at me. "But it's the Queen's birthday," he said, confused, the way I imagined most non-Driedish people would be about this most Driedish of holidays.

"Here in Drieden we celebrate Queen Elsa-Marie's birthday." I lifted my glass, recalling the toast I had learned at a very young age when I'd been served only water mixed with a bit of wine. "To Elsa-Marie and the homeland!"

"You'll have to educate an ignorant Scot . . ."

"Yes, yes," I said as I patted the ignorant Scot on his warm, firm arm. "Queen Elsa-Marie was Leopold the Fourth's wife. She was from Austria, off of that Holy Roman Empire branch of the family tree. Unfortunately, she and Leopold were crowned just as the French Revolution was starting." I waved my hand. "It caused a bit of a stir in Drieden, given the close proximity and relations between Elsa-Marie and Marie-Antoinette, not to mention Louis and Leopold."

"Good buddies, were they?"

"Actually, there's a letter between them where Leopold is scathing about the over-the-top construction costs of Versailles. The Driedish are a practical folk, as you know."

Nick raised an eyebrow, but I went on. "Anyway, Elsa-Marie was determined to keep her crown and her head, since she'd just gotten the crown and liked her head very much. She was not having any of that French Revolution nonsense. So she learned from Marie-Antoinette's mistakes and decided to be the most benevolent, the most charitable, the most beloved queen that Drieden ever had."

"And she obviously succeeded, if people are still celebrating her birthday."

"It helps that she gave the people three days off from work every year to do so."

Nick lifted his glass. "To Elsa-Marie and the homeland." We drank to that together.

"It's better than cheap whiskey," I announced, remembering the first time we'd drunk together. Nick looked thoughtful and opened his mouth to say something, but right at that moment the sky exploded above us. Fireworks in green and yellow, the colors of the Driedish flag, shot into the atmosphere, followed by red and blue and clear, sparkling white.

I'd never much cared for fireworks before. If I was watching them, it usually meant that I was at a political function, standing in uncomfortable starched clothes and careful about my posture and expression. I'd be smiling with restrained appreciation or clapping politely, but my feet were normally aching and I'd be dying to get home to relax and/or escape from some annoying family member.

These were fireworks I could finally enjoy. There, on the deck of a stolen boat, I leaned my head back against the hull, drank wine, and enjoyed the warmth and companionship of the most intriguing man I'd ever known. I felt like celebrating, I felt at home, and I felt like *me*.

"I'm in so much trouble!" I laughed as I heard someone on a nearby boat playing the Driedish national anthem on a radio.

"Why?" Nick looked down at me, and I realized that at some point I had rested my head on his shoulder. I didn't move it.

"Because I'm missing the celebration. I should be at Gran's side tonight." I chuckled again as I thought about the inevitable tabloid speculation about my absence and realized I didn't care anymore. "I should have done this years ago," I murmured in the space between explosions.

"What?"

"Run away. Run from it all."

For the first time, I had a taste of sympathy toward the man who might have run away from our wedding. I was still angry with him for the way he did it—not explaining, not saying good-bye, not saying . . . anything.

But if Christian had felt a sliver of what I'd felt over the years— being locked in, locked away, locked up—maybe he'd decided to take the chance and get as far away as he could from the prison known as the House of Laurent.

After all, given the alternatives I knew now, the fates of his Boson Chapelle colleagues . . . I hoped Christian *had* run away.

How many times had I slipped away from the palace? Those nibbles of freedom where I had tasted what it was like to be a normal person for a few hours had kept me sane through the years. And now I was on a crazy trip with a once-presumed dead man. How could I blame Christian for doing the exact same thing that I wished I had done?

Given it all up.

Ignored duty.

But it was duty that had called me on this journey. It was duty that still made me say, *I'm going to do everything I can to find you.* Even though he didn't deserve it. Even though he'd embarrassed me in front of the entire world.

I felt something warm cover my chilled fingers. Nick. He was holding my hand.

"If I find your brother, I'm going to punch him," I said through gritted teeth.

"You're fairly violent for a princess."

I sighed. "I know. It's my only flaw."

Nick squeezed my fingers.

"What's it like?" he asked suddenly.

"Having flaws? It's rather annoying for princesses, to be honest."

He squeezed again. "Being at your gran's side on a night like tonight."

It was the last thing I'd expected. A personal question. A real question.

I wanted to give a serious answer, but the habit of not talking about my family was strong. "Well, as you know, my grandmother is also a monarch."

"So I've gathered."

"There's a lot of standing straight and tall. Waving for long periods of time. And it helps if one has a good pain tolerance."

He frowned at me. "This sounds barbaric."

"Biting one's tongue all the time can become rather gruesome."

"Too bad you're not any good at staying silent."

"Are you suggesting I have yet another flaw?"

His eyes sparkled under the fireworks. "No, Princess. It so happens that I rather like that mouth of yours."

My cheeks warmed. I brushed my thumb against the back of his hand, contemplating making a move. On Nick. Here on the deck. Outside. In the middle of a crowd of boats on the Queen's birthday.

"If I were with Gran tonight, I couldn't be with you," I whispered. "Not like this."

"No boy toys allowed?"

"Family only," I confirmed. "For years, we would all gather for the Queen's birthday. It was my parents and siblings and cousins. And Uncle John's family and Aunt Beatrice's. But no one who wasn't connected by blood or marriage."

"Sounds crowded."

"I suppose the system rewards fecundity."

"Careful now."

I startled, gripped his arm, and looked around as if we were about to be boarded. "What?"

Nick chuckled. "I only meant using that word. With that mouth," his lids dropped low as he stared at my lips, "I might forget who your family is."

An unforeseen weight dropped into my stomach. "You say that like my family is a bad thing."

"Aren't most?"

"Well, *I* haven't pretended to die to avoid mine."

He gave me his wry Nick smile. "You can't tell me you haven't been tempted."

I looked down at our hands still intertwined. Thought of my impossible mother, my distant father, my messy siblings. My scary grandmother.

I sighed and settled back against the boat hull. "I'm here, aren't I?" I said. Nick lifted my hand and kissed it as though he understood my meaning perfectly—even if I wasn't quite sure of it myself.

We stayed silent for a long time, watching the grand finale of the fireworks and then the return of the night as the world around us went inside, turned off their lights, and slept.

At this point in the summer, the sky never truly went black. It turned a velvety, lit-from-within, hazy purple. It seemed appropriate for two people like us. We weren't midday or midnight. We were dawn, dusk, and midsummer. Caught in the middle of time and space, ever so fleeting. Blink and you'd never see us—the runaway princess and the dead spy.

If we could have stayed in this in-between Neverland, I think we both could have been happy. But the sounds of a marimba ringtone came from below deck.

"What. In the hell. Is that," Nick growled, and I shivered. Not because he sounded scary.

But because . . .

"That's my secret cell phone."

twenty

NICK WAS FURIOUS. "WHERE DID YOU GET THIS?" HE demanded as his knuckles turned white from the grip he had on the cheap phone.

"At Ceillis House," I told him calmly. There was no need to be so brutish about it. "It's just my old phone."

"Did you turn it on?"

"No, it was dead. I was charging—" I broke off when he ripped the back off the cheap cell phone and tore a small card out of it. "No! Don't!" I launched myself into him before he could do anything irreversible.

I just wanted to knock the phone out of his hand, but I smacked my open palm against his hard shoulder instead when he turned quickly away from me. The man had superhuman reflexes, but he couldn't see behind him when I planted my boot firmly in the back of his knee. He buckled for a moment but seemed to catch his balance, so I followed up with another kick to his ass.

Nick toppled forward, his arms outstretched to catch himself, and I jumped on his back as he fell to the floor. He outweighed me by quite a bit and he could have easily tossed me off, but he froze when I said in his ear, "Christian called."

By some miracle, or maybe because he was that good, Nick still had the phone and chip in his hand. "What the fuck are you talking about?"

"He's the only one who has that phone's number. He's calling us." *He's calling me.*

I felt some of the tension go out of his back and shoulders, but not all. "Tell me everything, as quickly as you can."

After scrambling off Nick's back, I sketched out the details. "Christian bought us secret cell phones right before the engagement was announced so no one could trace our movements or our calls. He bought them in Amsterdam on holiday. No one knows about them but us. This is mine. I gave it back to him at Ceillis House the night of the ball because we weren't going to need them anymore once we were married, but I found it in his room when we were there. It was dead, but I thought I might use it to call my sister, so I found a charger in the galley and . . ." I made a useless gesture. "What are the odds? Christian could be calling me! We have to call back!"

Nick had stayed on the floor, sitting with his forearms on his knees, staring at the phone while I'd explained. Strangely, he didn't seem as excited about the fact that his missing brother had found a telephone to call me. "No one knows about these?"

"No."

Nick didn't seem convinced. "And just how do you keep a cell phone secret from your staff?"

I thought about it for a moment. "I mean, they might have been around when I used it." Nick looked skeptical. "But they never asked about it and I never discussed it with them. They don't have the right to interfere with—"

That pushed him over the edge. "If you don't think your security personnel didn't know all about this, then you're a bigger idiot than I thought. Cell phones can be traced; they can be tracked; they can be *hacked*. Using this device was a huge breach of security."

"It never left my possession!"

Nick got up with grim resolve on his face. "It needs to be destroyed."

"But he just called! We need to call back and see where he is!" Apparently he didn't understand that we had a vital clue. A literal lifeline. He couldn't destroy it.

"And what if it's not Christian who's using the phone?"

That made me stop in my tracks.

"Who knew about his secret phone?"

I shook my head. "I don't know," I finally said, not really understanding why this was relevant. "His security detail, maybe."

"His friends? The people he worked with at the law firm?"

"Maybe," I allowed. "But what does that have to do with anything?"

"The probability that Christian has left you a detailed message that will not only clue us in to his location but also leave you emotionally fulfilled is very small. Which means it doesn't outweigh the probability that someone in your palace, or other unknown agents, will trace this phone as soon as we turn it on again to find you."

"I don't care!" I cried, angry that he was trying to use probability of all things. Nothing about my life at this point was probable. There was no statistician in the world who could have predicted that Princess Theodora of Drieden would be abandoned by her possibly kidnapped fiancé four months ago, and there was no one who could have calculated the chance that Christian would call my secret phone once I'd retrieved it from Ceillis House. "That's a chance we have to take."

Nick was unmoved. He crossed his arms and stared, waiting for my next outburst, which I was happy to provide.

"And another thing! How dare you minimize me and infer that this is about my 'emotional fulfillment.'"

"Isn't it? You were going to marry him."

"I'm so tired of you throwing that in my face," I said, disgusted, "when what you're really mad about is that I didn't meet you first."

It was meant as a petty slap. But the stunned look on Nick's face was almost as if I had really slapped him, open palm and stinging.

"I'm sorry," I rasped, but I really wasn't. Now I knew something true. Maybe Nick had developed certain feelings for me, as I had for him.

And we were both dealing with the specter of Christian between us. One of us duty-bound to a brother, the other to an ex-fiancé—this road was unmarked and treacherous territory for both of us.

Nick didn't deny my accusation. He ignored it, though. "I'm going to take this and turn it on several miles from here. I'll listen to the message and come back when it's safe."

"I'm not scared of being found."

"Then you're an idiot. My brother disappeared; you can disappear, too."

"I'm a princess."

"And you haven't been seen in public for nearly a week. Think how easy it could be to tell the world you've given it up."

I saw the tabloid stories in my head and knew he was partially right. The "Princess Theodora in Seclusion" headlines could go on for a long time. Hell, the newspapers could say I'd been sent to a convent in the Andes and people would believe it.

Nevertheless, it still felt like a defeat when I asked him, "How long will you be gone?"

twenty-one

AN HOUR AFTER SUNRISE, I HEARD STEPS ON THE deck and crawled up as fast as I could. I had to know if Nick had discovered anything. Was it Christian on the phone? What had he said? Could we find out if he was okay, where he was?

But it wasn't Nick on the boat.

"Tamar?" First relief flooded through me. Then an alarm sounded between my ears. The last time I'd seen Tamar, she'd disobeyed me and had shot bullets in my direction.

And now she was standing here, her brown curls softly stirred by the breeze. There were no mixed feelings on her face, only joy. "Your Highness!" She lowered her head. "I'm so glad I've finally found you."

As someone who didn't want to be found, I wasn't sure how to answer that, and a million other questions sprang to my mind. Why had she come? How had she found me?

Was I safe?

As if to answer that question, I heard another familiar voice. "Looks like we have a visitor."

Nick was at the end of the gangplank, his hands shoved in his jacket pockets, a halfway pleasant expression on his face. Since Nick didn't do pleasant, I was quite certain there was a gun in one—or both—of his pockets. Pointing straight at Tamar.

That thought was confirmed when he said, a moment later, "Why don't we go down below and have breakfast? I'm sure Thea has prepared something delicious."

"There's some cheese," I said.

"See?" Nick said gamely.

With a careful glance between Nick and me, Tamar moved down the stairs, her arms loose by her side, and I prayed she'd keep them there. I had no doubt that Nick would enjoy taking his revenge on one of the people who had shot at him in the museum, and I really didn't want that to happen.

"How did you find us?"

"How many others are there?"

Nick and I asked Tamar our questions simultaneously as soon as we reached the galley. She looked at Nick and then at me, answering mine first.

"I triangulated the signal on your phone, when you finally turned it on."

I didn't have to look at Nick to know that he'd have "I told you so" written all across his dark glower.

"My secret phone, you mean." I had to point that out, but Tamar looked confused.

"Yes, the one you used to talk to His Grace."

Nick had been right when he'd said I was naive about that secret phone. I didn't want to be naive any longer.

"Are there others out there, Tamar? Who else did you bring with you?"

She shook her head. "I came alone. The search for you was focused on Ceillis House. Now they've gone up to the Claytere summer cottage."

The last two places that Nick had found black discs tucked behind paintings. My brain shied away from the obvious implication of this news.

But Nick didn't. "Is the palace searching for my brother, too?"

Tamar threw him a challenging look. "Why would they do that?"

"Tamar . . ." I murmured. "I have learned that Christian might not have returned to Scotland, as I was told. Have you heard anything?"

She looked indecisive for a half second before answering me. "We've been very occupied looking for you, Your Highness. But I know that the two guards who were assigned to His Grace recently returned from abroad."

"So they thought he was in Scotland, too," I said, wondering whether that should be comforting or not.

Tamar interrupted that thought. "They didn't go to Scotland."

"Where did they go?" Nick demanded.

"The Cayman Islands."

I met Nick's eyes.

Finally. A clue. A direction we could go in. It had started to feel as if Christian had just disappeared into the ether and now we had a starting point, which had led us straight back to the Cayman papers. "Would you like a drink? Some water?"

I moved toward the refrigerator, intending to be a little more welcoming to Tamar, but I had taken only a few steps out of the way when my two squabbling guard dogs made their moves. Faster than a blink, Tamar brandished a sidearm and pointed it at Nick. And nearly simultaneously, Nick had a firearm in his hand, pointing it at Tamar.

"What are you doing?" I cried out. "Tamar, put that down!"

"Your Highness, you're safe with me now."

"Over my dead body," Nick snarled.

"If that's how it has to be, then I'll do so gladly."

"Nick, please, this is crazy!" I threw up my hands. "Both of you, just stop!"

"He's working against you, Your Highness."

"Me? I'm not the one refusing a command."

"I took an oath," Tamar sneered.

"To shoot at your princess?"

"I was shooting at *you*." Another snarl from Tamar.

Nick lifted a shoulder casually. "Well, since you missed me the first time, I'm feeling decidedly more confident now."

Tamar smiled slightly, a chilling sight from my usually deadpan bodyguard. "I won't miss this time."

"No one is shooting anyone!" I tried sounding regal and authoritative, but it was coming off as a little panicky.

This wasn't happening. No one was getting shot today. And if they wouldn't obey my orders (or desperate pleas), I'd have to figure out another way to stop the madness.

I walked forward until I was in between the two barrels.

Nick growled my name. Tamar muttered a Driedish curse.

I held out both my hands. "Give them to me." I wasn't taking the chance that they'd lower their weapons and then shoot as soon as my head wasn't in the way.

"Your Highness, I—" Tamar started to protest.

I cut her off. "I don't trust you. And *you*—" I threw a look over at Nick, whose face could have killed me faster than a bullet. But I couldn't finish that statement. He cared for me, and that was why I knew I couldn't trust him.

Because he would kill Tamar if he thought it would protect me.

"Hand both of them over, *now*," I said.

Grudgingly, they both did as they were told, but I had an Israeli-trained former soldier and an ex–Royal Marine MI6 agent in close quarters. Tamar could probably kill someone by jamming her fingers up his nose. Nick would definitely have no problem throwing Tamar's head against the wall. I could rule nothing out.

I pointed Tamar's gun at my own head. "Check her for more weapons," I ordered Nick, and he responded with mouthing, "You're crazy." And then he did what I said and patted Tamar down, finding nothing.

Now what did I do? I had Nick's gun in my left hand and Tamar's pointed at my temple. Nick was right; I *was* crazy. If I ever returned to the palace, I was going to get trained on tactical handgun techniques. But for now, I would do what I could to make sure no one died on this boat tonight.

"All right, both of you above board. Tamar first." I followed her, gun still to my head, with Nick behind me. The fact that he didn't try to pull me down probably meant there was a high likelihood that I was about to accidentally kill myself. When we were all on deck, I went straight to the railing and threw both guns into the river.

I brushed my hands. "Like I said, no one is shooting anyone."

Tamar and Nick both crossed their arms and glared at me like children who had been told they couldn't play their favorite game anymore.

"Tamar, why are you here?"

She frowned as if I'd asked the question in another language. "You disappeared from the museum and didn't return to the palace. No one's heard from you and you were with *him*." She wrinkled her nose at Nick like he smelled bad. "We assumed you'd been kidnapped."

"But you came here alone. You said royal security are searching other areas. Why are you not with them? Or why did they not come with you?"

Again she gave Nick the side eye. "I thought a large group might alert this one."

Nick didn't look happy with that answer and I can't say it sat well with me, either, but none of this had felt right, starting with Christian's disappearance.

"Did you think you were going to rescue me by yourself and bring me back to the palace?" I tried asking gently, because at that moment I wasn't quite sure where I wanted to go, if I wanted to go anywhere at all.

"Your Highness. It is vitally important that you return with me tonight. If you do not, Her Majesty plans to request formal military support to search for you tomorrow morning. The Prime Minister will have to be informed of your absence, and your family will be informed as well. The cost of a national search will . . ." Tamar's dark brown eyes were clouded with worry. "The palace will subjected to intense scrutiny."

I understood the implications of what she was saying. After the exorbitant costs of a royal wedding that never was, the Liberals in Parliament would seize the opportunity to once again illustrate the wastefulness of the royal family, the irresponsibility of the Crown, and the uselessness of supporting a group of people who couldn't lead functioning, normal lives without hand-holding.

"Thank you, Tamar." I gestured toward the gangplank. "I need to think about this."

"You want me to leave?"

"You can wait on the shore. I promise you, this boat can't go very fast. I won't be able to escape you again."

Tamar didn't move for a minute, as she seemed to assess the potential risks of my directions. Then she reluctantly walked across the gangplank and back onto the grassy bank of the canal.

I avoided Nick's gaze and went below deck. He followed a few minutes later and entered my cabin without knocking.

"You can't go back there. It's not safe. Your own security took shots at you, Princess."

"Tamar said they were shooting at you."

He made a face as if he didn't care. "They disobeyed your order to stand down. Someone was trying to stop you from talking to me."

"You heard what Tamar said. Tomorrow the whole country will be looking for me, even if we manage to get away from her today."

Nick scowled. "Bullshit."

"Which part?"

"She came here alone? Without backup? Without notifying her superiors that she had a signal on your cell phone? Something isn't right."

"You're just mad she got by you."

"Only because you turned on the damn phone!"

His voice rose, and that reminded me.

"Did you want to kiss me?"

"What?" He shook his head, giving me a why-are-you-bringing-this-up-when-your-life-is-in-danger look.

"When I had a gun pointed at my head. It was a dangerous situation, don't you think? Did you feel the urge to kiss me?"

"I had the urge to bash your head in with a frying pan."

"I think that's illegal."

"It's funny that you think a law is the reason I didn't do it."

"I don't know what you want me to do." I reverted to our first debate. "We can't leave. Tamar would have helicopters on us in minutes."

"Oh, I can make sure she doesn't."

"No shooting!"

He lifted his hands. "Who said anything about shooting her?"

"No poking your fingers in her nostrils, then."

He looked alarmed . . . and confused. "What?"

Ugh. I couldn't explain it now. "I'm going back."

That didn't make Nick happy at all. "Several people who Christian worked with have died or disappeared in the last six months. What's to say you won't be next?"

"Why would anyone try to kill me? I didn't work with him at the firm. I didn't know those papers existed the entire time we were together."

"What if the people who were targeting Christian's firm don't know that? What if they assume two people who were getting married told each other everything?"

I had no answer for that.

Nick continued, "What if it's not about the papers at all?"

That got my full attention. "What else would it be?"

"A thousand things, Princess." His voice had softened. "You can't go back."

"We've exhausted our avenues out here." I shook my head and grew more determined. There was no other option. Once my grandmother made the search for me public, finding Christian would be impossibly complicated. My ability to move around basically undetected would vanish in a heartbeat. The monarchy would once again be a target for Anders and the Liberals in Parliament. I was thoroughly boxed in between duty and my thwarted desires. I felt the weight of a nation as I shrugged. "Any information we need to know about Christian's last days in Drieden can only be found in the city. Inside the palace." It was our last and best chance to solve the mystery.

From the resigned expression on Nick's face, I suspected he'd already thought through this, too, but he still protested. "You're a fish in a barrel there."

"Not if I have someone looking out for me."

He made a disgusted face and nodded toward the canal bank, where Tamar presumably waited for me. "You trust her to watch out for you? When she didn't listen to your orders?"

"No, I don't."

He sighed in relief.

"I trust *you* to watch out for me," I said.

He stilled. "You speak perfect Driedish," I continued. "As far as anyone in the family knows, you're additional security that my father hired to watch me. No one will call Father to ask, and if they do, he'll remember that he saw you with me at Ceillis House and assume that it was all his idea. If Tamar and Hugh have a problem with it, I'll remind them that you're Christian's brother. Why wouldn't you be doing everything in your power to find out what happened to him?"

"Thea . . ."

I stopped him with a princess hand held up. "As my new security officer, you'll have access to the records about Christian. We'll be able to piece together that end."

"And what will you be doing?" His crossed arms and furrowed brow told me he wasn't convinced. Yet.

"The Driedish government has access to the Cayman papers."

"So does the British government, Princess. You don't think I have people who can look into this?"

"Once I'm back, I can determine what Christian knew and who else knew about the papers."

"And who would want to keep him quiet."

Last chance to run away.

As if he could hear the voices inside my head, he touched my cheek with the back of his hand. "Are you sure? Remember our conversation last night?"

I nodded, my throat suddenly raw.

"Sometimes it's a lot simpler to pretend to die than to deal with your family."

If there was the slightest chance that Nick was right, that the palace had orchestrated Christian's disappearance, then I couldn't in good conscience let this go.

I looked into his eyes and felt the internal rush he always triggered. "Nothing is simple," I said. "Not anymore."

Then I reached up and did the most complicated thing. I pulled his head down and kissed him.

After a moment, he kissed me back and I knew we were both in way over our heads.

As much as I didn't want to believe it, no one could have planted a bug in the Crown Prince's house without someone on the inside, and only someone inside the palace could find out the truth.

It had to be me.

twenty-two

WE ARRIVED AT THE PALACE A FEW HOURS LATER. This time, there was no sneaking in. The gates opened when Tamar's dark sedan pulled up and the guard took one glance at her, and then at me, and waved us through.

It was a bit anticlimactic, to tell the truth.

Tamar excused herself to go check in with the security office, but Nick stayed glued to my side as I went up the back way—through the administrative offices to the West Wing elevator, taking a right, and then standing face-to-face with the retina scanner.

"I'll let you in this time, but I'll have to get the staff to set up your retina scan," I told him.

"It's not my first rodeo, Princess."

After we went through the scanner, we headed to my apartments, where Nick started unpacking a selection of technological devices from the knapsack he'd brought from the houseboat. In less than five minutes, he'd scanned my rooms with his gadgets, and since he hadn't gone straight to the Renoir over my bed or my Grisden hanging above the mantel and extracted a matte-black disc, I supposed I was in the clear.

My apartments were fairly simple. As a single woman, I didn't need much space, especially when I had ten acres of grandeur around me. There was the living room, my bathroom, my closet-slash-dressing room, my bedroom, my office, and a tiny second bedroom that had a single bed shoved in a corner.

At some point, my apartments had been occupied by Princess Carlotta, the young widow of Prince Franz-Gregor, and the tiny second bedroom had been the nursery for her children when they were ill. Because things were practically never remodeled in the palace, this tiny nook with a single bright window had remained, even though Carlotta's children had been in St. Julien's graveyard for nearly a century.

This is where I took Nick next, opening the door and gesturing toward the neatly made bed, which was freshly changed by the maids every week despite the fact that I hadn't had a guest here in . . . ever. "You can put your things over here," I told him. "If you need an étagère, I can call a steward."

"No." Nick turned around and went back to my bedroom. He dropped his pack. Eyed my bed.

"No!" I said.

He lifted his eyebrow. "You didn't have a problem sharing at Sybil's."

"If you thought it was too dangerous there, you haven't met Hugh yet."

"Hugh?"

"My lead security officer."

Nick crossed his arms. "And this Hugh regularly invites himself into your bedroom?"

He had me there. But I refused to give in so easily. "Well, he would. If there was an emergency. A fire. Or a bomb . . . or some other sort of explosion."

Nick gave me a look that showed he wasn't impressed. "And this very protective Hugh, why wasn't he the one who came to get you instead of the woman?"

I didn't know, and for some reason, that bothered me slightly. "I'm sure he was working elsewhere," I said, yet another lame answer, which Nick didn't acknowledge. He jerked a thumb at the guest room. "No exterior door there. I'll take the couch."

"The couch?" I echoed as I followed him back into my living area. My couch was tiny, hard, and narrow. It was meant for meetings with my stylist and secretary. It wasn't designed for a tall, broad Scotsman to lie on.

Not like my antique, four-poster canopied bed literally meant for a queen.

"You can't sleep there."

Nick dropped his backpack on the couch.

"It's pink."

He lifted his shoulders. "I like pink."

"It's uncomfortable."

"I've had worse."

He seemed a bit more distant after that, more professional, and when he asked me where the security offices were, I called an aide immediately to show him down.

I could have done it myself, but it seemed like we both needed some space. If life on the boat had been tight, I knew that life in 700,000 square feet could be suffocating.

Nick returned hours later, after I had already readied for bed. My door was closed, and I was tucked in when I heard the knock and his low voice.

"Yes?" I called out.

He didn't answer and I didn't hear his voice again.

LUCY ALWAYS HAD HER PRIORITIES STRAIGHT. SHE RUSHED into my sitting room the next morning, first crushing me in a tight hug, then pouring me a cup of coffee and giving Nick the stink eye. "Who are *you?*"

"I'm new."

Lucy looked at me for a more thorough explanation. "Father had him assigned. To keep an eye on me."

She nodded approvingly before launching into an expected scolding. "What were you thinking, Thea, really? A royal princess can't just take a vacation without anyone knowing about it."

She looked back at Nick. "And you. Haven't you been trained? Her Highness is standing. One does not remain seated while Her Highness is standing."

Nick reluctantly rose from the chair he had been comfortably slouching in.

"We have standards in this palace. I expect you to keep a very close eye on Her Highness and immediately inform me if she tries to do anything reckless."

"Yes, of course." Nick did a very good job keeping a straight face when he replied. He was already well acquainted with my reckless streak.

"Lucy's quite protective of me," I told him.

Her head whipped around at my words. "Me? *He's* the one who needs to be protective. I don't know why your father didn't hire four more guards to keep an eye on you."

"She's only got the one couch," Nick said offhandedly.

Lucy's mouth dropped open. "Wha . . . ?" Yes, Nick had agreed to my return to the palace only if he stayed in my apartments with me, but I hadn't planned on telling anyone. No one would have really noticed, as long as he got up early and put the blankets and pillows away before Lucy or a maid came in.

But Lucy's order to stand must have ignited Nick's contrary streak. "Father's orders. Twenty-four/seven protection," I said with a rush to distract her.

Lucy harrumphed. "She should send you back to Perpetua," she said, speaking of my grandmother. "But with Anders making so much noise, she's calling the troops into action."

"The troops?" Nick echoed, and I tried sending him a mental order to shut up. Lucy wouldn't understand a bodyguard who wouldn't stand and who wanted to speak, too.

Sure enough, Lucy shook her head disapprovingly and went to the canvas bag she'd set down when she first came in. "Sophie's not happy, and neither is Henry."

"So Gran asked everyone to come back to Drieden to appear at royal events," I summarized, hoping that would satisfy Nick's blatant curiosity before he did something as gauche as talk again.

Lucy heaved the bag onto a table and removed a pile of newspapers. "I think I got all of the ones that you asked for. If this is going to be a new habit, I'll have the press office send up extra subscriptions. My newsstand isn't convenient for my driver to stop at."

Nick strolled over and started leafing through the newspapers I'd ordered for him: *Le Monde, The Wall Street Journal, The Driedener.*

"He's checking for weapons," I told Lucy when she looked affronted at his impertinence.

"He's very thorough."

"You have no idea," Nick said.

Lucy blinked several times. I turned my head so she wouldn't see me biting back a smile.

"About these events, do you have the details for me?"

Lucy removed her leather-covered planner from the bag. "Some. Her Majesty's office is still finalizing the schedule." Her finger landed with a thud onto today's page. "She wants to see you."

"Who?"

Lucy had known me too long to play that game. "You can't pull stunts like this, Thea. Not anymore."

Nick flashed a quick look at me when she said that, but thankfully, Lucy was in efficiency mode.

"She'll expect you at noon." Lucy pulled a sheet out of her calendar and laid it on the table. It was cream with my light blue coat of arms embossed at the top, but it was Lucy's feminine, crisp handwriting that filled the page. "And here are the next week's appointments."

After ordering me a full Driedish breakfast and calling Roberto to "do something" about my hair, Lucy left, and Nick made a quick bee-line toward my calendar.

"No. No. No. No." As he switched back into English, he ticked off each of Lucy's neatly drawn dates with black sharp slashes of the fountain pen she'd left behind.

I stole the pen from his hand. "You can't say no to all of these."

"This was a bad idea."

"You didn't have a better one."

Then I took my calendar back. "One doesn't say no to an audience with Queen Aurelia."

Nick's expression suggested otherwise.

"You can't be serious. She's my *grandmother*. She's seventy-five years old! How could she possibly be a threat?"

"According to you, she was one of the last people to see Christian alive."

My head jerked and then I remembered—he was right. That night at Ceillis House, when Big Gran had called Christian and me to speak privately. "What are you saying?" I put a hand to my throat. "I should interrogate my grandmother?"

"Do you want me to do it?"

"No." I don't think I'd ever said a word that quickly before.

Nick loomed over me, his face deadly serious. "Someone has murdered and kidnapped Christian and his associates—or ordered it done."

The realization slapped me in the face as if I'd run into a brick wall. "You didn't want to come back here because you thought my *grandmother* was behind this?"

He picked the calendar out of my hand again and started to scribble.

When he was done, he handed it to me calmly.

"Sophie, Henry . . ." I read aloud the names of my brother and sister next to each appearance. "I don't understand."

"As soon as they're in town, you're doing everything with one of them."

He turned and moved toward my small study, newspapers under his arm.

"Why?" I asked his retreating back.

"Because Grandmama's men probably won't want to kill a second heir in the cross fire," he called out.

Dumbfounded, I stood with my mouth hanging open. This is what my life had come to. Using my younger brother and sister as human shields. Just like mad Prince Hugo had done in 1476.

History really did repeat itself.

twenty-three

BIG GRAN HAD SCHEDULED OUR MEETING AT NOON. Since she always took luncheon at one o'clock, I'd assumed this would be a cursory interview. A quick chat with her granddaughter before a civilized bite to eat.

I was wrong. Very wrong.

It wasn't Her Majesty Aurelia, Queen of Drieden, I spoke with. It was an angry, worried grandmother, which was so much worse.

She lectured and railed and lectured some more. I was reminded of my upbringing, my duty, my responsibilities. She laid the guilt on thick: my family loved me, my country needed me, my legacy depended on my reliable reputation.

"You're nearly thirty years old, Theodora. You are second in line to the throne! Your time for gadding about on your little adventures is over."

I let her have her say. Now it was my turn. I had some questions that needed answers, too. "Two nights before the wedding, you told me that you and Father were changing the order of succession. That I would be first in line."

Big Gran's gaze shot to the window, where the late-summer day was gray and gloomy. "Yes?" She asked vaguely.

I guessed I had to be more direct. "Has that changed?"

"It was never made public."

"That's not what I asked."

Her eyes flared at my impertinence.

"I think it's a fair question. Was the initial decision to make me first in line because of me, or because of Christian?"

Now she really looked insulted, but her expression quickly returned to ferociousness. "Your marriage to Christian would have strengthened our position significantly."

"Our position?"

"With the vote. I have been informed that in five days, Pierre Anders will call for a vote in Parliament regarding the creation of a republic and the continued support of the monarchy."

I stood, suddenly frustrated with the way the conversation was going. It said something that I was able to handle her half-hour harangue about every negative aspect of my character, but as soon as my grandmother started pulling puppet strings, I could not sit still.

"What does Christian have to do with it? We all got along fine before he came along."

Gran's eyes widened as she realized that I'd stood while she sat—a breach of every etiquette rule I'd ever learned.

But she quickly got over my manners in order to lecture some more. "We've gone over this. A stable, well-adjusted family with a clear expectation of succession is what will ensure the future of the Crown."

"Well-adjusted? Have you met our family?"

"Theodora! This is exactly what I meant. Your impetuousness and impromptu trips are simply inappropriate for any princess, let alone the heir apparent."

I understood now. "So you're saying I can't be queen without a husband who's going to keep me in line."

Yet again, she refused to be baited. "I'm saying I've changed my mind. For the time being."

We could keep arguing about this, but I had a feeling a tantrum would only reinforce what she believed about me. That somehow I was not yet worthy of being named the next monarch.

I remembered Nick's crack about interrogating my grandmother. She wasn't taking my questions very well. But if I didn't do it, who would?

"Did you see him again?" I blurted out. My grandmother looked taken aback, but once I started talking, I couldn't stop. "After the ball at Ceillis House, did you see Christian again before he escaped the loveable clutches of our well-adjusted family?"

"No. I had heads of state to meet with; I didn't have time to pencil in bonding sessions with my new grandson."

Well. Big Gran had some sarcasm in her after all.

I walked over to her desk, pretending to look at the black-and-white snapshots I'd seen thousands of times. These were the only photos she kept in this room, the ones of her and her parents when she was a little girl. "I keep thinking about it. Wondering what I did wrong, what I could have done to make him stay." My eyes dropped to her papers. Unfortunately, there was nothing particularly incriminating there—just her usual correspondence and her tablet.

"I was thinking I would see him again." I ran a finger across the tablet screen, only to see her usual news websites pop up. Something about the Caribbean banking system. Something about global warming. "Maybe we'd be able to talk. Who knows—maybe we could be friends again."

She sighed. "Obviously, you weren't listening earlier. This impulsiveness and poor decision-making has got to stop, Thea."

She'd switched back to my family nickname. Interesting.

"One minute ago you said that my relationship with Christian was good for the Crown. Now it's a bad idea. Which is it?"

She smoothed her skirts, and for a moment I saw something I rarely saw on my grandmother's face: uncertainty.

My question wasn't that tricky, not for a wily public servant like herself, used to public pronouncements one day and political double-talk behind the scenes the next.

"It's the perception that you can't make up your mind that's worrisome. A future queen must not waver from the course she has set."

I thought about that for a moment, marveling at the scream that started welling up in my throat.

I was finally able to swallow that anger and speak. "I was going to marry him, you know. I didn't waver from *that* decision."

She was avoiding my eyes now. Maybe she knew she'd pushed me too far. Maybe she didn't want to look the crazy heir straight in the eyes, like a dog that just might bite.

I don't know why I said what I said next.

"I'll do everything you've asked me to do. I'll make all the appearances; I'll smile, stand straight, and simper. But I *will* find out what made Christian leave Drieden. I deserve that much."

When she finally looked up at me, the previous uncertainty was gone, replaced by another, thoroughly chilling, emotion: fear.

OF COURSE, I WAS ON EDGE AS I RETURNED TO MY APARTments. Sparring with Big Gran was not a soothing experience, and I never wanted to push her too far. The ghost of my disinherited sister was never far from my mind. As I entered my sitting room, I thought of Caroline. Maybe I could visit her. See where she lived. After Sybil had mentioned Caroline's astrological chart, I had meant to call her on my old secret phone. But that plan was ruined now.

I kicked off the stupid high heels that I'd worn to meet my own grandmother. What normal twenty-first-century woman dressed up in high heels to have a conversation with her grandma? I curled my toes into the thick white rug and wondered what would happen if I showed up in my running shoes next time.

What if I put my Nikes on now? My toes curled again. Nick wasn't here. I could easily slip out for a quick jog. No one would have to know.

Before I could finish processing that thought, there was a knock at the door. "Come in," I called out automatically, instantly disappointed that I couldn't escape out to the city gardens for a little bit.

Just for some fresh air.

Tamar walked in, wearing her usual button-down shirt and wide-legged pants. No gun that I could see. I wondered about the one I'd dropped into the Comtesse. Would it be hard for her to get another? Would she have to fill out paperwork?

"I'm sorry, Tamar."

She looked confused. After all, she'd just walked in. "For what?"

"For throwing your gun in the river. Do let me know if you get in trouble for that."

It only seemed to relieve her worry for a moment. "About that . . . Your Highness, may we speak?"

"Sure." I paced the perimeter of the rug. I was restless. I needed to move and talk at the same time. "Oh—have you seen Nick?" If I timed this right, maybe I could still arrange an hour or two of privacy. I needed to think. I could do that better outside.

"Mr. Cameron"—she grimaced as she said the name I had told her to call him while he was in the palace,—"is downstairs doing new-employee paperwork."

Oh, crap. Nick was going to love that. But what I said was, "Excellent," because that was surely going to take a while. "Do I need to speak with Hugh?" I asked, remembering my other bodyguard, whom I had not seen since returning to the palace. As the only other person who knew who Nick was, I should probably make sure he didn't reveal "Mr. Cameron's" true identity.

Tamar shook her head. "Ma'am, Hugh's been out this week. I heard it was the flu."

"Wonderful. I mean, not wonderful for him," I added hastily when

Tamar looked alarmed at my choice of words. "But it's a bit convenient for us, isn't it?"

Tamar did not look similarly relieved.

"What's going on?" I asked, stopping my to-and-fro across the room.

"Mr. Fraser-Campbell."

"Cameron," I corrected her.

"Pardon, ma'am, but I must speak plainly. It's my job to protect you and I don't feel comfortable with this man, this Scot, staying here, in your rooms, under false pretenses."

"I see," I said. Frankly, I was a little stunned. I had assumed Tamar would go along with my orders, as her employer and as her princess. But of course, after all that had happened, things had changed between us. It was good for me to be reminded that perhaps Tamar was not to be trusted. I had to play this carefully.

"Is there something in particular you're worried about?"

Tamar licked her lips. "He lied when he first met you. He used a false identity. He's lied for years to his family, to Christian." She rushed the words out and looked visibly concerned.

"He's not going to hurt me." I hoped that would soothe her. "There's no reason why he should hurt me."

"I still don't trust him. Why would he come back to see you, now? To live with you, no less? To continue lying about his identity?" She shook her head, her brown curls bouncing as if adding to a rising warning chorus. "When his own brother isn't even in this country? Ma'am, I know it's forward of me, but I have to be sure that you are safe. That there's a good reason for this man to be in the palace under false pretenses."

"I see where you're coming from," I said slowly. "And, as ever, I appreciate your loyalty and thoroughness. I can assure you that Nick is only here for the best interests of both his brother and me. Can you trust me on this?"

Tamar backed down like a reluctant German shepherd—still tense, yet obedient.

"I'm giving you the next few days off," I said as I crossed into my dressing room to change into workout clothes.

"Ma'am?" She sounded worried in the other room.

I stripped off my purple jersey dress and pulled on a warm-up jacket and running tights. I wouldn't go outside the palace walls, but it was imperative that I get some of this energy out. When I returned to the sitting room, Tamar was still there, standing at attention.

"Just a few days, Tamar."

"Is this a disciplinary action, ma'am?"

"No!" I cried, aghast. "It's a reward for good service. You worked night and day to find me while I was off . . ." I made a little hand motion in the general direction of the Comtesse. "You deserve to relax a few days. I'll be fine with the backup shift." And Nick. When she still looked uncertain, I explained, "I won't be going anywhere without Sophie and Henry and their guards, anyway. I will be quite well protected."

She finally left, admirably resigned to the fact that I was forcing her to take some time for herself. I made a mental note to tell Lucy to arrange something nice for Tamar. Maybe she'd like a spa day? And then I left an actual note for Nick on the entry table.

Gone for a run.

twenty-four

WHEN I CAME BACK FROM THE GARDENS, NICK was waiting for me. He shoved a large fruit basket in my hands and pushed me back down the hallway.

"What is this?" I asked, stumped by his behavior. "Where are we going? What are you doing?"

He led me to the service elevator and hit the button for the basement. "Your security officer is ill. You're bringing a card and gifts to cheer up old Hugo."

"Hugh."

"Sure."

At the door to the security office, he put his eyeball next to a red light in a box on the wall, and the door unlocked for him. I looked at him through the tower of oranges. "Why am I holding a fruit basket?"

"Because no one argues with a princess with a fruit basket."

It turned out to be true. How Nick would know that everyone in the security office would smile and nod and ask no questions, I wasn't sure.

Maybe that's what they expected of me—all they expected of me. A pretty face behind a bland display of cheer and charity. No one would suspect that the pretty face was accompanied by a British spy.

Hugh's office was a small, drab box, a shocking contrast to the gilt and ornamentation in the rooms just three floors above. "This doesn't make sense," I muttered after Nick shut the door. "If Hugh isn't even here, who is going to eat all these oranges?"

Nick pulled the rolling chair up to the desk and woke the computer. "Someone's picking up his mail." He pushed a turquoise envelope toward me. "Write him a nice note, will you?"

I stared at the get-well card and the ballpoint pen clipped to it. Then I looked at Nick, who was now expertly accessing the files on Hugh's computer.

"Aren't those password-protected?" I asked, suddenly worried about the security of the security office's not-so-secure computers.

Nick frowned at the screen and ignored my observant question. "We don't have much time. Have you finished that note?"

I grabbed the pen and card. " 'Please come back soon,' " I read aloud as I wrote. " 'The new guy is a jackass.' "

Nick's irritated expression showed in the reflection of the computer screen. He was not impressed.

"What does this mean?" Nick asked brusquely. He was pointing at the calendar program and it took me a minute to decipher what we were looking at.

"Those are personnel assignments," I told him. "Who is on duty for each member of the royal family. Here." I reached over and indicated a color-coded key. "Those are the family members."

"Cricket? Horntail? Grasshopper?"

"Sophie, Henry, Caroline," I said, explaining the code names of my siblings.

Nick analyzed the list. "Honeybee?"

"Me," I said.

"Let me guess: your grandmother is Queen Bee."

"Monarch, actually."

"What an uncrackable code," Nick drawled. "I suppose my brother's code name was Darter."

"How did you know?"

Nick pointed at the screen. "Darter stopped receiving security detail the day of your wedding."

"Ah." I popped the cap back on the pen and stepped away. "So we know who was assigned to him the day he disappeared, then?"

Nick was scribbling down the information; a series of numbers had been entered throughout the day. "I'm assuming these are initials and last names."

I read the names, some familiar, some not. E. Hejnstrom. T. Gruber. K. J. Charlet. "Yes, I think so. Will you be able to talk to these people?"

"Probably not," he said. "But I'll send the names to Max so he can get in touch. Apparently there have been a number of reassignments. A few retirements."

"Really?" I was surprised. Some of the security team were like extended family. They just seemed to always have been there.

"A lot happens when you're on a deserted island for four months, Princess."

I couldn't help but wonder if there was a connection. Sure, a presumptive prince disappearing right from under one's nose would be met with disapproval from superiors. But what if some of Christian's security had been forced out because of his disappearance? I rubbed my forehead, distressed at the thought. How many people had lost their jobs because of my aborted wedding? Because I was wondering if Christian's disappearance had resulted in people getting fired, I didn't notice what Nick had said until it was too late.

"Honeybee, you say?" he murmured, and it took me a moment to realize he'd said it in English. That alerted me to trouble more than the recitation of my code name.

Nick had pulled up a file, marked "Honeybee Incident Reports."

My stomach sank as I realized what he was looking at. Much like the file that Tamar and Hugh had shown me mere days ago on Nicholas Fraser-Campbell, my file was filled with reports, photographs, and records of past behavior.

A minute or so passed as Nick scanned the stories.

"We should go," I said.

"Sure." Nick didn't look up. Didn't move. Engrossed by my past.

"It wouldn't take me this long to write a card," I hissed.

Finally, he raised his eyes to meet mine. Then his eyebrow rose and I knew I had made a fatal mistake inviting Nick to be part of the security office, even undercover.

"I didn't know they kept records like that," I said nervously.

"It's their job to protect you. Of course, they're going to discipline those who let you get away."

"They're not supposed to," I said defensively. "When I was seventeen, my father told them that it wasn't anyone's fault when I ran off."

Nick gave me a look reserved for three-year-olds and drunk teenagers who should have known better when they backed their car into a bush. "It's their job. And you make it harder for them."

Guilt and shame crawled up my throat. My compulsion to skip out of the palace had been long-standing and, apparently, well documented. Once I'd passed into adulthood, I'd ordered people to stop following me at times.

But hadn't I always known there was no way out? Not really. Not until I'd stuffed myself into a trash chute with Nick Fraser-Campbell at the National Galleries.

"We have to go." I shuffled toward the door, with one last look at the fruit basket for my flu-stricken security guard. I hoped it would be delivered soon.

Before I could open the door, Nick's hand clamped around mine on the doorknob. He whispered in my ear, "If you run, you'll not get away from me that easily."

I half closed my eyes as a thrill ran up my spine. "Is that a threat?"

Nick smiled slowly. "It's my solemn vow as a Scotsman."

twenty-five

PRINCESS SOPHIE GAVE A DRAMATIC SIGH, PARADING into my apartments in patchouli and Prada. "My God, you're lucky. I'm in a tiny turret in the West Wing. All this space! And liquor!" She made a beeline for my silver tray of alcohol.

"I'm sure if you lived here full-time, you'd be allowed your very own ice bucket," I told my little sister.

"If I lived here full-time, I'd be a desperate alcoholic, incoherent with insanity," she said, considering the options on my bar. "Ooh, champagne!" She reached for the vodka instead. "I'm so jet-lagged, I couldn't even do my hair." She touched the multicolored scarf that wrapped her wild red curls.

"Vodka probably won't help with the jet lag."

"Oh, won't it?" she drawled, taking a sip of the drink she'd just poured over two ice cubes. Then she noticed the man in my room. "Well, now . . . *who* is this?" She batted her lashes.

"Nick Cameron," I said, barely holding back an eye roll. "He's just been assigned to me."

"Thea, you are the luckiest." She didn't stop staring at Nick when she said this, her wide blue eyes sparkling as she appraised him like one of Big Gran's racehorses. "Such a strong, capable man. He probably makes you feel very secure."

I made an apologetic face to Nick behind Sophie's back.

She cocked her head. "And he's sitting. How refreshing! It's always so uncomfortable to have security constantly lurking over one's shoulder."

Nick lifted an eyebrow. "I stand very quickly."

"I bet you do." Sophie's suggestive tone was inappropriate for a princess. And for my little sister.

"Sophie, please," I said.

But she ignored me and sat on my sofa, resting her chin in one hand and clutching her vodka protectively in the other. "You do know what you're getting into with Thea, don't you?" she asked Nick. "She has a reputation. I'm sure they've briefed you."

"Thoroughly," I inserted impatiently.

"I've reviewed her file," Nick said carefully. I wanted to reach back in time and drop the thick file labeled "Honeybee" on his foot.

"Mm-hmm." Sophie took a sip. "Well, I'm sure it's all there. Take very good care of my sister." She lowered her voice. "She's very quick. Blink and you'll miss her."

"I can handle her."

Sophie's hot-pink lips pursed in pleasure as she winked at me. "Like I said. Lucky."

I couldn't handle the innuendo anymore. "Did you get your calendar?" I asked her while heading toward the bar myself, pouring a glass of champagne to take the little-sister edge off while still keeping my wits.

Another dramatic sigh from my redheaded sibling. "Factory ribbons and cancer events and orphanage visits . . . I didn't even know we had orphanages in this day and age. Thea, what did you *do*?"

"What do you mean?" I topped off my champagne. Desperate times and all.

She swung her feet up on the pale pink upholstery. Her rainbow-painted toes peeped out of her high-heeled sandals. They would have to be toned down before she toured any cancer wards. "The troops haven't been called out like this since the last one of your incidents." She eyed me speculatively. "I thought marriage was supposed to make you behave."

"You might have noticed, I'm not married."

Sophie smiled naughtily. "And I'm so glad. But I was desperately worried about you on Perpetua all these months." She tilted her head toward Nick. "Make a note. Thea becomes a bit unpredictable when she's locked up."

"You make it sound like I was in prison."

"Perpetua *is* a prison." She looked at Nick again. "Have you been there?"

He shook his head no, saying nothing, but he still had that glimmer in his eye that meant he was way more interested in this conversation than he was letting on.

"It's beautiful in a haunted, freezing, isolated way."

"Sounds lovely," Nick drawled.

Apparently I was the only one who heard his sarcasm because Sophie continued to explain, "It's where they put us when they want us to disappear."

"Have you been sent there?"

A question from the bodyguard would have been unacceptable if any other royal were in the room, but Sophie found the novelty thrilling. "Oh, yes. I went through a phase, after I finished school. I rebelled, like we all do. It's practically expected of every member of the family. But still . . . Thea holds the record."

"That's in the past," I said, avoiding Nick's curious glance.

"Yes," Sophie agreed. "Except now I've been called back to Drieden to inspect the newest organic rutabaga farm. If you haven't misbehaved again, why is Big Gran requesting my presence at St. Francis's Home for Incontinent Dogs?"

This was much safer ground and a question I could answer. "It's Pierre Anders. He called for a vote on the republic issue."

"Oh, he's done that for years." Sophie waved a hand, dismissing Anders and his regular calls for dismantling the Driedish monarchy.

I realized that Sophie was right. This wasn't a new threat, and Anders had never come close to convincing Parliament before. So why was Gran so rattled this time?

I was distracted from that thought when another knock sounded on my door and my brother, Henry, boldly strolled into the room, his military posture as glaring as the Driedish football club jersey and garish plaid golf pants he had on. If he couldn't wear a uniform, the man had no clue how to dress.

"Henry!" I greeted him.

"Where the fuck did you find that outfit?" Sophie asked, echoing my own thoughts.

"There's liquor over there," I called out.

"Thank God," he muttered. Then he stopped, halfway to my bottle-topped cart, and stared at Nick. "Who are you?"

"That's Nick, Thea's new Hugh."

Henry took a minute to work that out. Likely, he had forgotten the names of my security staff, which was understandable since he flew fighter jets for NATO and probably had a lot of other details to memorize. "He's sitting," he noted.

"New protocol," I said.

"It's lovely," Sophie declared brightly. "It's almost like he's part of the family."

I choked a little on my champagne.

"You look familiar," Henry said to Nick, his eyes narrowing. "Have we met? Were you in the Army?"

"Marines," Nick said in such perfect Driedish, Henry would never have suspected that Nick had served in the *British* Marines.

"Ah." A gleam of respect shone in Henry's eyes. A royal prince he might be, but he was a military man at heart. "I'd offer you a drink, but I'm sure it's against regulation."

"It is."

Henry poured a shot of whiskey. "And you'll need to keep your wits about you around Thea."

I'd forgotten that little brothers were just as annoying as little sisters. "Shut up, Henry."

But that only egged him on. "She's impossible, really. And for a princess, she really hates being told what to do."

"I've noticed," Nick said drily.

It was the worst possible thing for him to say. Now Henry and Sophie were all ears and eager for more.

"Really . . ." Sophie drew out the word, pregnant with curiosity.

Henry chuckled. "You move fast, Thea. I guess there weren't enough diversions on Perpetua."

Sophie leaned forward and cupped her mouth. "Diversions are code for *men*," she said in a stage whisper to Nick.

I knew what they were doing. This was all to tease me. They didn't care about Nick or helping him manage the unmanageable princess, and they had no idea of the extent and depth of Nick's and my relationship.

I didn't know how to shut them up. If I protested, they would keep going. If I said nothing, they would goad me. My only hope was to get drunk. Or create a distraction.

"Gran wants you to open the new fishing museum," I told my brother.

He leaned his head back and groaned. "Isn't that what Father is for?"

"What the fuck is a fishing museum?" Sophie asked, again echoing my thoughts.

"I think it will be a joint appearance. Prince Albert and Prince Henry, tying hooks together. Filial fishing, if you will."

Henry fixed me with a baleful stare. "Let's get out of here. Like that night after your wedding."

Oh no. I spoke quickly. "We have the opera opening tonight. Sophie and I have hair and makeup in an hour." Ordinarily, a conversation about hair and makeup would be more than enough to distract my little sister, but something else had caught her attention.

"Wait. You two went out after the wedding?" Her red curls bounced indignantly. "And you didn't invite me? I was trapped between Aunt Carlotta and some dead-eyed, ancient Hapsburgs and you two were off cavorting *without me?*"

Henry grinned. Sophie waited for an explanation. And Nick's green eyes were watching all of this.

What the hell. "I had to blow off some steam."

Sophie lit up. "You *didn't.*"

Henry tilted his head in my direction. "I caught her in the east stairwell. What could I do? She needed a chaperone. She was in a bad way."

"Thea knows all the ways out of the palace," Sophie said in an aside to Nick. "Just watch."

Henry winked at me. "And let's just say, I have a mate who's still asking me when you're going to call."

"*Thea!*" Sophie squealed. "You were supposed to be married!"

"Ah, but I wasn't." I stood, checking my watch. "There's no law against a single woman having a good time."

"Except Gran's law. Going out on the town the night you were left at the altar? The scandal! Now I get why you were shipped off so fast."

"Perpetua." Henry shivered and nodded at Nick. "The next time Thea gets shipped off, pack extra long underwear. You'll be there for a while."

I leaned my head back and drank more champagne. A half hour with my brother and sister, and suddenly an isolated former convent in the middle of the North Sea sounded like heaven.

twenty-six

THE GILDED GRAND DAME OF DRIEDISH ARCHITECTURE, the Imperial Opera House, was built in 1798 at the height of the Baroque era. It was designed by Edouard Sharpe, the architect of the National Galleries and the ostentatious home of the infamous General Jacques Goueget. It was still considered one of the best examples of traditional Driedish design.

Opening night at the opera was always a lavish affair, drawing the titled and wealthy from around Europe who were bored by their yachts and summer coastal escapes. The Driedish opera season was the earliest in Europe. Some people thought this was to avoid the early winter storms that started rolling in off the North Sea, spoiling opera devotees' fashionable gowns and many a soprano's vibrato. But history told a different tale.

"I swear to God, if you start talking about the prostitute again, I will throw you off this balcony," Sophie muttered behind her clenched-teeth smile.

The four representatives of the House of Laurent—Big Gran, myself, Sophie, and Henry—stood in the royal box, waving at the crowd before the President of the Opera declared the season open (with the implicit permission of the Crown, of course).

The applause would continue until Big Gran lifted a hand and gestured at the podium for the President to speak, as she did now. The four of us stepped back into the darkness of the box so the guy could have his big moment.

"She wasn't a prostitute," I couldn't help saying to Sophie in a hushed voice. "She was the king's mistress."

"'Opera singer' was code for prostitute, and I can't believe you're pulling me into this conversation again." She looked at Henry. "She's the worst."

But our brother was having a Very Bad Evening. He was dressed in his formal cardinal uniform, dripping with braids and shiny medals, had just sucked down a flute of champagne, and was anxiously grabbing another off a waiter's tray. "*Opera* is the worst," he said under his breath while carefully watching Big Gran, who had stepped to the side of the box to greet her guests.

"You should try a Xanax," Sophie said a little too loudly. "That's what I do."

"There's no way you just took a Xanax," I observed. "You're entirely too worked up about King Philippe's opera-singer mistress."

Sophie swung around to Nick, who was hovering over me in the shadows, his face a fairly close approximation of Henry's horrified expression. "Does she do this when I'm not around? Or is it just to annoy the shit out of me?"

"Fuck, Sophie," Henry said quickly, looking at Big Gran, "lower your voice." Aw, the big military hero was scared of his grandma. So cute.

"Does she do what, exactly?" Nick asked my sister, pointedly ignoring my reminder from earlier this evening that he keep his mouth shut like a good little security guard.

"Ramble on with pointless stories about infamous Driedeners and inconsequential moments in Driedish history?"

"No," Nick said shortly. "Although there was an illuminating lecture about the Driedish printing press."

Sophie gave me a pointed look. "Illuminating."

I knew what my little sister was attempting to do. She was trying the same thing that Henry was: avoidance. We had been dragged to the opera, which none of us enjoyed, and each of us was trying to distract ourself from the quickly approaching onslaught of boring screaming we were about to endure. Henry thought he could ease the pain with alcohol. Sophie thought a good, old-fashioned sibling feud would be fun.

Me? I eyed Nick in his well-tailored tuxedo. I would settle for my second-favorite avoidance tactic. History.

"You see," I said, leaning toward Nick with a conversational tone, "the reason for the opera opening so early in the year was that King Philippe's mistress—"

"Was a very demanding Florentine who wished to return to her native land before winter."

It was none other than Pierre Anders who had finished my story. I turned, surprised to see the anti-monarchy government officer in the royal box. Especially since the only way he'd be here would be if he had been invited by the Queen herself.

Etiquette kicked in. "Mr. Anders." I extended my hand. "So lovely to see you."

The seventy-year-old politician bent his head, still full of thick gray hair. "I do apologize for interrupting your conversation, Your Highness. An unfortunate habit born from years of trying to be heard in Parliament."

"No doubt your skills are the reason for your years of success." I smiled politely even though my words meant nothing. Sophie slunk away, pretending to wave at someone across the box, and I was left with the politician who wished to render my grandmother unemployed. It was a good reminder that I needed to be very careful with Anders. "Are you a devotee of opera?" I asked. As far as small talk went, this was pretty much as small as it got.

"Not as much opera as history. I heard you discussing King Philippe and couldn't resist jumping in."

"Yes, he was a fascinating figure, wasn't he? Very important." This was a good opportunity to remind Anders of all the benefits that the monarchy had brought our nation. "Of course you know that he was called Philippe the Philanthropist for all he did. Such as starting primary schools. I recall that you are a strong proponent of public education."

Anders nodded thoughtfully. "Yes. Education, labor reform, the arts . . ."

Aha. "Another of Philippe's achievements." I lifted a hand to the magnificent building we were in. "He opened the opera house to the people for weekly performances."

"To encourage them to pay for the facility, he had collection boxes stationed at all of the exits after the show. And the primary schools, if I recall correctly, were for children of the aristocracy only."

He said all this pleasantly enough, but I felt the barb as he intended. This was the eighteenth century we were discussing, however. "Surely you can agree that these acts were steps in the right direction," I said.

"Surely you can agree that gilded halls and fine clothes do not put food into the mouths of Driedeners."

I reminded myself that I was a princess, we were at an official event, and my grandmother the Queen had obviously invited her key rival for a reason. "Well, fine clothes can, in fact, provide income to Driedeners," I said, invoking the serenity that Queen Elsa-Marie was known for. "This gown, for example." I ran my hand down the garnet silk skirt of my ball gown. "This gown was designed and made by Yolande Reobert, a Driedish designer with an atelier here in the city."

Anders eyed my beautiful dress—the one that had made Nick do a double take—with a glance that couldn't manage to mask his disdain. "Ah, yes. Wasn't that the same designer who hand-sewed three thousand pearls onto your wedding dress?"

I could see where this was going. It was so unfair. "Ms. Reobert and her staff were all paid in full for that dress. Which put food in their mouths, if you will."

"And the national treasury? Other wedding expenses were never reimbursed." I felt my face flush, in embarrassment or anger or both.

"I know the arguments of the conservatives," Anders continued. "The tourists bring in that revenue. The tourists that only come to this country because we have a beautiful princess in need of a prince."

I opened my mouth to spout off a charitable princess answer: that tourists visit Drieden for many other reasons—our beautiful landscapes, our culture, our history.

But then I realized I would be making his point. That Drieden didn't *need* the royal family for tourism. That the royal family was, in fact, superfluous.

The lights dimmed for a moment, a sign that the opera was about to begin. Sophie and Henry quickly selected seats in the second row, behind Big Gran, where they could tune out without her notice. It was my perfect excuse to get away from the awful Anders. But as I opened my mouth to explain that I must take my seat, something else entirely came out.

"You are wrong," I said in a low voice that only he could hear under the hustling and rustling of very important people being seated for a very boring event. "This princess has no need of a prince."

Anders pulled back, as if to see me better. "Then why did this country waste hundreds of millions of euros to prepare for your wedding day?"

"You could ask my fiancé that," I said bitterly.

"Next time I talk to him, I will."

"No one wanted to be married more than me," I assured Anders, but as soon as it came out, I knew it was a lie.

Christian had just happened to run away first.

twenty-seven

HAD LANDED IN MY SEAT NEXT TO BIG GRAN AS THE FIRST notes of *Aïda* had started playing when Anders's words sunk in.

Next time I talk to him?

Next time he spoke to Christian?

What. Did. That. Mean?

The next three hours were an interminable aria hell, one where I couldn't move, couldn't whisper, and generally couldn't do anything but applaud politely at the designated times. At Queen Aurelia's side, photographs could be taken at any moment, and God help me if someone caught a glimpse of not perfect Princess Theodora, but the real me, the one who ached to chew on her fingernails and rip her hands through the sprayed and teased crown of blond hair she wore.

Even in the limo back to the palace, I bit my lip as Sophie and Henry bitched and moaned about the evening. They wouldn't care about Anders's offhand remark about Christian, or see what it had to mean.

But Nick would.

An hour after I had returned to my apartments, he let himself in. I swung around. "Finally!"

He looked over my garnet ball gown, half-hanging off my shoulders.

"What?" I demanded. "I can't get it off by myself."

"Don't you have someone who helps you with such things?"

I could have called in a maid, but I had been anxious for privacy as quickly as possible. "I need to talk to you."

"You're half dressed."

"Could you focus, please? You're like a fourteen-year-old boy who has never seen a girl naked before."

He opened his mouth as if to argue but then shut it with a sardonic smile, which would have distracted me if I weren't bursting to talk about Anders.

"Did you hear him? What he said to me?"

"What? Who?"

"Pierre Anders. You were five feet away; surely you heard."

"I zoned out somewhere between the history of Driedish opera and fashion talk."

"You're supposed to be my bodyguard."

"And if he'd taken a knife out to stab you, I would have dealt with it."

"Dealt with it?" I was shocked. "What? Would you give him a stern talking-to?"

"No, he's a leader of Parliament. I'd put him in time-out."

"For stabbing me."

Nick's voice softened. "What did he say, Princess?"

I repeated the conversation to Nick, who paused for a moment before replying, "So?"

"Don't you think it's strange? As far as I know, he'd never spoken to Christian before in his life."

"I think we've established that you didn't know everything Christian was doing in the last year."

"I didn't think he was talking to Pierre Anders."

"No, he wouldn't have."

"How do you know?" I demanded.

"Because I know my brother."

I nibbled on my thumbnail. "There was something about the way Anders said it, though."

"Made you think that Christian was secretly lobbying Liberal members of a Parliament that wasn't even his?"

"Yes, that's it exactly."

"Perhaps you didn't notice I was joking, Princess."

I'd caught his sarcastic tone but had dismissed it, because maybe he was on to something. "The entire conversation was like he was trying to send me a message. Anders chose his words very carefully, making a case against King Philippe."

"Who is very dead, if I'm not mistaken with my Driedish history."

I threw my hands up. "He was making an argument against the existence of the whole royal family."

"He's trying to dismantle the monarchy, remember? That's his job. He was just trying to get under your skin."

I shook my head and twisted my arms around my mid-back, trying to reach the hook between my shoulder blades. "This was something else," I insisted.

With a muttered curse, Nick moved behind me, pushed my fumbling fingers down, and took my dress into his own hands. A moment later, a rush of cool air blew across my back as my gown pooled into a lush froth of silk and netting around my legs.

"He was just trying to get under your skin," Nick said yet again.

"You just said that," I said, hyperaware of his magnetic masculine presence behind me. The way I could almost feel his gaze on my skin. The way I wanted his hands on places so recently covered by red silk.

"It's still true." Nick's voice came from farther away; he had moved out of the danger zone. I stepped out of my dress and turned to see him studiously examining an enamel box on top of my writing desk.

"I never knew Scots were such prudes," I said, refusing to be

ashamed about standing in the middle of my own home in a corset and
stockings.

"I'm very good at my job, Princess."

The non sequitur made me jerk my head back. "Excuse me?"

"I avoid distractions. There's a time and a place for everything."

"So I'm a distraction?"

He lifted his green eyes to meet mine. "Very much so."

"There's a time and a place?" My question came out a bit more
breathless than I liked, and when he smiled a soft, rueful smile, I shivered with delicious anticipation.

Princesses weren't usually good at delayed gratification, but it
seemed Scottish spies were masters of it.

OVER THE NEXT WEEK, IN THE MORNINGS, SOPHIE AND I
visited hospitals and took photos with children suffering from leukemia.
In the afternoons, Henry and I opened new train stations and toured ex-
hibits at the military museum.

Then I would go back to the palace and read acres of the papers
Nick kept downloading and bringing to my apartments. After finding
nothing interesting in Claytere's private documents, Nick thought a
pair of fresh princess eyes might catch something in the publicly available files. He was so wrong. It was relentless, pointless work. There
was nothing there. Nothing at all to connect Christian and the Boson
Chapelle firm with the monarchy, Big Gran, or the Driedish government.

The routine was numbing, and I probably should have realized that
I was in trouble when I'd started wandering the halls of the palace.

I was in the South Wing, in the viewing gallery above the garden
portico, when they found me.

"Thea! There you are!" Lucy tutted, feeling my forehead as soon as she got within range. Nick was close on her heels, his face as dark as a Driedish winter storm.

"I'm fine," I told her.

"You're warm," she said. "She's warm," she repeated to Nick.

"I'm sure she is." He somehow managed to make a mumble sound sarcastic.

Lucy threaded her arm through mine, a secure lock as though I was about to make a break for it. "This is what happens when you're pushed too hard."

"She wanders off without telling anyone?" This time Nick's voice was a full-out Scottish growl that somehow escaped the notice of my germaphobe secretary, fussing over me as she was.

Lucy tugged on my sleeve. "It isn't right; you can't worry your staff so."

"I was within palace grounds. Perfectly safe," I said as she started leading me back toward the residential wing.

"Very reasonable."

"Not so much," I heard Nick say behind us.

"He has a point," Lucy said with a squeeze of my hand. "You don't want your father to put more of him on you."

Nick's snort bounced off the three-hundred-year-old wooden parquet floors, but Lucy retained her sangfroid.

"You should stay in tonight. I'll call Her Majesty's secretary and tell her . . ."

"No." I cut Lucy off, irritated by her suggestion. "I'm not sick."

"But you need—"

"I need to go out and see people."

"You saw people yesterday."

In the stuffy basement of a training center for developmentally delayed adults. Rewarding work, of course. But there had been security and expectations and a decided lack of . . . windows. Sunshine. Fresh air.

If I said that to Lucy, she would overreact. Obviously, I was ill when I started counting windows. Obviously, I was about to . . .

Make a run for it.

As if he could read my mind, Nick barely let me out of his sight when we returned to my apartments. I was allowed to use the restroom and change into a black wool dress. Lucy had set out a perfectly sensible pair of sturdy black shoes for my event tonight, but when I came out of my dressing room, Nick's eyes fell to the cherry-red lace-up, four-inch heels I had slipped into.

"At least I know you can't run in those."

"Not very far," I said, chagrined.

I don't know why I got these impulses. I really didn't want to run anywhere, literally or figuratively, but I was so frustrated with not making any progress on finding out how the Cayman papers might have gotten Christian kidnapped—or worse. That, combined with my complete lack of power in the palace, probably made the events of the night that followed inevitable.

It should have been easy enough. A formal dinner party in the China Ballroom, attended by the closest friends of the Queen and esteemed members of Drieden's political parties, honoring the European Union president.

It shouldn't have been a recipe for disaster. And yet . . .

There they were.

The usual set of potential acceptable husbands for Princess Theodora. Alexander of Bayern. The Duke of Manse-Rader. Hans DeGerald.

Sophie was holding court with a few other men I didn't recognize. Maybe they were backup husband material, ones that would be suitable for the next eligible granddaughter of the Queen.

And then on the other side of the room, Pierre Anders stood talking to the other distinguished politicians. The ones with power and influence.

It was as if two versions of my life were laid out in front of me. To the left, stability, domestication, duty.

To the right? Curiosity. Adventure.

Control.

I took two steps toward the right, to where Anders would certainly answer my questions about his connection to Christian, when I heard my name called out by Harald. "HER HIGHNESS, PRINCESS THEODORA OF DRIEDEN."

Damn. Harald could boom when he wanted to. The room's focus shifted toward me. Postures changed. Smiles appeared. Ladies dipped. Gentlemen bobbed.

I acknowledged the room with a slight nod, still fully intending to go speak to Anders, but then who hopped next to me and clutched my arm but my dear Lucy, pulling me straight to the Approved Future Husband Brigade.

I couldn't pull away from her tight grip without making a scene, so I resolved to talk to Anders later in the evening and find out when exactly he had spoken to Christian last.

As soon as I got within ten feet of the Eligible Aristocratic Bachelor Club, fawning and preening commenced from every gentleman who had been born to the country's elite. Were they under some sort of mass delusion? Did they sign a contractual agreement with the palace? Because there was no way I was as delightful, as charming, or as beautiful as they swore I was. Especially since I kept darting my eyes to the other side of the room. To where the real conversations were happening.

Suddenly, Hans DeGerald pulled me off to the side for a semiprivate chat.

Hans and I had known each other for years. In fact, he had been at the ski party where Christian and I first met. Hans wasn't a royal or any sort of aristocrat, but his family was one of the richest in Drieden, which made him almost as acceptable as someone with a great-great-

great-grandfather who had been the younger brother of a king's illegitimate cousin.

He started off asking about the recent work I'd been doing. I returned the favor and asked about the job he kept to maintain the appearance that he was contributing to society.

"Hell of a hard time finding a new law firm for Father's consulting start-up." He must have misinterpreted my expression. "Oh, of course—I apologize for even bringing it up. You know we pulled our business from Boson Chapelle the day after the wedding. I mean, the, um . . ."

"It's fine," I said abruptly, but Hans still felt he had something to apologize for.

"You know our loyalty is to the Crown. The DeGeralds and the House of Laurent have a relationship that goes back centuries. In fact, as soon as I knew what Christian was about, I told Father we needed to speak with him. His behavior was not appropriate."

The back of my neck tensed. "You spoke to Christian after the wedding?"

Hans was appalled. "Good God, no. I told you our loyalty is to you. We cut him off immediately. And that firm of his."

"When did you speak to him, then?"

He was so transparent. Caution crept back over his face. "You're better off without him," he said with perfect urbane neutrality.

"What was Christian 'about,' Hans?"

"Look," he ducked his head and said in a confidential tone, "it doesn't matter to anyone what arrangement you two worked out, but to carry on with another woman during his engagement showed that he lacked a certain . . . discretion that anyone would require in their corporate lawyer."

"Christian was cheating on me," I said evenly, though my heart was jumping into my throat. But Hans misunderstood my calm tone.

"I know you're a woman of the world, but it still doesn't excuse the way he conducted himself. And to run off with her? Instead of marrying you?" Hans shook his head. "But that's what you get with a Scot, I suppose."

"Did you know her name?" I asked, still surprisingly cool about it.

"No." Hans took a sip of his drink. "I never could see the caller ID when he took her calls. But he wasn't exactly subtle about what was going on," he finished with a grimace. Hans really was a loyal friend.

"Let me guess—the same phone he used with me?"

He thought about it. "I guess so. It probably wouldn't do to use his firm cell phone."

I briefly closed my eyes, remembering Nick's lecture about cell phones. He had been right. People had noticed our so-called secret phones; they'd just chosen to pretend they hadn't so as to give us privacy.

Although I had managed to stay composed, thanks to many years of training, the revelation that Christian had cheated on me shocked me to my core. There had been a lot of speculation in the magazines and online about the causes of our breakup. Some had even gossiped that I had been the one cheating and suggested that Christian had gotten fed up with my infidelities and left the country in disgust.

Many of the nights on Perpetua, when I had gone over every possible reason for Christian's desertion, I had, of course, considered a third party. What woman wouldn't? But when no grainy photos had appeared of Christian with his bimbo, I suppose I'd dismissed it. No one was looking harder for that angle than hundreds of reporters, who scoured all of our local haunts. And if they hadn't found any evidence of another woman, I'd thought she probably didn't exist.

While Hans took my hand and kissed it, murmuring about his sincere feelings, I realized that while this confirmation of Christian's infidelity was yet another blow to my increasingly fragile princess ego, it was also something that Nick and I had been searching for: a clue.

"Excuse me for a moment," I told him, intending to go find Nick to tell him what I had learned. But again, Hans assigned another meaning to my words, and he clamped my fingers tight and pulled me closer, my hand through his arm.

"I cannot let you leave upset. Theodora, we've known each other too well for too long. I insist you stay and enjoy yourself. *He* doesn't deserve your tears."

The last part was definitely true. And Hans was right—we had known each other for years. In fact . . . I examined the other gentlemen that some aide on Gran's staff had diligently researched before adding them to the guest list. There were many faces I knew quite well. Several, actually, who had been in Christian's circle.

Maybe someone else would drop some information about Christian. What he'd been up to. Where he was. Most important, who this other woman was. If we could find her, we'd find him, surely. All I had to do was work the crowd like a good princess.

With a keen eye for pedigree and social connections, I quickly homed in on my prey: Jonas DeKregg, a distant relative on my mother's side. Five minutes later, I'd determined that Jonas hadn't known Christian as well as I'd thought. Next up, Alexander of Bayern. I remembered he had studied law—perhaps he had known the Boson Chapelle crew.

I circulated like that for the rest of the evening, flirting, inquiring, letting every eligible bachelor there believe that he might have a chance with a princess.

Finally, I had to take a break. Stepping out into the barely lit corridor on the east side of the ballroom, I took some deep breaths and started to piece together what I had heard.

"I thought you didn't need a husband."

The voice jolted me out of the thoughts that had consumed me since Hans mentioned Christian's side piece. I turned and was surprised to see Pierre Anders—the man I had wanted to speak with all night long.

"I don't," I said, trying to cover my surprise at seeing him.

"Then why are you flirting with every eligible bachelor in the country?"

I bristled at that. "Is it a crime for a woman to have a nice evening?"

Anders tutted. "No, of course not."

"I'm surprised you notice such small details as my whereabouts, being the leader of a major political party and all."

"I'm a leader *because* I notice small details."

His matter-of-fact tone struck me as significant. "You and my grandmother are alike in that way, I think."

Anders cocked his head. "I must respectfully disagree. Your grandmother is not interested in the details."

I wasn't used to people pointing out Gran's presumed failings to my face. She was the Queen, after all, and while no one believed in her infallibility anymore, it really wasn't polite to criticize her in the presence of another royal.

"Her Majesty is deeply involved in this country."

Immediately, I saw that I had made a mistake. It was an almost imperceptible change in the politician, but his eyes lit, his mouth twitched. I had walked into a trap, but hell if I knew what it was, and Anders didn't seem inclined to share that with me.

I thought quickly, remembering why I had wanted to speak with Anders again, and I was suddenly desperate to change the topic. "I enjoyed our conversation at the opera," I said.

"Really?" Anders looked amused.

"I do admire your work in this country."

"You do."

It was a strange, vague response, but I was being sincere. "Yes. I hope to have as great an impact on Drieden's future as you have."

Now a true smile broke over the man's face. "You do realize that I mean to abolish the monarchy."

"I know you have scheduled a vote."

"A vote that will pass."

He was smug. I hated smugness. For all my family's faults, good manners had been drilled into us from the cradle. Manners that did not abide smugness.

"Once Parliament abolishes the monarchy," he continued, "I'm afraid there will be no role in Drieden for an unemployed princess."

Well. That was how it was going to be, then.

"You seem awfully sure of your abilities to win a war you've been losing for thirty years," I pointed out.

That barb didn't de-smug him. It only sharpened his grin. "I have new weapons that strengthen my case."

Weapons. The word was harsh and reminded me of the pool of blood at Tomas Claytere's country home. "Driedeners will never support a violent rebellion."

Anders's white brows lifted. "Who said anything about a violent rebellion? In the twenty-first century, it is far more likely that people will discover the truth for themselves. Information is out there, everywhere, being uncovered every day by both patriots and rebels. Surely even you watch the news. Read the internet." His lips twitched. "All it takes is one determined hacker and the House of Laurent will crumble under the weight of its tyranny."

I laughed coldly. "Hackers? That's what your strategy is? That something like the Cayman papers will suddenly reveal a reason to abolish the monarchy? I've gone over the Cayman papers, Mr. Anders. You won't bring down the House of Laurent with those."

Anders's smile melted, replaced with an expression of fury that seemed demonic on his genteel, elderly face. "You've spoken with him, then."

"Who?"

"You tell him I expect delivery or there will be hell to pay."

"Who is 'him'?"

"Tell Aurelia that I know all about her schemes. And soon everyone in the country will, too."

"But you said you'd spoken to Christian—"

I was interrupted by a rough hand on my arm and a "Your Highness" spoken in Driedish but spiked with a Scottish accent. Anders looked quickly at my bodyguard and his features went smooth again. I tried pulling away from Nick, but his grip was unyielding.

"Party's over, Princess."

twenty-eight

A SOON AS THE DOOR TO MY APARTMENTS CLOSED, we both let loose.

"How dare you!" I clenched my fists, angry beyond belief that Nick had escorted me out of the function before I had gotten more information about Christian from Anders.

"What did you think you were doing back there?" he demanded, looking at me like I was the crazy one.

"I was doing what you couldn't. That was the point of all this."

"Making a fool of myself with brain-dead aristocrat suitors? Yes, I'm sure that's something I wouldn't be doing."

I blinked two, three times. "*That's* what you're mad about?"

"I'm mad about all of it, Princess."

"Your Highness." Tamar's voice came from my bedroom door, the sound of it equivalent to someone throwing Nick and me into the Comtesse River in January.

Still, Nick drew his weapon faster than I'd ever seen. The fact that Tamar did not reciprocate was more chilling than if she had.

I moved to step forward, but Nick stepped in front of me. "Don't move," he growled. I didn't know whether he was talking to Tamar or to me.

Unlike me, she was unfazed and held her hand up. Something was between her fingers. It wasn't a gun. It was much smaller.

"I found this in your room."

It was a small black disc.

"He needs to be removed from the palace, Your Highness."

"I'd like to see you try." An ominous click came from Nick's gun.

"I told you he couldn't be trusted," she said, not taking her eyes off me. "Your rooms are scanned regularly for listening devices. This wasn't here before he came."

"She already knows it's not mine," Nick growled.

"Does she? How would a princess know about such things?" Tamar asked in a sly, soft voice. "Unless she's already found your other devices and believed your lies about them, too."

There's an expression—feeling like the rug was pulled out from under one's feet. Right there, at that moment, I had that sudden, strange feeling. A quick drop, an irreversible change in altitude, in perspective, one that shifted everything.

My brain flashed back to when Nick had found those other two devices . . . He had known *exactly* where they were. Had that been a trick? A simple sleight of hand? I had never questioned it before.

I circled around until I faced him—not in front of his gun; I wasn't being that stupid this time. When he saw me, something subtly switched between us. I had questions, and I could see from his eyes that I wasn't going to like his answers.

At that moment, I didn't care at all for my safety. Which is why I held my hand out and told Tamar to give me the bug.

After she did, she murmured that she would call the palace guard. "No," I said with a sharpness that caused her head to jerk.

"But Ma'am . . ."

"You're dismissed, Tamar."

I didn't thank her as I usually did when she left the room. I wasn't feeling especially grateful for anything as I turned and faced Nick again with the bug.

"Explain this," I ordered him.

"Destroy it first."

"Who's listening to us?"

With a scowl, he snatched it from my fingers, held it against the wall, and smashed it with the butt of his gun. Black plastic crumbled down the wall, now marred with a jagged six-inch hole in its hundred-year-old plaster.

As if in slow motion, and with the freakish control of an exotic martial arts master, he turned and stared at me. "You cannot believe her." His voice was a Scottish splice of barbed wire.

"What else am I supposed to believe?" My throat hurt. "No one else has been in here since you searched the room."

He snorted. "No one else? Your staff? Your maids? Lucy—"

I cut that off immediately. "Don't you dare speak of Lucy."

"You spend a lot of time telling people what not to do."

"When it's appropriate, yes."

"Facts aren't appropriate to you, Princess," he sneered.

"Facts?" I cried. "Let's talk facts, please. Give me some facts, some reason to believe that you weren't the one who planted all those bugs—here, at Ceillis House, at Claytere's house. Some reason to believe you at all!"

"What about her? Do you also demand facts to believe her?" He threw a hand to indicate the door where Tamar had just left.

I felt overwhelmed. There was no black and white anymore. No hard evidence. Only my instincts and intuition. Of course I was going to cling to any semblance of fact that I could.

"She has been with me for years. I have no reason to doubt her," I said, as much to calm myself as to explain to Nick.

"No? How about the fact that she shot at you at the museum?" Nick's voice had gone low and deadly. "Why is that not a problem for you when all I've ever done is save your bloody life?"

"My life never needed saving before you came along!"

"Your life has been in danger since your wedding day."

"That's ridiculous!"

"You just didn't notice because they were keeping you on that bloody island. Afraid of what would happen if they let you off."

"Who is this 'they' you speak of?"

He gave me a pointed look, as if it were so obvious. But I wasn't letting him get away with innuendo and open-ended answers anymore.

"Just tell me: Who put the bug in my room?"

His jaw clenched. "Someone in the palace."

"You're in the palace; was it you?"

"Once again, you're back in la-la land."

"Don't patronize me. Stick to the facts. Explain them to me."

I was reaching for anything, anything at all that would sound true.

Nick rubbed his forehead. "You keep asking the impossible. I can't explain why criminals do the things they do."

"You and I made a deal on the boat. That we were going to tell each other the truth. I've upheld my end. I've brought you here, shared everything. I've done what I needed to do to find Christian. And you can't even tell me one fact!"

"Ask me something I know the answer to!" he yelled, not even bothering to use sarcasm as a defense.

"How did you know I'd be there that night? At the bar?"

That stunned him into silence.

"It wasn't a *coincidence*, was it?" My accusation made my voice shake. "We didn't just happen to run into each other at a random dive bar in the theater district."

He opened his mouth to respond but stopped when I spoke again. "Don't tell me it wasn't planned." I wouldn't believe it, anyway. Not now.

"What do you want to hear, Princess?" Nick's voice was hoarse when he finally answered. "That I'd seen your face for *months*, paired with my useless brother in magazines, on every television? That I'd wondered what the hell kind of woman would take him on for a husband when it seemed like she had everything on the planet? That maybe when I looked across that bar and saw you for the first time, I couldn't help myself from talking to you, even though you were the last person in this damned country I needed to get involved with?"

"Why did you talk to me?" I half-whispered, partially hypnotized by what he was describing.

"Because maybe you were the one responsible for my brother's disappearance."

It took me a second to realize what he had just said. What he was accusing me of.

Me.

"You were the last person to see him. You had motive, opportunity, a security force to help you cover it up."

Rug. Pulled.

The world was flipped upside down.

I saw what he saw. And he was right. It could look like I was involved in Christian's disappearance.

It could look like Nick had been sent to investigate me.

From somewhere deep down, I summoned the strength to say, "You have no right to speak to me this way."

"You wanted to talk facts."

My face burned as though I'd just been slapped. "Get out." I turned on my heel and marched toward my bedroom, slamming the door behind me. I realized that what Nick had observed his first day in the palace had been right.

There was only one exit route from this room.

THERE WAS NO WAY I COULD SLEEP, NOT WITH THE WORDS that Nick had said barreling through my brain. Neither of us were happy, or knew what we were doing, or where we could go from here. The proverbial dead end was tall and wide, and I could see no way over, under, or around it.

Except . . .

As I lay in bed, I saw, as I had seen so many other nights, the lights of Drieden City sparkling below. My feet hit the carpet seemingly of their own accord. I drew the white satin draperies wider and pressed my palms against the cool glass of the window. All those times I had crept out of the palace onto the streets below, I'd been looking for an escape from the rules. The expectations. The life to which I'd been born.

What was stopping me from going now? From walking out and never looking back?

As steady and familiar as my own heartbeat, I heard Nick's footsteps behind me. He stopped mere inches from my body. I could feel his heat, his strength, calling me to him.

I didn't fall into his arms. Instead, I whispered, "We can go. Tonight."

"Where?" His deep voice sent a shiver down my spine.

"Wherever you want; I don't care." Couldn't he see? I couldn't be here anymore. But I could be someone else, someplace else . . . with him.

My hair was lifted and moved across my neck, as if a ghost were behind me. His breath was warm against my neck and there was the barest pressure of his lips.

Then it was gone.

"I'm sorry for earlier." My whisper was hoarser now. "Let's go. I feel like I'm going crazy here. I don't know what to think, what's happening."

The lightest touch caressed my shoulders, down my arms, and I almost sank into him, but my desire was far outweighed by my pride, that straight steel structure that had encased me from birth.

"Let's go," I said once more. Leaving was the only way I knew to handle this situation.

The curve of his palm fit right on my hip and I wondered if this was it. The moment where he took what he wanted, to hell with the consequences. I wanted that for him. And I wanted it for me, for entirely different reasons. Then he said the words I hadn't known I'd desperately wanted to hear.

"I'd rather stay."

He spun me around, swept his hands slowly up the sides of my waist, and then lightly circled my wrists with his fingers, pulling them up over my head, pressing them against the cool glass of the window.

I was stretched out for him. On the windowpane, I was completely on display both for him and the city. I could barely breathe, every fiber of my being waiting for what he would do next.

Slowly Nick tilted his head forward. My mouth opened, craving the taste of him. But he didn't kiss me. Instead he pressed his forehead against mine.

A sharp inhale.

"We should have stayed on that goddamned boat."

Only Nick could make me laugh at a time like this.

Then he took another shaky breath. "Tamar was wrong. No matter what happens, Thea, I will never hurt you."

The rough, raw promise made me tremble with need.

"Tell me you believe me," he demanded gently.

I found myself nodding. *Yes.* "Always." Inexplicably. Time and time again it came back to that. My heart telling me that I was safe with this man.

He continued as if he hadn't heard me. "I promised myself, that first night in the bar, that I wouldn't have you."

"That was a stupid thing to do." I arched into him, needing to feel something hot. Something hard.

He nodded. "I told myself after we were at Sybil's that I was being an idiot—"

"You were."

"For wanting you."

"You weren't." I arched again, as much as I could with Nick still holding my hands against the glass.

He finally kissed me, as slow and sweet as syrup. "I'm sorry," he said against my lips.

"No."

"I'm sorry I dragged you into this."

My eyes shot open as a chill ran down my spine. "Don't say that. I'm not a pawn that you're playing with. I'm a fully grown woman making her own decisions."

Maybe respect was why he released my hands then, letting his hands come back down and cup my head, his fingers twining with my long hair. I thought he was going to kiss me again. I wanted him to kiss me again.

"Thea." My name on his lips was something like a miracle. Like I was hearing it for the first time. I pressed my lips against his as if I could seal my name there for eternity. Keeping all of his promises to me, there would be no more talk about investigations or bodyguards or running away.

It was just me. Thea. And Nick. Two people who had found this space. This night. This fire.

His hands grasped my ass, jerked me tight against him. My mouth parted in surprise and he took control of our kiss. It was just like him, really. Always trying to get the last word.

When he'd left me breathless, he continued kissing my neck, my collarbone, nudging my camisole strap down my shoulder as I ran my fingers through his thick, dark hair, clenching my thighs to hold on as tightly as I could.

There was a moment, right after he'd lifted me to the edge of the bed and right before I'd intended to lift his sweater over his head, that he said my name again. This time there was a question mark after it. Slight, but meaningful, that inflection was so many questions in one.

Will you?

Can I?

Are you sure?

But I was tired of talking. Even more tired of debates and arguments. Tonight I just wanted to act. To run off the edge. To take a wild, crazy leap.

Instead of his sweater, I reached for his belt. Met his eyes and pulled on the buckle. Three, four quick moves and we were both bare to each other, and I finally had answers to all my unspoken questions about Nicholas Fraser-Campbell. I saw Nick's scars, his wounds, his tender side, his demanding edge. And they were all mine.

For that privilege, even if it was just for the night, I was willing to jump with him into the unknown.

twenty-nine

WE HAD ONE LAST SHOT. I MARCHED INTO MY sitting room the next morning and laid it all out on the table. "We have to find Christian's phone," I said, after I'd explained what I'd learned from Hans. And Anders.

Nick looked exasperated at my perfectly reasonable conclusion.

"It will show us," I continued, ignoring his scowl, "if Christian was definitively talking to Anders or kidnappers, or if he's shacked up with his girlfriend in Tahiti."

"Looking for a cheap unregistered cell phone is like a looking for a needle in a haystack of needles."

He was always so negative. I was not throwing this shot away.

I went on to the next thread. "You said you searched Christian's apartment; what did you find?"

"Nothing. It had been cleaned. Like he'd never been there."

Christian's apartment had been a set of rooms at my uncle's palace on the east end of the city. As a royal property, the palace would have cleaned it out as soon as it became apparent that Christian was not coming back. And knowing my family as I did, I knew that we kept everything. Nothing would have been thrown away.

I picked up my phone and called Lucy. Ten minutes later, Lucy called back confirming that all of Christian's things had been collected and delivered to the same facility where the wedding gifts were sent.

"Can you arrange for someone to make them available for me, please?"

Lucy paused. "Yes; I'll just have to find a phone number."

That surprised me. "I didn't think there was a number in Drieden you didn't have."

"Well, there are quite a few Scottish phone numbers I don't have."

"Excuse me?"

"When we returned the wedding gifts, we sent Christian's things back to his house in Scotland."

A PLANE WAS WAITING FOR US AT A SMALL PRIVATE airfield five miles from the city. Nick had ordered it as soon as I told him what Lucy had said.

The flight to Scotland took less than an hour, but we didn't waste time. As soon as we were airborne, Nick handed me a tablet to review the new data that he had received from the manufacturer of Christian's vehicle GPS system, courtesy of Nick's "colleague" Max.

"This is a waste of time," I muttered as I stared at coordinates and a map of Drieden City. "It's telling us nothing." I'd thought that perhaps we could find Christian's girlfriend from his driving patterns, but Christian's Land Rover seemed to go in a predictable, safe loop: his office, to the palace, to his apartment. Nick ignored me and kept working. He certainly seemed to know things about my city that I had never learned. Maybe he knew which hotels were especially conducive to conducting illicit affairs.

Not convinced that the coordinates would help at all, I looked out the window and watched the green fields of Scotland float below us. "Are you excited to go back?" I asked Nick.

He made a grumbly sound.

"I'm sure they'll be very pleased to have you back. Prodigal son of Steading. The return of the Duke and all."

There was a long pause. "Will someone be waiting for you? Christian said you had aunts and uncles nearby?"

Finally Nick shut off his tablet. "I'm not returning."

Given that the landing gear had just dropped out of the plane, I wasn't sure what he meant by that. Then he said the next part. "We'll have rooms at a hotel a few miles away."

"What about Christian's things?" I asked. "Lucy said they were sent to his house. To Brisbane Castle."

"We're working on those."

"Working on them? What the hell does that mean?" The plane hit the tarmac with a loud jolt and my fingers found Nick's as if they had a mind of their own. While the sound of the airplane's brakes crescendoed, I realized what Nick wasn't saying.

"You're not letting anyone know you're alive, are you?" I asked quietly. "You're not claiming your title."

"I couldn't care less about the title," Nick nearly snarled. It did not intimidate me.

"You're going back to your ancestral country and keeping up the ridiculous charade that you're dead?" It was unbelievable and unconscionable. "Christian could use your influence right now."

"Christian's probably dead." Nick sounded so cool and unaffected right then, I knew it had to be an act.

Wasn't it?

"If he's dead, then why are we even here?" I nodded at the door to the plane. "We should just turn around and go back."

"We have to know for sure. And we've exhausted all of our resources in Drieden."

"And you said British analysts couldn't figure out any connection to Driedish interests in these damn papers," I said, holding up the tablet in my lap. "And if you're not here to reclaim your title and actually help Christian, then we've exhausted everything *everywhere*."

A muscle in Nick's jaw worked, and for a second I thought he was going to nod and tell me I was right. Or tell me I was missing something. Or thank me for my words of wisdom.

Instead, he unbuckled his seat belt, grabbed his backpack, and stalked to the exit.

If that was going to be the way he handled this, fine.

I followed him down the stairs of the plane to a dark-windowed Range Rover. Nick had already taken the front passenger seat and a man in similar black tactical clothing was at the steering wheel.

The driver rolled down his window when I knocked on it. "Hi, I'm Thea."

He shook my hand. "Max."

Aha!

"Max Cornelius?" I asked pleasantly, loving the frown on Nick's face when I did.

The driver nodded carefully.

"So nice to finally meet you. I borrowed some clothes from you in Drieden." Then I pointed at Nick. "I think Nick stole your boat."

The men exchanged another careful look and I wondered what classified information I had just said aloud.

The drive was twenty minutes through rocky hills and verdant pastures. This was Scotland, Christian's home. If we had been married, I would have come back here for visits as his wife. Now I was to be hidden in a cheap hotel room as Nick's . . . what? Marginally helpful assistant?

At the hotel, Max showed us up to our suite, which was already filled with boxes labeled with bilingual delivery instructions in Driedish and English. I decided not to ask Max how he'd acquired and/or retrieved the boxes from Brisbane Castle, choosing to believe it was all legal and aboveboard.

We got right to work.

Everything that had been in Christian's apartment was here in half-organized boxes. Clearly, someone had tried some system, probably devised by a harried post-wedding Lucy.

We started with his mail and the contents of his desk.

Credit card statements had some charges I didn't recognize, but those weren't a red flag. Christian had records from a Boson Chapelle credit card, too, which Nick carefully set to the side and that I grabbed, praying for something highlighted and marked with a Cayman Islands flag. But there was nothing besides charges for expensive dinners and hotel rooms, none of which were in the Cayman Islands. Maybe they'd been for his girlfriend.

"Have you ever been there?" I asked, sorting through ancient bank deposit slips.

"Where?"

"The Cayman Islands," I said. "They're a British territory, correct?"

Nick frowned at a bill from a Savile Row tailor. "Yes. With a governor appointed by the Queen."

"And what makes them so popular for offshore banks?" I asked, with the weary voice of someone who had reviewed far too many bank spreadsheets the past week.

"No taxes there, for one thing. It's a good place to shelter offshore accounts."

"And the British Crown thinks that's a good thing?" In my extensive reading of history, monarchs tended to like taxes. The more, the better.

Nick's eyebrow cocked at me. "I suppose Liz gets something out of it."

We fell into a silence as I tried to remember what else I knew about British territories around the globe. The remnants of a vast empire, the United Kingdom had strategically retained control over certain holdings while granting independence to others. Of course, some had always been independent, like a few of the Channel Islands . . .

Shock, sudden and irrefutable as a lightning strike, skidded through my skin.

"We've had it all wrong." I pushed back from the table and left the piles of paper sitting there. I wouldn't need them again. "I need the Boson Chapelle files."

Nick glanced between me and the papers I'd just left behind.

"Not those. The firm's clients, that paperwork. That's the key to the mystery. Don't you see?" I stalked over to Nick and looked into his stern, confused face. "Your analysts were right. There's absolutely nothing in the Cayman papers about Drieden."

thirty

SYBIL ANSWERED ON THE THIRD RING.

"Sybil, this is Thea."

A pause. "Oh. Am I allowed to call you that again?"

I rolled my eyes. I didn't have time for her drama. "I need some information."

I briefly went over what I required.

Another pause. "It may be impossible."

I wouldn't accept that. "Find a Boson Chapelle secretary, a part-time intern, their IT guy. Hack into their system. We need a list of their clients. You know Drieden better than anyone, Sybil. I saw you hacking all those secure files on your computer. I know you can do this for me."

"When do you need it?"

"As soon as possible."

THIRTY MINUTES LATER, SYBIL CALLED BACK WITH AN AD-ministrator's password to the Boson Chapelle network.

"What are you looking for?" Nick asked in frustration as I searched the firm's client files on his laptop.

I held my breath, and then . . . *there*. I pointed at the screen and read aloud, "Incorporated via the Territory of Perpetua."

"Perpetua? Your women's prison island?"

"Perpetua is a distinct legal identity, like the Channel Islands. In 1543, The Holy Roman Emperor wanted to give it to Drieden for complicated political reasons. He had the Dutch Crown and the French kept declaring war, but he also wanted to keep a legal string on the barrier islands guarding the continent so he didn't have another Ottoman Empire invasion scenario from the west . . ."

"Princess . . ."

". . . so he actually transferred the title to the Royal House of Laurent. It's a technicality, but since the Holy Roman Empire doesn't exist anymore and Drieden doesn't legally control Perpetua, it's sort of like—"

"Gilligan's Island. An invisible place no one can find on a map," Nick finished.

He was almost right. I focused back on the document I'd found in the law firm network. "According to this, Boson Chapelle incorporated a shell company, Magdalena Energy International, which is solely owned by the Territory of Perpetua."

Nick scanned the screen as I scrolled through the information, and then he jumped to grab his tablet with copies of the Cayman papers. I suppose I knew what he would find before he did, because I was not surprised when he whistled under his breath and read the numbers aloud. There were billions of euros in offshore Cayman accounts connected to Magdalena Energy International.

Tax-free. Untouchable. Unknowable to 99.999999 percent of the world's population.

The only people who could have put the pieces together were those who knew of Magdalena Energy's existence.

And those who knew who controlled Magdalena Energy.

Which Nick put together in an instant. When he didn't call me Princess, I knew his internal alarm system had gone off. "Thea, who controls the Territory of Perpetua today?" His voice was purposely casual, his question surgically precise.

There were times in my life when I could have chosen an entirely different path. Sometimes I was aware of the significance of these waypoints. Sometimes I only recognized them later.

I saw this one for what it was.

My life would never be the same after this moment. What I said would affect whom I could trust, whom I could love, whom I could grow old with.

In the end, it was the memory of betrayal that made me choose. Christian had somehow gotten involved in this web of danger and deception. Even though I was still looking forward to (hopefully) shoving his head into a muddy pigsty, I couldn't stay silent, not if this information meant we could still find Nick's brother alive.

"The treaty between the Holy Roman Empire, Perpetua, and Drieden delineates that the head of the House is the guardian of the territory."

Nick regarded me with serious eyes. "The House?"

"Of Laurent," I clarified.

He tapped the screen without looking at it, seeming to weigh what he should say next, so I decided to help him out. "That would be my grandmother."

After another moment in which he thought through the ramifications, he said, "Is there any way—"

"No." I cut him off. "Unless someone was impersonating her or acting without authority, there is no way she wouldn't know about the existence of Magdalena Energy International, founded in the first year of her reign, thirty-nine years ago."

Finally, he stood, and gently took me by the shoulders. "You know what this means?"

I nodded. My grandmother, Her Majesty Aurelia Victoria of Drieden, was an embezzler. And someone was committing murder to cover up her crime.

thirty-one

WE KNEW THE WHY. NOW WE NEEDED A WHO.
And we still needed Christian's phone.

Or some other evidence pointing to someone who had started committing violence to keep my grandmother's secret.

Nick's bad mood only seemed to grow as we started ripping open more boxes that Lucy's capable staff had shipped to Scotland. Since some of Christian's belongings were familiar to me, I found myself lingering over certain items. Some held memories, while some I wanted to make sure had no hidden significance. One of those was Christian's black leather-bound calendar.

I traced his handwriting with a delicate fingernail and carefully went over each entry, every appointment.

There were business meetings, visits to his tailor, haircuts penciled in every three weeks. Nothing seemed out of order, but there were some mystery notations I didn't understand. They could have been nothing, of course, but I reviewed and double-checked them to the best of my ability, to try to glean whether they referred to the mysterious mistress. Or something far more sinister. That's when I noticed Nick slamming something into a box and the resulting crackle of glass.

"What was that?" I asked, getting up to see what had broken. In the empty cardboard box lay a silver frame, the remaining glass jagged over a snapshot of Christian and me, one of the few that hadn't been sold to the hundreds of magazines and newspapers that had clamored for exclusive peeks into our so-called storybook romance.

"Was there something that offended you?" I asked. "Perhaps you thought it was a snake and were afraid it might bite you?"

"Perhaps you should get back to mooning over his diary."

"Mooning?" I echoed in disbelief. Had he really just used that word with me? "I'm trying to find a clue."

Nick reached into the box, grabbed the snapshot, and shook the glass shards off before handing it to me. "Here. You can kiss it good night."

"You're ridiculous."

He moved on to another box, nearly ripping the entire top off with his bare hands.

"This bothers you, doesn't it?" I held up the snapshot he was refusing to look at.

"I'm just wondering how you got over your boy toy so fast."

Not this again. "What's up with you?"

"And who knows how many of your brother's friends."

"Need I remind you that I was the dumped one?"

"So?" Nick snarled at the contents of the box, taking fistfuls of Christian's clothes and tunneling through them.

"So that means I can do whatever the hell I want," I told him. "And I certainly don't have to explain it to you."

"No, you don't." Nick muttered at a pile of Christian's cashmere socks as if they'd offended him as well.

But somehow that was an unsatisfying answer. So I kept pushing. "And for the last time, stop calling Christian my 'boy toy.' "

"Why? That's what he was, just a prop, a useless cock to do your bidding."

"Not that useless," I retorted with a sharper meaning than I'd intended.

Nick paused. His jaw worked but he didn't lift his head, which angered me. He didn't get to poke at me and then ignore me.

"You're jealous, is that it?"

That did it. Nick lifted an eyebrow at me. "Of what?"

"Christian and me. You keep putting him down for no reason, calling him a boy toy when you have no idea what our relationship was like." I shook my head. "Maybe I was going to marry him for my own reasons. But it was you who I invited into my bed."

While he stayed silent, the energy shift was palpable. Finally, he spoke, his voice halting and hoarse. "I'm not jealous of my useless brother. I don't respect a man who would take and take from a woman, never giving her something worthwhile in return, and then abandon her in front of millions of people." He stopped and started again. "Maybe the idea of him hurting you pisses me the hell off."

Well. My heart jumped into my throat. That was an unsettling new perspective. Maybe Nick wasn't jealous, even though my ego would have loved to believe he was. Maybe there was more to his grumpiness since we'd landed in Scotland.

"Why did you die?" I blurted before I lost my nerve. "Why did you fake your death, I mean."

His hands stilled over Christian's carefully rolled silk tie collection. "There has to be a good reason," I pressed, "or else you'd be at Brisbane Castle now, reacquainting yourself with your extended family and your title."

Nick stared coldly at the strips of silk in rainbow colors, a contrast to the dark storm cloud reflected on his face. "I can do whatever the hell I want, and I don't have to explain it to you."

Okay, this was a topic that was clearly none of my business. Perhaps it was even classified, given what I knew of his employer for the past six years.

But I still felt hurt.

I picked up Christian's calendar again, intending to continue my examination, but the weight of Nick's anger was making it difficult for me to turn the pages.

Strange.

Had I ever felt someone else's emotions before? Had I ever wanted to walk across a room, throw my arms around someone's waist, and comfort the person? Soothe away the person's mysterious pain or palpable fear?

Of course, I loved my family. And the friends I had, while few, were true and dear to me.

But I couldn't remember another person whom I'd felt so connected to, yet so unbearably distant from.

Somehow, I had come to care deeply for Nick Fraser-Campbell. And as I flipped randomly through Christian's calendar, I realized what I had to explain to him.

"We led separate lives, Christian and me." My voice sounded hesitant and scratchy in the chilly room. "Before the wedding. There's really no way around it, I guess. There's no protocol for a princess and her fiancé to live together, combine households or finances." I took a shaky breath as I realized the journal had opened to March, the month of our wedding.

Christian had not written anything on the page for our wedding day.

"I expect we would have continued on in the same fashion," I said. Nick had stopped refilling a box with sweaters and jeans, but his head hung low so I couldn't see the expression on his face. "We would have met at dinners, occasionally in the bedroom, at our children's events. Maybe that qualifies as a boy toy, I don't know, but he wasn't my partner. Not in any sense of the word. I chose him because we got along well, our families approved, and he was handsome and charming and good with people."

He had filled out other dates in the month of March, but not our wedding date. Had he known all along that he wasn't going to make that appointment? Or was it simply unnecessary? If we never found Christian, maybe I'd never know. But I knew one thing.

I ripped out the month of March and crushed it in my hand.

Nick's head jerked up at the sound of paper tearing and crunching.

"I won't do that again," I said with a clearer, stronger voice. "From now on, any partner I have will be a true partner. In every way."

I left him in the room and went outside to get some fresh air. I stayed close to the hotel's door, even though I knew there were probably more eyes on me than I realized. The Scottish wind was cool and dogged, sort of like the man who was driving me crazy inside.

Similarly, the sharp Scottish air did nothing to clear my frustration. We had reached a dead end. After going through Christian's things, there were no other places to search. No more bread crumbs to follow. If Christian was still alive, it was at the hands of someone who wanted to destroy my country. If he was dead . . .

My heart felt like granite. Then what was this all for?

When I returned to our rooms, I met Max, who was carrying in great plastic sacks of traditional Scottish curry. The smell was sweet and cloying, and after spooning some plain rice onto a plate, I retired to my bedroom.

Nick did not look up when I left.

Their voices carried through the door until late into the night, and they were still talking when I went to sleep. I tuned out their rough English words and found my thoughts drifting home. To Drieden and the people I had known all my life.

Once again, I dreamt of Christian.

In the dark, tunnel walls dripped with foul water.

Christian ran away from me. I couldn't understand why he didn't stop when I called his name. Why he didn't want to be found. I tried ordering him to stop. He didn't obey.

I tried cajoling; I tried pleading; I tried invoking the law. I tried every feminine wile I knew. He still didn't stop, didn't shout back in his charming Scottish brogue.

He kept running; I kept chasing. The headlights of an oncoming train blinded me. I fell to my knees, scraping them in the filth. I couldn't breathe and I knew time was up. For me. For Christian.

Then suddenly, I heard my name, dragging me out of a tunnel.

"Thea."

I opened my eyes. The lights were off in my room but there was enough moonlight for me to see that I was on the floor, with Nick kneeling in front of me.

"What happened?" I mumbled, aware of the hairs on my arms standing up. I was ice cold.

"You screamed."

My fingers brushed the short pile of the carpet under me. "Did I fall out of bed?"

"No." He paused. "I pulled you out."

I shivered and wrapped my arms around myself, remembering that all I wore was my camisole and underwear. "Why would you do something like that?"

Nick's voice was gruff, but as matter-of-fact as ever. "You scream. I try to carry you out of places. It's become our thing."

I was still drowsy, but what he'd said didn't make sense. "So why am I on the floor?"

"You kicked me and I had to put you down."

"You mean you dropped me."

His hand reached out and caught my chin, as if to examine me for injuries. "I would never."

I shook my head and chuckled softly, but then I saw his expression. *I would never.*

It had sounded like one of his jokes. But what I saw in his eyes was a promise. Something caught in my throat. "Nick."

"You're better now?"

I nodded and went to him, the only man I had ever allowed to wrap his arms around me and carry me back to bed.

WHEN THE BUTTERY SCOTTISH SUNLIGHT BRUSHED MY face the next morning, I opened my eyes and realized that I had just enjoyed one of the best night's sleep I'd had in months. Even with the nightmare, I felt rejuvenated and alert enough without coffee to notice the small changes in the room. Like the indentation in the pillow next to mine.

And the sprig of heather on top of Christian's journal on the bed-side table.

Nick came through the door from the bathroom, wearing shorts and a nondescript gray sweatshirt. His hair was damp, his cheeks flushed under the scruff of his two-day beard.

"Where have you been?"

He seemed surprised by my question. "You're awake."

"Is it late?"

"No."

I slid out of the sheets in my camisole and underwear.

He reached down to the floor where his black sweater lay and handed it to me. "You're cold," he said simply. It was true, and I couldn't help a smile as I slipped the rough wool over my head. It smelled like him, which distracted me.

"I went for a run," he said suddenly.

The way he said "run" sent a shiver down my neck, as his Scottish burr had been thickening since we'd landed in his native country.

"Looks like a good one," I said, referencing the sheen on his skin, as I walked toward the en-suite.

"Thea." My name, sudden and intense. *Not Princess*.

I stopped in my tracks. "Yes?"

"I grew up in these mountains." He started to speak in a hurried, uncertain voice. "Spent more time outside than in, exploring, going on adventures, hunting. That was real to me. Not the future that was presented to me at birth, wrapped up in a ribbon.

"Military service is a noble calling," he continued. "No one batted an eye when I said I wanted to serve. I suspect your brother knows something about the usefulness of that. When I arrived in Afghanistan, I . . ." He paused. "Let's just say I was very good at my job."

I waited patiently, ignoring the chill of goose bumps covering my bare legs.

"I was missing in action. That part wasn't a lie. But when I returned, I was offered a new position within the government. I knew at that point that my father had died, and . . ." He shrugged. "It seemed like a gift. The title suited Christian better, anyway."

"So you decided to let him have it. To disappear and let him assume the mantle of Duke of Steading."

Nick hesitated for a half second. "Yes."

"Did you not think he might need his brother?" I asked softly.

"We were never close."

"Okay."

"He was a grown man. I was serving my country."

"I understand."

"Do you?" The Scot had turned accusatory. And a little defensive, even.

I held his eyes and didn't back down. "I know something about feeling trapped. About family, and duty. And about wanting to run away."

We held each other's gaze and then Nick swallowed hard. "But still you think I should return to Brisbane Castle."

Suddenly, I was exhausted. Ten minutes into my day and all I wanted to do was crawl back under the warm duvet and sleep for another ten hours. Or force Nick back under the duvet with me. Things were so much simpler when we didn't have to use words to explain ourselves. "You have to make that decision yourself, Nick." Then I pushed past him toward the bathroom. I would dress, get coffee, and we would return to Drieden and the castle Nick would lock me up in, even when he wouldn't subject himself to the same prison.

That was the plan, anyway. Until Max brought the news that changed everything.

thirty-two

THE BODY IN THE PHOTOGRAPH WAS GRUESOME. AND instantly familiar.

I cried out, a mix of shock and horror. I had fully planned on marrying the man in the photograph, who was now cold and dead.

Nick had grabbed the photo as soon as Max brought it in. "How sure are we about this?"

"Our people found it on a secure server outside of Drieden."

Nick frowned at the photo, showing no signs that he recognized his own brother. "And is anyone taking responsibility?"

Max lifted a thick shoulder. "No. We caught it before it was broadcast. Erased the file."

"What do you mean, erased it?" I asked. It sounded barbaric. Unfeeling. This was a murdered man. Surely his death deserved some sort of acknowledgment, not erasure. I snatched the photo out of Nick's hand as if that were going to protect Christian now.

Max looked at Nick, deferring to the breathing Fraser-Campbell heir. "She can have it. It's fine."

"*Fine?*" I grabbed at Nick's sleeve, demanding that he pay attention to me. "This is not fine. This is your brother. Dead!"

Nick's eyes were on me. "Which we already knew."

"No, we did not!" I was fully aware I was reaching hysterical levels, but I didn't care. "What was all this for, then—what was the search for, what was the . . ." I flung my hand back toward his computer, where we had pulled up the Magdalena Energy files.

And then it hit me.

"You used me."

Some silent command passed from Nick to Max, who quickly left the room and shut the door behind him with a decisive click. Nick was going to regret sending Max out of the room. Privacy was only going to encourage me.

"You used me to get information on my country. On my own grand-mother!" I had given sensitive information to a foreign national, and I'd known he was a spy.

Which made me . . .

A traitor.

"What did the British government want?" I demanded. "How did you know Christian was dead? Did you know about Magdalena Energy? Did you know all those people at the law firm died, too? Has everything you've told me been a lie? Was this entire search for Christian all a ruse? Have I been confirming everything you've known all along?" Even now, I had to know.

"It's not like that."

"What's not 'like that'?" I decided to circle back to the most important question. "How did you know Christian was dead?"

After a long, painful pause, he answered. "Boson Chapelle employees were dropping out of sight. Christian exited the world stage in a very loud way. He didn't show up in Britain . . ." He shrugged. "People don't just hide for four months."

"*I* did." I took a sharp, deep breath that hurt. "On an island that England has been trying to claim for centuries."

Nick didn't blink. "That wasn't the goal here."

"It's just a useful benefit, that now I've given you key information about a strategic territory in the North Sea . . ."

"Christian was a notable British citizen who was ascending to another nation's throne. With his connection to the Cayman papers—"

"And to the next Queen of Drieden . . ."

"Of course we were going to try to ascertain what happened."

"I've ascertained that you are full of bullshit."

Nick's eyes half-closed. "Thea . . ."

"Don't use that name," I snapped.

"You're doing that? With *me*?"

It was my only defense. Retreating into princess mode slammed walls between me and others. And it had to be done now. I remembered what my grandmother said the morning of my wedding. That there would be no more tears for Christian.

And indeed, even as I looked at a photo of Christian's lifeless form, I shed no tears.

Everything inside me, everything I knew, said to walk away from this now. All the rules of propriety and etiquette and fucking common sense had screamed at me to leave Nick alone.

But I hadn't.

Ever since I had met him, I had sought him out, followed him. Had I known, subconsciously, that Nick would give me the answers I was craving?

Or just the adventure I had always wanted?

Looking for answers about Christian's disappearance—any woman would want to know why she'd been thoroughly humiliated on the international stage.

Itching for adventure—it wasn't uncommon for people to seek thrills on the top of mountains, behind steering wheels, plunging to earth with only a parachute for safety.

But when the climber started leaving oxygen tanks behind; when a seat belt was ignored; when the parachutes weren't double-inspected—then the adrenaline junkie had a serious problem.

Seeing the photo of a dead man had shocked me into sobriety.

"It's time to end our partnership," I said, packing as much regality as I could into that short sentence.

I don't know what I expected, but I certainly hadn't expected him to stand, crush me in his arms, and take my mouth in a desperate, hard kiss.

I savored it for a split second, one last hit for a woman addicted. Then I came to my senses.

I slapped him. Hard. Then I shoved him away.

Nick stepped away, his green eyes flashing.

"I'm Theodora of Drieden. When I say something's over, it's over." I lifted the printout of Christian. "And people are going to know what happened to him."

"What are you going to tell them, Thea? How are you going to explain it when you don't have a body? Or a motive? Or a murderer, in fact?"

They were questions I didn't have answers for.

Nick leaned closer in, and his voice dropped. "What are you going to say when they blame it on you?"

"Like you did?" It hurt more than I thought it would to say it.

He was unflinching; he didn't look away. He didn't deny the accusation.

"It doesn't matter," I said. "I'm Theodora of Drieden—"

"It doesn't matter how many times you use a title; it doesn't make it important."

I opened my mouth to tell him what an ass he was being, but then I realized something. His argument was pointless. "I'm Theodora of Drieden. And you're the Portuguese."

"What the hell does that mean?"

"In 1678, Queen Marie-Theodora led the Driedish fleet through a hurricane to defeat the Portuguese."

Nick crossed his arms. "You and your history lessons."

I continued with my story. It was a good one. "Marie-Theodora was recently widowed. She had survived an attempted coup from her own son, executed him, and decided to sail with a tiny fleet to directly address the Portuguese who had aided her son's coup d'etat. She ordered the cannon attack, directed the strategy, and lost eight of eleven ships, but seven days later, she won."

"Your point, Princess?"

I lifted my chin and showed him my true colors. "You have manipulated and used me to gain incriminating information about my family. And by doing so, you've become my enemy. Like Marie-Theodora, I will do everything I can to protect what's mine."

"What are you protecting? A grandmother who's been slicing herself a few billion off the top for the last forty years?"

Rage roared through my ears. "How dare you! You dare preach to me about what's important? About what I should protect? You're a coward!"

"Which castle were you living in when I was fighting the Taliban? When I nearly had my head shot off my shoulders every night?"

"A man who won't face his own family is a coward. A man who serves his country by lying to a woman before he gets her into bed. That's not honor in any language."

A bitter, harsh laugh came from Nick. "Oh, such a brave little princess. Such scary battles ahead. Dear Grandmama, whatever shall we do with the billion dollars you stole?"

His mockery made my stomach turn. There was truth in it, perhaps, but the larger truth was that he didn't understand me at all. I was going to explain myself only one more time. "I've spent my whole life in the cross fire between freedom and duty. My parents picked their sides. You picked a side. But those with true courage, those who want ven-

geance, justice, won't stand in no-man's-land. They use their power to
effect change. So you can either be at my side when I take my vengeance
against those who killed Christian, those who threaten my family. Or
you can run away like a coward, afraid to take what you want from life.
The choice is yours."

A thick silence filled the room. "*Vengeance* is an awfully strong word
for a princess," he finally said. "Take it from someone who knows."

"I'm going home," I spat, turning and heading toward the door. I
didn't have to explain anything else to him. A lioness doesn't explain
herself to a mouse.

"Will you be telling the world about my brother?"

The way he said that melted my stone heart a little. Maybe I was
imagining it, but there was something rough and authentic there. Something that would have made me turn around if I hadn't already decided
my course of action. I didn't want to admit he was right, but . . . in so
many ways it wasn't right for me to announce Christian's death.

"That's the Duke of Steading's responsibility," I said scathingly.

Then I went home to Drieden to follow the example of my ances-
tors. And to defend my country against those who threatened it.

thirty-three

MY GRAND PLANS FOR MY RETURN TO DRIEDEN were, as usual, ruined by a man.

A dead man, in my case.

Somehow the press had found out about Christian, and by the time I landed in Drieden, they were calling it a suicide. How they got this information, or who told them, I had no idea, but a fresh uproar was waiting for me and the palace had assigned double the usual guards to meet me at the airport.

To anyone else, it would appear that they were protecting me from the mob of photographers. But I suspected there was another explanation. Big Gran wanted to keep me under her control.

Her secretary met me as soon as I exited the armored car and informed me that Aurelia would expect me in an hour.

I ignored that directive.

And the next two.

Lucy came to see me and threw her arms around me. She offered sympathy and condolences for Christian's passing, but I saw other thoughts on her face, shadows that she probably thought were well hidden.

Fear, worry, doubt.

For Pierre Anders, Christian's death was a political tool, and it seemed he immediately was on every station, telling the country his views on abolishing the monarchy. "Another casualty of a corrupt enterprise," he said on prime-time television with a shallow show of sorrow.

"You didn't even know him," I muttered at the TV, after Lucy had forced me to sit down and eat a sandwich for dinner.

"There's been another call from Her Majesty's secretary—" she began.

"Nope," I said with my mouth full.

"I know you're overcome with grief." She hit the off button on the remote just as yet another engagement photo of Christian and me flashed on the screen. "But this rebellious streak will not be tolerated for much longer."

I half-laughed at the thought. They all thought this was a rebellion, that I was so insane with grief I couldn't simply tell my grandmother "no."

I wished it were my typical Thea rebellion, where I snuck out of the castle just to show I could.

The truth was, I was scared.

Now that I had the facts about my grandmother, about how she'd embezzled billions into private offshore accounts, I had no idea what— if anything—I should do about it. While I had invoked her legacy, the ghost of my namesake Marie-Theodora hadn't yet come to explain to me what my brave next steps should be.

And it wasn't just Christian's death that was giving me pause. There was, of course, the unexplained slaughter and disappearance of those who had access to Magdalena Energy International files at Boson Chapelle.

If my grandmother was behind the murders of these people . . . Well. Let's just say I had a lot more than permanent exile on Perpetua to worry about. She could cut me off completely, like she did Caroline.

Or she could cut me down permanently, like Christian.

I stuffed the remainder of my sandwich in my mouth and started toward my door. "I'm going to the library," I said.

"Again?" Lucy wrung her hands. "This isn't normal."

"I love the library. And I can't go anywhere else," I pointed out. "Not until everyone forgets about me and Christian."

I wasn't allowed outside the palace gates. All of my public appearances had been canceled and/or reassigned to Sophie. Needless to say, I had heard through the grapevine that my little sister was not thrilled.

I had pulled the door open when Lucy decided to get serious. "But what about Her Majesty?"

"If my grandmother wants to see me, she can walk her butt down to the library."

The palace library was actually a series of rooms, interconnected in a line along the North Wing. Three hundred years ago, they were assembly rooms for politicians and courtiers and aides. Factions would camp out in their designated chamber until the King could disperse them or negotiate compromises that would please the majority. In the late 1800s, they were remodeled into an extensive library under Queen Wilhelmena, who allowed scholars and artists free entry. Public access to the palace was restricted considerably during World War I—after Franz Ferdinand was shot, the monarchies of Europe grew understandably more concerned with their safety—but the thousands of books remained.

And it was in these that I had been losing myself for the past week.

The history of my country had always fascinated me. Now it was my lifeline. Every tiny detail, every small fact I absorbed, as if these collections of paper and leather and thread were going to tell me how the hell I would get out of the situation I was in.

My nose was buried in *A Nautical History of the Driedish Coast, from 1615–1824* when the wide doors of the library opened and the current queen of the land strode in.

So this was where our confrontation would take place. It seemed appropriate that I would accuse her of criminal acts here, where only history would witness it.

I stood, more to prepare myself than out of respect. And then my stoic, proud, regal grandmother burst into tears.

This I had not prepared for.

Never in my wildest dreams had I imagined Big Gran sobbing, approaching me with outstretched arms. "Thea, my child," she moaned as she embraced me.

I was stunned into silence. When was the last time she had clutched me so? It must have been more than a decade ago. Since primary school at least.

"I'm so, so sorry," she said when she let me go and patted my cheek with her cool, violet-scented hand. "Such a tragedy. Poor Christian. His family . . ." Her voice drifted off as she removed a linen handkerchief from her sleeve. "I would like to call someone, but Lucy wasn't sure who would have been closest to him."

"He had a brother," I heard myself saying. "But he's gone, too." As far as I knew.

"What do you need? What can we do?" Perhaps it was the suggestion of the royal "we," but I felt my defenses lock into place again.

"Drop the act, Grandmother." I took three steps back and crossed my arms. "I know you're involved in this."

She was a better actress than I'd realized. If I hadn't learned about all her secrets, I might have been fooled by her shocked face, her bleak eyes.

"I know about Magdalena Energy," I said.

The Queen of Drieden inhaled a sharp, full breath and her eyes cut into me like the talons of an eagle. But all she said was, "I see."

And in that moment, I had never been so afraid of my own grandmother. In my mind, I saw the pieces click into place. How she had grown a secret fortune, locked it away, and when Christian's firm became the key to discovery, ruthlessly eliminated everyone who could reveal her scheme.

I had to take action to ensure I wasn't the next victim. "Other people know."

"Really."

"If something happens to me, they'll publicize it."

"Who?"

I thought quickly. Who would give Queen Aurelia pause? "Pierre Anders," I replied.

Her eyes narrowed. "I knew it."

"You did?"

"Why else would he move now for the vote against the monarchy? He had to have something that he could take to the people and to Parliament." She turned and stooped over a nearby chair, her hand across her mouth, thinking. "What are we going to do to stop him?"

This "we" wasn't a rhetorical, royal "we." She was asking *me* what she and I were going to do to stop Anders from disclosing a secret I wasn't sure he knew.

And if she had been murdering her political enemies, I'd just put Pierre Anders on the chopping block.

"We're not doing anything to Anders."

Gran's ice-blue eyes lifted to give me a chilly glare. "Think about this carefully, Theodora. Magdalena isn't just mine. It's yours."

I coughed. "What are you talking about? I had no idea about the company or your billions."

"Did you think the money was for me?" She laughed softly. "Oh, darling. It was quite apparent from the moment I took the throne that the world was changing. That land, that oil, belonged to our family."

I must not have looked convinced, because she continued. "What will you have, what will your family have, after Anders gets his way? Magdalena is our insurance policy."

"You stole from Drieden."

She shook her head, stubbornly. "I won't just let him destroy our birthright."

Her words were seductive, but the thought of Christian's lifeless body prompted me to fight back. "There are more important things."

Gran lifted a dramatic arm at the books that surrounded us. "More important than a history, a culture? A way of life?"

"Yes!" I cried out. "Human lives are more important than our culture! Christian's life was more important than all of Magdalena's holdings!" I lifted the closest book and slammed it across the room. "Why did you do it? If you cared so much about our family dynasty, then why did you risk it all and form Magdalena?"

"I was ensuring the future of *your* family. It was insurance, not risk."

Maybe I could understand her reasons forty years ago. "I just don't think it's worth murdering people over," I said, heartbroken.

Gran frowned and straightened her posture. "Murder? Who was murdered?"

"Christian," I choked out. "To keep him quiet about Magdalena . . ." My voice faded to nothing as I watched genuine shock blossom across her face.

"Who would do such a thing?" she demanded, her voice shaky with outrage.

I knew my grandmother was skilled at many things. She was a canny queen, an experienced politician, a skillful manipulator of the family. But looking at her now, I knew, deep down in my bones, that she had nothing to do with Christian's death.

Facts, as Nick had shown me, were useless. All I had now was instinct. And a whole lot of history to uncover.

thirty-four

SOPHIE SET THE CHOCOLATE CAKE AND VODKA IN front of me. "Austrian chocolate and Russian vodka," she said. "It seems appropriate, given the circumstances."

I had no idea what she was talking about.

"Heartbreak. Loss. Devastation," she said, as if that explained it. "Austria . . ." She let that dangle out there, a strange carrot. Her hands went in the air. "Oh my God, you really are upset. You didn't even start lecturing me on King Vladimir or Empress Alexandra of Salzburg."

I shook my head at her. Those people never actually existed, but I appreciated her trying to cheer me up with a faux historical topic of conversation. "Thank you. The cake looks delicious."

My sister served two neat triangles and dug in. "How are you doing, really?" she asked with her mouth full. "The news was so shocking. I couldn't believe it. Suicide. That explains everything, doesn't it?"

I pulled my feet from under me and stared at my sister in shock. Christian's death explained everything? For me it only raised a hundred more questions. "How do you mean?"

She made a gesture with her fork. "Well, he was obviously unbalanced. Makes everything much clearer. I mean, the leaving-you-at-the-altar bit. Who would do that? A crazy depressive, that's who," she said, answering her own question. After another bite, she continued, "And that's why I'm still so pissed off at Caroline."

I had not expected Sophie to bring up our other sister, so I was more confused than ever. "What did she do now?"

Sophie's voice rose. "Has she called you? Has she shown that she cares about anyone besides herself? Selfish, that's what she is. Eloping and leaving the rest of us to carry all the burdens; using your situation to cover for her own."

"I hadn't thought of it like that," I murmured. It was true that Caroline's elopement two months ago had benefited from the media craziness that had surrounded my canceled wedding. In any other year, a Driedish princess running off with a race car driver would have been splashed all over every newspaper. This year, one-half the population was exhausted by royal coverage, and the other half was glad that at least one of their royal princesses had found love.

Sophie was still rambling about Caroline shirking her responsibilities, which was only because Sophie would now have to do a little more work. "And that's why this is so unfair!" she cried dramatically. "You're the heir. You deserve happiness! And Christian was such an asshole to you!"

My lungs tightened. I had spent the last four months calling Christian that and worse. But now I knew that he'd been the victim. All because of my family. Because of me.

"Don't be mad at him," I finally managed to say. "It wasn't his fault."

Sophie's expression was pitying as she crossed over to wrap her arms around me. "You're too good," she said. "You're the glue that holds us all together, even when you go off on your little vacations." Sophie shook her strawberry curls at me. "You're not like her."

"Mother?" I guessed.

"No, Caroline!" Sophie shrugged. "But Mother works, too."

She was right. Both our mother and sister had left us behind.

As I let my little sister hug me tight, I have to say I felt the same pang of resentment against Caroline that was tearing apart Sophie. Why did she get to escape? Why did she get to leave?

It would be so lovely if I didn't have to worry about my duty, my legacy, and my family anymore. Hell, I was even worrying about a dead man who'd left me at the altar.

If Caroline could leave it all behind . . . could I?

The memory of a houseboat flashed before my eyes. It wouldn't be too hard to disappear. Not in Drieden, though. Perhaps . . . America. Or Canada! More open spaces, people too nice to ask me questions. I could dye my hair, live in the mountains, find one of those nice police officers in a red coat to keep me warm during the winter . . .

It sounded blissful. And possible.

My big speeches aside, nothing was keeping me in Drieden. Gran had this queen thing covered, and then it would be father's gig. I wouldn't have to worry about a crown for years. Driedish hospitals would just have to invite some other high-profile Driedener to visit their terminal patients.

For the first time in weeks, maybe months, I felt a hint of relief. The tenuous promise of a life of my own washed over me, and it was that sweetness that caused the tears to flow. The release of expectations and worry flooded my nervous system.

Liberation was so close, I could taste it.

"Oh, darling." Sophie squeezed me. "Don't cry. It's going to be all right, I promise. There are other perfectly acceptable men out there. Ones who hopefully don't have mental illness in their family tree."

I nodded, thinking of that brawny Canadian lumberjack I was going to meet at the . . . saloon? The hockey rink? Where does one pick up Canadian hotties?

I distracted myself with that thought as Sophie prattled on with her sympathetic nonsense. Something about Lucy bawling in the stairwell and hundreds of bouquets piled at the palace gate. And then she said something that didn't quite fit.

"Excuse me?" I asked. "Who was upset about Christian?"

Sophie pulled away and reached for her chilled vodka glass. Clearly we had moved on from the chocolate phase of this memorial service to the vodka portion of the evening. "I was asking you how Tamar was taking the news. Since they worked so closely together, I imagine one would be attached, even if it was just a service-type relationship."

"Service-type relationship?" How long had she been drinking, anyway?

But Sophie's eyes were clear and direct when she explained herself. "You know what I mean—she was his bodyguard. I know they're our paid employees and all, but we do get to know them quite well. I would imagine she would be upset by the news. Speaking of which, where is that Nick fellow? He was quite lovely to have hanging about, if you didn't mind the scowl and the scary scars."

Nick . . . I wouldn't think about what his scowl had done to me. Or Tamar . . . "She wasn't Christian's bodyguard; she's been assigned to me for several years."

Sophie frowned at an ice cube in her glass. "Are you sure? I saw her coming out of his room at Ceillis House after your wedding ball. They seemed quite cozy . . ." Sophie's voice trailed off before an understanding smile flitted on her lips. "Ohhhh . . . I see. You sneak! You probably used her to set up your assignations, didn't you?" She sighed. "One of these days I'm going to have a torrid affair and I'll call you for all the tips. I haven't had a proper date in almost a year, not since . . ."

She veered into some story about a Turkish billionaire's yacht, but I couldn't pay attention.

Tamar.

Christian.

I had never asked Tamar to involve herself with any so-called assignations. And certainly not the night of the ball at Ceillis House.

What would she have been doing there? With my fiancé? I didn't recall her presence at all. Even though my father generally kept a shoe-string staff at Ceillis House, at an event such as that, the entire house would have been protected from the exterior. All security personnel would have been required at the gates and doors, with just a few inside the residence.

A slick black oil spill of suspicion slid through my gut.

thirty-five

TAMAR IN CHRISTIAN'S ROOM?

There were a thousand reasonable explanations.

Tamar and Christian acting comfortable around each other?

It was only Sophie's opinion, after all, and she read into everything, inserting drama and innuendo where there was none. Like when Nick was here and she insinuated about me and him.

Which she had been correct about . . .

Sophie was flighty and creative, but she was also smart.

It was past time for me to be smart, as well.

Ten minutes later, I was walking down the hall to the service elevator. Stopping at the basement. Down another hall, I carried the leftover chocolate cake that Sophie had brought me. My eyeball was scanned and the door to the security offices was unlocked.

No one was going to argue with a princess bearing chocolate cake. It was far superior to a fruit basket. When I asked for Tamar's office, I was immediately given directions. "Thank you," I said with my very best demure smile. "I'll make sure she shares the leftovers."

"I didn't know it was her birthday," the young man with the close-cut dark hair said to me as he unlocked Tamar's door.

"You know Tamar," I said vaguely, to which he nodded automatically, not seeming at all as if he knew her. When I was safely inside her office, I had to wonder if *I* knew her.

How long had she worked for me? Three, four years? There should have been something of hers I recognized in that gray box of a room, but it seemed sterile and chilly down there. Remembering the last time I was there with Nick, I pulled up a chair and easily logged into the palace network, using the same password that Lucy had provided me to access my social appointments.

I knew exactly what I was looking for. The same assignment calendar that Nick had needed to find the guards assigned to Darter—Christian—the night before the wedding. I was also looking at the guards assigned to Darter at Ceillis House.

That was all I needed to see, I told myself. Once I saw that Tamar had, for some official reason, been assigned to Christian the night of the ball, then Sophie's story would make perfect sense.

I opened the calendar. Pulled up the month of March. Scrolled to the date.

There it was. The location, Ceillis House, was entered in everyone's column because the whole family had been there: me, my mother, my father, my siblings, and my grandmother. As I had expected, most of my family had not had individual bodyguards assigned to them.

Christian had been no exception. According to this calendar, no bodyguard had been assigned to Darter that night, and that included Tamar.

Sophie's words raced through my head like the high-speed rail that ran through Drieden.

They seemed quite cozy . . .

I closed the program and gazed at the icons on Tamar's computer. Nothing particularly incriminating jumped out at me. Nothing was marked "Christian's Secret Birthday Presents for Princess Theodora," for instance. Or "101 Possible Reasons to Speak to My Employer's Fiancé Two Nights Before the Royal Wedding."

Think, Thea.

Pretend this is research.

There was rarely one document that thoroughly explained a historical event. Historians had to piece a story together through letters, contemporaneous accounts, and items that belonged to people of the time.

I clicked on Tamar's email. Lots of internal memos. I searched for Christian's name. Lots of internal memos about the days after his disappearance.

Nothing from before the wedding.

All right, then. No letters or contemporaneous accounts to study. I pulled open her desk drawer and half-heartedly pushed a few items around—plastic packets from fast-food restaurants, random office supplies, feminine products . . .

This wasn't right. This was her personal space. I had no business invading her privacy.

The drawer was half-closed when I stilled my hand, praying that I hadn't seen what I thought I did.

I inched the drawer wider.

It was not a stray black button that had fallen off a winter coat and something that Tamar had meant to sew back on one day.

It was a matte-black disc.

Some would call it antiquated technology.

Some would call it evidence.

I fought the urge to slam the drawer shut, run out of the office, and forget I had ever seen the damn things. They tended to bring a disproportionate amount of trouble.

But I'd been the one who had called forth the spirit of Queen Marie-Theodora, that awful domineering woman. I'd had to make a big speech to Nick. I'd had to declare that I was going to seek vengeance on Christian's killer.

With all that grand talk, there was no way I could leave this item in the bottom of a desk drawer.

My hand was shaky when I picked it up and my hands hadn't stopped shaking when I reached for the door handle and nearly ran headlong into Tamar.

thirty-six

MY EXPLANATION WAS SORT OF REASONABLE. I WAS checking on Hugh, I'd said. I was deeply worried since he had been so ill for so long.

Tamar's eyes went to the partly eaten chocolate cake. "Is it someone's birthday?"

"Oh, that." I couldn't think of a lie that would be better than the truth. "Sophie brought it to me. She thought I needed a little chocolate therapy after the news of . . ." My voice broke off remembering Sophie's questions—whether Tamar was close to Christian, whether she was upset at the news of his death.

"I thought I'd share it with some of the security staff," I continued, thinking fast. "Those who had been close to Christian may also need some comfort."

If Tamar was grieving or even remotely sad, she didn't show it. "How very kind. I'll show you where you can put it."

I followed Tamar to the fluorescent break room and left the cake on a table. Tamar walked with me back toward the door. Was she a little stiffer than usual? Maybe. But maybe she was upset about Christian's death. Maybe she was uncomfortable with me being around the security offices. And what about the bug? Had she placed the one in Christian's room at Ceillis House? Or had she found this one here? Were there more that had been hidden around royal residences?

Right outside the door, I stopped short and said, "Tamar, I want you to know, about that night in my apartment—this situation with Mr. Cameron has been very complicated."

"He didn't return with you from Scotland."

Of course she'd know that, given the number of guards that had greeted me at the airport. "No. He didn't. You were the only other person besides me and Hugh who knew his relationship with Christian. Suffice it to say, it was complicated and difficult, and I truly appreciate your discretion. We were only trying to help Christian."

Tamar pursed her lips like she was trying not to say something before coming out with, "He wasn't trustworthy. Look at what he did."

The bug in my room. Nick putting it there did seem like a plausible scenario at this point, but it didn't really make sense why he would have pretended to put one in Christian's room at Ceillis House. Or at Claytere's house.

Now I had to address the big bug in the room. "When I was in your office, I was looking for a pen to write you a quick note. I found this." I pulled out the device from my pocket. "Where did you find this? Are we sure Nick placed these?" When she didn't answer immediately, I continued with my stream of consciousness. "Because I'm worried that something else is going on. Maybe with Anders and his vote. Maybe he's resorted to desperate means to try to get some information about the family."

Tamar finally shook her head. "I don't know, Ma'am. Hugh found that one. Gave it to me the day he got ill. Said the maids picked one up in Lady Lucy's office."

"So that's why you searched my room?" It made a little more sense now. Tamar was dedicated to me, to her job. She wouldn't be intimidated by Nick.

"I can't be too careful."

Because of my staff's diligence, we had uncovered two listening devices in the palace. The implications were enormous, but there were still some huge blanks I needed to fill in. If it was Anders, who was he dealing with? Did he know about Gran's Magdalena enterprise, or was there yet some other bombshell that was going to be dropped on the monarchy? And what had happened to Christian? Was it suicide? Murder? It was surprising how a photograph of a dead body yielded so little useful information.

"Do you know anyone at the national police?" I asked Tamar. "Anyone who can be trusted with this?" I held up the bug. "Perhaps they can trace it to see where it's transmitting—"

"Yes, but I would need to talk to Hugh first," she said, talking over me in her businesslike fashion. "I wouldn't want to go over his head with the national police."

"Of course," I agreed immediately. "Is he well? How is he doing? It must be a vicious flu."

"Much better, Your Highness. In fact, he's been trying to get out of bed, he's so anxious to come back to work."

"Would he be able to stand a visitor?"

Tamar looked overcome. "It would be too much to ask, Your Highness."

"Not at all." I put a hand on her arm. "You and Hugh are like family to me. And this way we can consult with Hugh about our next steps and he can still recuperate."

The decision made, Tamar and I walked to the underground garage, where she selected the keys to a white palace Fiat, in which we would both ride in the front to keep a low profile. On our way to Hugh's apartment, I asked if we could stop to buy him a few things: a bouquet of flowers, some fresh bread, a selection of magazines.

We had been driving east toward the port for ten minutes before I realized we were going the wrong direction. "Has Hugh moved?" I remembered distinctly that he lived in the Koras district, as he had for all his life. He was a proud of being from a neighborhood known for its strong blue-collar, traditional values.

Tamar turned on her blinker and made a left turn—but not back toward Koras.

"Is he staying with a friend?" Maybe Hugh had a partner who was helping him during his illness. "Are you sure this is the right way?"

Tamar sighed, reached into her jacket, and took out her gun.

"Tamar?" I asked, confused for only a half second before she reached out and rammed the butt of her gun in the back of my head.

thirty-seven

MY FACE HURT LIKE HELL. IT WAS ALSO WET, COLD, and sticky. And when I opened my eyes, I saw nothing but pink.

Shades of blush and magenta and rose surrounded me in a suffocating swirl of sweetness.

Had I died? Was this heaven?

I closed my eyes. Opened them. Yes. Still inside of what seemed to be a giant piece of bubble gum. Slowly, my eyes focused and I realized I was in a bedroom that appeared to be trapped in the mid-twentieth century, with pale pink organza curtains over the shutters, a raspberry satin duvet covering the queen-sized bed I was on, and coral wallpaper. Even the lamps were shaded in peony.

I wiggled my toes. My fingers. Everything seemed to be heavy but functional.

So. Not dead, then. Good to know.

It hurt to push up from the uneven mattress, and when I did, I discovered a nylon rope was tied around my wrist. I ran to the wall heater, which the rope was tied around—which also, funnily enough, was the only thing not painted pink in the room. Unfortunately, the heater didn't seem to be working, as my fingers felt like frozen fish sticks. There was no way I could attempt to work these knots with two hands, let alone one.

I sat on the edge of the bed and fought the impulse to lie back down on the threadbare salmon sheets, close my eyes, and give in to the throbbing pain in my head. It wouldn't take much to cause me to pass out again.

Two names kept me upright.

Tamar.

Nick.

If I passed out, Tamar won.

If I passed out, Nick would never respect me. I tried my best to summon a memory of him. Something he'd say in his Scottish growl, something that would give me the strength to get through this.

"Hullo, Thea."

Male. Scottish. Here. *Nick?*

I blinked and tried to focus through the dim strawberry haze. A man, ten feet away.

"Christian?"

My head swam. I was about to pass out. Or maybe I already had. This was a dream, a surreal nightmare.

"You're dead." I managed to croak out the words.

"Not yet," he said. It was an echo of something another Fraser-Campbell would say.

"Where are we?"

"Believe it or not, it's a very pink prison."

He came forward and I could focus again. Tamar's gun had really done its job on my brain. "It *is* you," I said in disbelief, the haze slowly wearing off.

"I wish I could say I was glad to see you."

"I wish I could kick you in the balls," I said.

He chuckled with little humor.

"I'm serious."

"I know." Christian sighed.

"Have you been here this whole time?" It was shocking. Here? In a time capsule of faded femininity? "Who put you here? Tamar?"

"So many questions, as usual."

Yes, and asking them had sucked the small jolt of energy seeing him had given me. I collapsed back on the shabby pillows and willed the blissful blackness to suck me back into peace. Thankfully, it worked. I passed out.

When I gained consciousness a second time, I heard a female voice. "What did you do?"

Then Christian's. "Nothing. She just rolled into a ball. Darling, I have no reason to hurt her."

Darling?

"She's our last chance. What if she's found the documents? We need her alive."

Yes, you do.

"Let her rest, love. What if she remembers wrong? We can't afford another mistake."

Love?

In my half-conscious state, I imagined jumping up and doing some kung fu moves on Tamar and then kicking Christian in the balls as an encore. A deep, instinctual warning bell sounded in my mind and I stayed where I was until all was quiet.

Or maybe I passed out again. Hard to tell.

The sound of silver against china was the bell that signaled another pain that my body instinctively knew: hunger. I pulled myself into a half-seated position. Christian was sitting in a spindly chair in the corner. I was reminded of the chair of doom in Big Gran's office.

"There you are. I was beginning to worry about you."

I could only focus on the plastic bottle in Christian's hand. "Water."

He walked to the bedside and gave me the bottle. I drank nearly half the bottle before he spoke again. "Careful, there. Don't want you to be ill."

I stopped drinking, the water dribbling down my chin. "Fuck you." I had waited months to say that to Christian.

"Thea." His tone was patronizing even here. I couldn't help myself. "Don't fucking use my name."

He paused, and it was possible I imagined the rueful look on his face. "It was never supposed to turn out this way."

"You called her 'darling.' "

"Yes, well." He nodded, an efficient, businesslike gesture incongruent with the situation we were in. "I have a strange attachment to my life."

The grimness in his voice snapped me to attention. What had he said? We were in a prison? Were we in danger?

"What's going on, Christian?"

He smiled tightly. "I want you to hear it from me. Tamar and I are in a relationship."

"Did you know she bugged your rooms and office?"

"That's not surprising. She believes in complete honesty between couples."

When we were together, I found that dry humor charming. Now I found it terrifying. "You can't mean that you're still together."

A look of real pain crossed his eyes. "Thea, you would be surprised what you would do if someone threatened to murder every coworker you had."

I supposed I would be more horrified at the thought of Christian being manipulated by Tamar in some sort of twisted love affair if I weren't tied up—and a victim of them both. After all, how much sympathy was I supposed to have toward the man?

"How long were you cheating on me with my own security officer?"

"From almost the beginning, I'm afraid. It was always so hard to schedule alone time with you."

I tried not to show what I thought of that ludicrous statement, but my head was woozy and I couldn't help but make a face at him. "What sorts of drugs was I given?"

"Nothing that should do any permanent harm." Christian picked up a bowl off the bedside table and placed it on the bed next to me. It was half full of some lumpy stew. "If you're hungry, you should eat. There's more—don't worry. You're not being starved."

I weighed the option of eating possibly poisoned or drugged food and decided against it. I was currently locked up with my ex-fiancé and my obviously insane bodyguard. I needed to keep my wits about me.

With that thought, I tried to assess my surroundings. There were thick antique shutters over the windows, but they were locked with small padlocks. Even if I could find something to smash the locks or splinter the heavy wood, it didn't look like my ropes would stretch that far. I eyed the rope around my wrist. I would need something to cut through the nylon. I tried to think creatively, but I was a princess, not an escape artist.

The bowl Christian had given me was made of thin, cheap porcelain. If I could break a shard off, could I use that as a weapon? Or . . . there was the spoon.

Hot tears flooded my eyes. A freaking spoon was my only tool to cut through ropes, pick a padlock, break open a window, and fashion a device to lower me however many stories down into the streets of what I hoped was still Drieden City. While a murderous, highly trained ex–army officer was on my trail.

"Any chance there's a knife or an ax around here?" I asked Christian, because one never knew. Perhaps he could be easily convinced to let me go.

"Oh, I wouldn't want you to get hurt." He held up his right hand. A moody purple gash was healing across his palm. "Tamar only uses the highest-grade ropes for the people she loves."

I shook my head and picked up the water bottle and finished it off.

Hopefully that would help flush out whatever narcotic Tamar had given me and I could start working on Plan B. Whatever that was.

"Tamar's just gone to the store. She'll bring back more water." Christian took the empty bottle from me and then grabbed my hand. I wanted to jerk away, but I wasn't clear on how much sociopathy I was dealing with here.

"Why are you doing this?" I asked, trying to keep the hysteria at bay by focusing on facts.

Christian's eyes went watery. "I'm so sorry, Thea. I'm so sorry that I did this, that I started all this."

"Are you going to kill me?" I heard the question as if it were coming from someone else's mouth.

Now he looked almost offended. "I'm not a murderer. You know that."

I did *not* know that. I did not know who Christian was or why I was here. Even though I had a hundred more questions, I had to save my precious energy until I knew how I was going to get out of this.

Sometime later, Tamar returned with a basket.

"She won't eat," Christian explained to her.

Tamar looked concerned. "It's been over a day since you've eaten."

A day? Since I'd had chocolate cake for lunch with Sophie? What was my family thinking? Someone must have realized I was missing— Lucy, my maids, even. Surely they were coming to get me soon.

Of course I could say none of this to my kidnapper. "I'm not feeling well," I said vaguely, placing a hand on my stomach.

Tamar crouched down and looked at me closely. "They think you've run off again. You sent Lucy a text that you wanted to mourn Christian in private. 'Get some closure,' I think, were your exact words."

My brain was still operating on a delay, so it took me a moment to realize what she had done. "You used my cell phone?" I asked, in horror.

She stood, brushing her hands off. "I'm doing my job, protecting you."

"How?" I lifted the arm that was tied to the wall. "How is *this* protecting me?" Then I pointed to Christian. "And sleeping with my fiancé? Was that protecting me, too?!"

"He's a cheater. You deserve better."

"And you deserve him?"

Tamar shook her head in resignation. "The heart wants what it wants."

And that was when I fully understood that I had to be very careful around this psychopath.

She kneeled down in front of me and said frankly, "We'll let you go as soon as you tell me what we need to know."

My stomach churned. This was not good. Not good at all.

"Where are the Cayman papers that show how Aurelia has cheated this country?" Tamar's question was calm and straightforward, and I feared that as soon as I answered her, I would end up like Tomas Claytere. Missing, with nothing but a dried puddle of blood across a fuchsia satin duvet to suggest my demise.

But how could I get out of this? What would I tell her? Should I try to delay this? Could I lie? Misdirect?

"I kept hoping you and the brother would find something." Tamar sounded irritated. "But you came back from Scotland with nothing."

Christian's head hung back. "Ah yes, Nicholas. I could hardly believe it when Tamar said that he was alive. We were so hopeful that he'd help you find the documents for us."

I stared at Christian's lengthened neck, his profile, searching for any similarities between him and his brother. Maybe they were more alike than I could see, but I was blinded by the violent emotions that were overtaking me. Still, I managed to sound mostly calm when I asked, "You *wanted* us to find the Cayman papers for you?"

Christian barked a strangled, dry laugh. "Not just the Cayman papers. Those mean nothing without the firm records. Anders won't pay us our money until we give him the proof that'll end the monarchy.

And Boson Chapelle practically closed down after Tamar killed every-one who knew what they were doing."

Tamar threw up her hands. "I was protecting you!"

"She was eliminating the competition," I said. It was simple supply and demand. The fewer people who could provide the incriminating documents, the more the price went up.

"Yes! Thank you!" She flashed me a triumphant look before turning back to Christian. "Thea understands what I do for you."

"Thea's very understanding," Christian said with a distant note in his voice that Tamar didn't seem to catch.

But I did, and I understood that there was a very dangerous game being played here and Christian had, knowingly or unknowingly, just laid out the rules for me.

This was a scavenger hunt. Once someone found a clue, Tamar killed the person to make sure she and Christian were the only ones at the finish line with the prize.

"Now." Tamar faced me again, all her trained-assassin attention on me. "Where are the papers that will bring down the House of Laurent?"

thirty-eight

PRETENDED TO PASS OUT.

"What the hell is wrong with her?" Tamar muttered.

"Some people don't handle tranquilizers well." Christian sounded resigned. "And the ones you have are for horses."

Tamar swore, and I heard the toe of her boot smack something hard. "We only have two more days to get those fucking papers."

"Anders won't take back the offer, darling. He needs us too much."

"And he won't make the deposit until we hand over the documentation, idiot."

"*I'm* an idiot? You're the one who's made it impossible for me to get the right papers!"

"You were going to leave me for her."

"I was engaged to her."

Tamar might have made a snorting sound—it was hard to tell with my face pressed into lumpy goose down again—and soon it was quiet.

Until Christian spoke.

"You can get up now. She's gone."

I opened one eye, and through the matted curtain of hair that had fallen over my face, I saw that there was no sign of Tamar. When I pushed back into a seated position, Christian nudged a tray toward me with his foot. "You need to eat."

"Is it laced with anything?"

"Could be." He sounded tired. "But if the choice is between starving and being drugged—"

"I'd rather die with my wits," I snapped.

Given the dim light of the room, I felt more than saw Christian's gaze, heavy with meaning. "We'll see when you're here a few months."

"I won't be here long," I said, as much for him as for me. "I'll have the entire country looking for me."

"You? The disappearing princess? They'll figure Honeybee just took another little flight."

I wanted to argue with him, but the sinking feeling in my gut was because I knew he was right. How many days would it be until Lucy grew suspicious of whatever lies Tamar had told her? And Nick . . .

I couldn't count on Nick to rescue me. He'd already gotten what he'd wanted. I was no longer of any use to him, so why would he try to come find me?

In the silence, I began to hear other noises. The street outside. Water pipes and furnace hisses. Soon the sounds were integrated in my head, reminding me that there was a vibrant, busy world out there. A world that I wasn't ready to leave yet.

"So what happened, Christian?" I finally asked. If I was going to die, I wanted to know all the answers. After all I'd been through to get them, he owed me that much. "I could have handled you with another woman. You could have sold secrets to Anders. But leaving me at the altar?" I forced a brittle laugh. "That was unconscionable."

He thought for a moment. "It was all Tamar's fault."

"Of course it was. You were her weak little pawn. You had no control over your actions."

"Yes, we had an affair. Which was useful, I suppose."

"*Useful?*" I hoped my disgust was clear.

If Christian noticed my repugnance at his word choice, he didn't seem chagrined in the slightest. "She was the one who helped me put the pieces together. You see, I'd been going through our client files, trying to understand what might have been made public in the Cayman papers disclosure." He raised his eyebrows. "When I saw that much money? From a Driedish corporation? It could only mean big oil or the government." Christian smiled ruefully. "Tamar told me about the times she'd visited Perpetua with you after university, and it all clicked."

"A useful mistress indeed." I tried to sound haughty, but the words tasted bitter on my lips.

"And then Tamar went to Anders. Told him what she had seen. That there was a secret corporation based on royal lands that was taking money from the Driedish people," Christian finished. "He offered her millions, so we decided to give him what he wanted and to use the money to run away together."

"And you left me at the altar."

"Well, I tried breaking up with her before that."

I didn't believe it. "Sure you did."

"When Aurelia offered the change in succession," he smiled ruefully, "becoming a king before the age of forty seemed like a better deal than Anders's offer."

"I bet she didn't like hearing about it from a bug," I said, thinking of the black disc in Christian's room at Ceillis House.

Christian looked impressed. "Yes, when I told her the plans were off, we had a big row. It got a bit . . . heated." He winced and put a hand under his rib cage. "Then I promised she would still be my mistress. She pretended to forgive me. I'd had a headache after the whole thing, and she gave me one of those horse pills, said it was a pain pill. Fast-forward twenty-four hours and I had missed the big day. And the whole world vilified me as the man who abandoned their precious princess . . ."

"At least you had a backup plan." My voice was filled with spite and exhaustion.

"True." He seemed very matter-of-fact. "I have goals, Thea. If that means I tell Tamar what she needs to hear, then that's what I'll do. If that means I fake my own death to get my brother off my trail or help her recover those papers . . . I'll do what I have to do. Do you understand?"

And with that hanging in the air, Christian went quiet so I could process the new information. More than ever, I was certain that I was going to die. If I didn't give them what they wanted—or if I did. They'd kidnapped a princess. They couldn't afford to let me go.

I had only one chance to change the outcome of this story.

"Tamar! Tamar! Tamar!" I screamed her name as loudly as I could, praying that I was making the right decision.

The history books had never prepared me on how a princess should betray her queen. But they *had* taught me how to manipulate an enemy.

I heard her footsteps in the hall and thought of Nick, wondering how a woman half his size could sound twice as heavy. And when she said, "Yes, Princess?" I heard an echo of Nick's voice, except when he used the title it was gently sardonic. When she used it, the title now seemed loaded with threat.

Christian narrowed his eyes and rubbed his stubbled chin. "You couldn't just tell me?" he murmured.

"You're a team, aren't you?" I shot back, which made Tamar give Christian a wary look.

Christian flashed her a meaningful smile. "Tamar knows how I feel about her."

I had to say, his declaration of devotion was scarily authentic, and I had to smash down a wave of doubt that rose over me. What was I doing, playing into the hands of these criminals?

"I wanted you both to hear." I turned my attention to Tamar. "I found the files when I was looking for Christian," I told her. "The ones that Anders wants. The ones that will link my grandmother with Magdalena Energy and will help destroy the monarchy."

"Where?" Tamar clenched her fists. "I've followed you for weeks and you haven't had anything."

"We found them in Scotland."

She made a frustrated noise. "I knew it!" She turned on Christian. "I told you they were in your apartment." She turned back to me. "They're in his boxes at Brisbane Castle?"

I hesitated. This was where things were going to get tricky. "Yes."

"I didn't have any firm files in my apartment." Christian's nostrils flared. "You're making this up."

"I didn't say they were actual papers, you idiot. I found them on the Boson Chapelle network."

Tamar looked at Christian. "Do you know what she's talking about?"

I didn't want to give Christian another chance to speak. "One can't access the firm's client files without either a network computer or administrator's privileges. We didn't have either, so one of Nick's colleagues found us the admin password."

When Tamar looked unconvinced, I doubled down. "I saw the client lists and drew the connections. How else would I know about the Magdalena Energy accounts and the foreign incorporation agreements?"

Christian was triumphant "Yes. See, darling? I told you having Nick looking for them would be good for us. He's quite ruthless when he wants something."

While I hated agreeing with Christian, the truth of that statement was like an arrow through my heart. Nick was ruthless, even cold, when the situation demanded it. I only hoped that he could spare one last thought for me when the time came.

Tamar pivoted to me. "And you were able to get in with this administrator password."

"Yes, but I left it in Scotland, on a piece of paper in Christian's agenda. I had no reason to want to get to the files again, not after we saw the photo of Christian's body."

She paced, three steps then back, quick, jerky steps. "I can get in from the palace network. No one will track me there. But first I need to get my hands on that book."

I had to jump on that opportunity. "I'll help you. We'll go to Scotland together. Princess Theodora will want to pay her respects to the home of her ex-fiancé. While we're there, we'll get the password and you can get the firm records to sell to Anders."

Tamar was looking between Christian and me, speculation clear on her face. This could backfire badly.

Then she made her decision. "No. You will stay here with Christian. I'll go to Scotland and tell them I'm representing you, and you can tell me where to look for this agenda."

I nodded and thought quickly. "Of course. You'll have to call ahead, give them some excuse that there are items of his that I want."

"Who do I call?"

"There's a card in my top desk drawer. Plain, with just a number on it. Call it and ask for the Brisbane Castle butler. Then tell him who you are, and that you'll be visiting to pick up some items for me. Specifically, you'll want Christian's journal."

Finally, she smiled slightly at me. "Thank you for this information. This search has been exhausting."

"Yes, I know," I said faintly.

After she left to go make her calls from a safer location, Christian gave me a long, searching look, and I didn't know what else to say to him. "Good luck storming the castle" would be insincere. And I hadn't reached the point where I felt the need to dramatically beg for my life.

So I stayed silent and when Christian left me alone, I reached for the tray and the sandwich that Tamar had left hours earlier.

She may have drugged the food, but I needed all the strength I could get for what was coming next.

thirty-nine

THE SANDWICH HAD BEEN LACED WITH SOMETHING. I slept fitfully, as if a voice in a dark corner of my mind were yelling at me to wake up and take notice of something I had missed.

Finally, my eyes creaked open. The rose and salmon and coral clouds hovered around me, like the bloated innards of some hungry monster that had swallowed me whole.

An unknowable stretch of time had passed; my head swam, my stomach ached. I tried to make myself vomit, then nearly passed out from the effort. I floated in an ocean of anger at Christian's betrayal. It was strangely soothing, a life force that I could cling to, a reason to stay conscious, to live.

I listened to the sounds of the city outside, as if it were my last chance at communing with my people.

The history books might never know how I ended up here in this grotesque fantasy of a princess bedroom—if I was ever found in the first place, that is. If Tamar and Christian both disappeared, who would tell this tale?

My one fading spark of hope grew fainter with each hour. There was no other plan or ploy for me to make. So I closed my eyes and treasured the sounds of trucks, tires, and sirens. It was all I had left to cling to.

I tumbled into darkness and the sirens grew louder.

My heartbeat grew louder, too, like the sound of a *thump, thump, thump* I heard from far away—a sound that was soft, yet firm and determined. The sound was an echo of a footstep I had once learned well on a boat.

There was a distant boom, much like the sound I'd once heard in the National Galleries as Nick tried to protect me.

Another set of footsteps. A loud profanity. My eyes snapped open when my arm was yanked. Christian was standing over me, a knife glinting in the rose-tinted dusk. He held a finger to his lips, which would have been funny if I'd had any ability to make any sort of noise at all. Then the knife sliced down, landing inches from my arm, making a soft *zing* as the rope was cut.

Although he was smaller than his brother, Christian was strong enough to carry me out of the bedroom. As we went down a hall, another explosion went off, this time louder.

Shouts came from below, and a roar of movement followed. So did another string of curses from Christian's lips.

Another ten feet and we entered a tiny library. There was no pink here, only antique wood-paneled walls and dusty, empty bookcases. A small cot sat in the corner, with piles of blankets and a neat stack of clothes on a narrow table. That was where he dumped me like a sack of dirty laundry. I groaned.

"Can you shut up, please?"

"No," I managed.

"Fucking horse pills," Christian muttered as he bent over and grabbed something that rattled like another medication bottle. He shoved something inside his mouth, and I saw the slick shine of the gun barrel that he slid into his waistband. He took two steps, kicked the door to the room closed, and came back to the cot, pulling me onto his knee like a ventriloquist's doll.

Then all hell broke loose.

The slamming of the door to the room must have been a signal to what sounded like hundreds of soldiers storming the apartment. Then the door flew off its hinges.

Nick stood in the doorway, an assault rifle pointed straight at us.

Christian stood, me along with him, his arm wrapped around my middle. "Look who it is, darling. My brother's come to rescue you. Isn't that sweet?"

Nick's expression was cold and deadly. Christian used his free arm to pull his own weapon out. He pointed it at Nick. "I really didn't want it to come to this. Brother versus brother. It's so . . . I don't know. What is it, Thea? What's the word I'm looking for?"

"An unfair fight?" I managed.

Christian chuckled in my ear. "Oh, you *are* smitten, aren't you? Something about the men in our family must really do it for you."

"You call yourself a man?" Nick snarled. "Hiding behind a woman? Let her go and then we can deal with this like we used to back in Scotland."

"I call myself a duke, actually. I have your title, your princess, and I'm afraid I'm not doing anything like I used to." Christian caressed under my breast. "Unless Thea asks me to. Then I'll consider it."

Nick's lip curled and he sighted his rifle. "One last chance before I blow you away. Let her go."

Christian snapped off his safety. "We have some terms to negotiate first."

"Don't do it, don't negotiate," I said to Nick. "Shoot him."

Christian sighed. "Okay, fine." He pulled the trigger. I screamed over the ringing in my ears.

Nick was on the floor clutching at his right shoulder, his rifle strewn across the floor. Blood was smearing across his palm as he tried to sit up.

My knees sagged. Christian dug his fist into my stomach to hold me tighter.

He addressed Nick again in that calm, almost smug voice. I wanted to turn around and claw his eyes out. "I suggest you be a good boy and let me leave. You've got one good arm and you'll need it if you want her out of here alive."

Nick immediately looked at me and I just shook my head a little. I didn't know what Christian was talking about. I was a little loopy, yes, but I didn't feel on the verge of imminent death.

Then Christian spun me around and kissed me, forcing my mouth open, pushing his tongue inside. And something else. The pills. I gagged, then swallowed without meaning to. I choked as he let me go and fell to my knees.

He leapt to the back of the room as I continued coughing. Gagging. Trying to get whatever it was out of me.

The corners of my vision started going black.

"THEA!" URGENT AND ROUGH. "THEA! I'M GOING TO KILL the fucking bastard, so help me God."

Warm and solid.

"Come on, Princess. Don't give up. You hear me? Don't you fucking give up."

Sweet and hot. Warm and safe.

I died in Nick's arms.

WHEN I OPENED MY EYES, ALL I COULD SEE WAS NICK leaning over me, his hand clutching mine. I whispered his name, not sure if this was heaven or hell.

"I'm here, Princess. You're going to be fine." From the ferocity in his face, I believed him, even though it felt like my head was in a vise.

"Christian—"

He cut me off. "Shhh. Don't talk."

"Where is he?"

Nick put a hand on my forehead and yelled at the driver of the vehicle we were in the back of. "For Christ's sake, she needs a doctor!"

"No, Nick."

He kissed my fingers. "Stay with me, Princess."

"Your arm?"

He ignored my question, choosing to stroke my hair instead, and then, after I closed my eyes again, I felt his lips on mine. Fitting that the last kiss I would ever receive would erase the last kiss his brother would ever give me.

EFFICIENT AND REASSURING, THE DOCTOR INFORMED ME that Christian had forced me to swallow an overdose of the tranquilizers Tamar had been giving me. My heart had indeed stopped, and I had been brought back to life by what she called "emergency procedures."

"You were very lucky." She smiled warmly.

I supposed it could've been luck. But I'd bet it was having Nick by my side.

"Where am I?" I asked. The room had all the hospital paraphernalia, but the environment was eerily silent.

"You're safe here," she said with another too-nice American smile. "It's a private medical facility."

I wondered whether my government knew the CIA and/or MI6 had private medical facilities in Drieden. I made a mental note to learn more when I had the energy to think of such things.

Fading back into sleep, I had to ask, "Where's Nick?" But I'm not sure I was coherent, or maybe the doctor's American-accented Driedish wasn't perfect, because she answered, "Max will be here soon."

When my eyes opened again, it wasn't Max Cornelius by my bedside, but Nick. He was in his standard all-black shirt and cargo pants. How people didn't see the military experience in their midst, I'd never know. He had tough-as-nails written all over him . . . except his expression, gazing down at me.

As weak as I was, recovering from a heart failure and the general emotional trauma of being kidnapped, it was Nick's face, full of concern and deep regard, that buoyed me. When was the last time someone had looked at me this way? Had it happened when I was a child, even? I was a princess of Drieden, surrounded by every luxury. I had a big family, devoted subjects, enamored fans around the world. But not even Lucy looked at me the way Nick did. Like maybe I was a real person—a real woman—at last.

"Hi," I said softly.

"Hello there." His smile was tense. "Were you enjoying your nap?"

Thank you. The words were on my lips but I knew he'd bat them away, and I didn't want to be rejected. Not yet. "I had a hard day," I said instead.

"You did. Taking tea and painting watercolors and whatever else you princesses do."

"I'm sorry I got you shot."

He frowned. "Yeah. That keeps happening around you."

I knew he took refuge in the jokes. Teasing me was safe, for some reason. I didn't have the energy to keep up with him right now.

"Tamar . . ."

He put his hand on mine. "We're not talking about her."

"Christian?"

His jaw audibly clicked. "We're not talking about him, either," he said through gritted teeth.

"What happened after I went down?"

"There was a secret door in the paneling. Probably left over from Leopold the Fifth's reign."

The joke fell flat. Partially because he hadn't put his heart in it. Partially because that reference made no sense—everyone knew the last Leopold had been Leopold the Fourth.

"So he got away?" I asked.

Nick's eyes dropped to where our hands joined. "I'll find him. And he will pay."

On the one hand, I couldn't understand what Nick had gone through during the past few hours. Threatening to shoot and then being shot by a brother seemed traumatizing. As dysfunctional as my family was, neither Henry nor Sophie nor Caroline would ever shoot me, I was fairly certain. But being from that same dysfunctional family, I could understand some of Nick's possible issues. After all, just a few days ago I had thought my grandmother had ordered my fiancé murdered. It was going to take me a while to work through that.

"Do you want to talk about it?" I asked softly.

"You nearly died today. I think me going into the details of the torture I intend to inflict on my brother would be detrimental to your recovery."

"Another time," I said. "We can brainstorm ideas."

He laughed a little at my joke. Probably because it wasn't really a joke.

"Tell me what happened. With Tamar," I said.

"She called me, asking to make an appointment at Brisbane Castle." He rubbed his chin absently. "Gave her name and everything. Said you were looking for a journal that I knew for a fact was tucked safely in your own room." His green eyes met mine. "I had to come see what you were up to this time."

"How did you know where I was?"

"We traced her call and cross-referenced the unidentified GPS coordinates from Christian's Land Rover. We apprehended Tamar shortly thereafter." He lifted his shoulder. "Let's just say my colleagues convinced her to draw a map to your location." His voice was bland, but I had an idea of the persuasive methods used on my former bodyguard.

I sighed and leaned my head back on the pillows. My plan had worked. Sending Tamar to that number was the only thing I could think of that could have possibly alerted Nick's Batman senses without alerting Tamar's Spidey ones.

When I had finished updating Nick on everything that happened before he and his team of commandos had raided the building, I realized something. At the end of all this, Anders still did not have the papers proving Big Gran's embezzlement.

When I pointed that out, Nick replied, "Well, at least you got your happy ending." I couldn't help but notice it didn't feel happy. And that Nick didn't look happy. Instead, his expression could only be called brooding.

"Does your arm hurt?" I asked.

He tried to shrug my question off but couldn't quite hide his wince.

So I made him lie down next to me in the narrow hospital bed. Both of us had things we needed to recover from.

But I couldn't stop my brain, even while lying there quietly with Nick. My thoughts circled and twisted until they finally reached their terminal destination.

Drieden still was not safe from Christian Fraser-Campbell. Even if he was on the run, all he needed was a hacker as talented as Sybil and he could still get information to bring down the monarchy.

"Nick," I whispered to the large form that had draped itself around my side.

"Yes?"

"I need to do one more thing."

"No."

"You don't know what it is."

"Unless it's staying in a horizontal position, preferably under me, the answer is no."

"We can do that after I meet with Anders."

He groaned and sat up, then fixed me with a very stern glare.

"I have to talk to him," I insisted.

"If you haven't noticed, you're in a hospital gown. In a hospital bed!" he snarled.

"I'm the only one he'll speak to."

Nick tried very hard not to roll his eyes. "And why is that?"

"I'll explain everything after you call and give him a message for me."

"No." He gave me a look of frustration as I shook my head, a slow smile growing across my face. "What?"

"Let's make a deal."

forty

A NDERS'S PARLIAMENT OFFICES WOULDN'T BE PRI-
vate. The palace wasn't exactly neutral territory, either. So after much debate, Anders and I agreed to meet at a gazebo in
the middle of the Jubilee Caterina Park, a beautifully manicured garden
within walking distance of the Comtesse River. I didn't doubt that Nick
had escape routes plotted.

We were joined by Max and a small crew of men in black, possibly
the "colleagues" who had helped convince Tamar to reveal my location. I was allowed to dress in the same black weatherproof gear as Nick
and the rest of his squad, as much for safety as for convenience. Nick
personally strapped me into a Kevlar vest, grumbling the whole time
about how much trouble I was.

Even in tactical fabrics, we didn't attract attention moving down the
grass pathways to the prearranged meeting spot. Fifteen minutes after I
sat where Nick had told me to sit, Pierre Anders joined me in the gazebo.

"Your Highness," he said with a courtly nod of his head.

"I'm surprised you still call me that."

Anders straightened and looked me in the eye. "Your titles won't be
stripped. Europe is full of hereditary princesses with no formal role."

The idea irked me. It was going to take me a while to get used to it. But in the meantime . . .

"I thought you should know that my ex-fiancé will not be fulfilling the terms of your agreement."

Anders cast a quick glance at Nick, who was standing a scant six feet away as totally normal bodyguards do. He tilted his head. "You know what's in the papers they wanted to sell me?"

"Yes." I had to smile. "I have them. My security guard, however, the one who negotiated with you? She's currently detained by law enforcement. And my ex-fiancé soon will be. So they won't be bringing you a thumb drive."

Anders's smile faded at the realization that all his big plans for a republic were now somewhat weaker. "I know, I'm disappointed, too," I said. "I really don't think they deserve all that money."

Although his displeasure was evident, he still said, "I'm sure you'll understand why I sought them. For some principles, no price is too high."

"I agree with that," I continued. "I've always admired your principles. Your commitment to Drieden's poor and to its children is particularly inspirational."

His lips turned up slightly. "I appreciate the royal approval, even if I have never sought it."

I put my hands in the deep pockets of the black cargo pants that Nick had "loaned" me. They were far more comfortable than anything I'd worn during the previous occasions I'd addressed a member of Parliament.

"I know you haven't," I said. "And truthfully, I wasn't speaking on behalf of the Crown. I'm not sure what my grandmother's opinion of you is, beyond, well, her dislike of your attempts to abolish her job, evict her, and demolish her entire way of life."

"I'm sure I'll be even less popular after I succeed. Mark my words, I will expose your family's misdeeds one day."

"About that—"

"Is that why you called me here, today? Did you think you would be able to talk me out of this?" Anders let out a dry bark of a laugh. "Driedeners have had enough of the corruption of the House of Laurent. The monarchy will be abolished. History will not be denied its inevitable conclusion, Your Highness."

"Yet you still use my title."

Anders was imperturbable. He shrugged. "Habits. Manners. I'm an old man. And besides, what else should I call you?"

I saw concern in Nick's glance out of the corner of my eye. But I could handle myself.

"You could call me partner."

Anders stared.

"The papers that Christian promised you would probably help you bring down the monarchy. But what of your other concerns? The issues you fight for in Parliament? Job training. The environment. Early education. Nutrition programs. Even though you're trying to destroy my family's entire way of life, surely you must care—at least a little—about the people."

"Those causes will benefit automatically because the government will no longer have to support you and your family."

"True." I folded my arms, confident in what I was about to explain. "But they could benefit more if the Driedish government kept its oil revenues."

He smiled. "And what would a princess know about such things?"

I was really tired of men assuming I didn't know anything.

"Let me explain it in simple terms. The majority of the Driedish pipelines go through Perpetua's waters, not to mention the drilling sites that are located in Perpetua's territory."

"I don't see what that has—"

"I know, it's practically forgotten history. You may not have learned in primary school that Perpetua is a separate legal entity from the country of Drieden. Its ownership was granted directly to the House of

Laurent by the Holy Roman Empire. Any oil between Perpetua and Drieden goes right through my grandmother's hands."

Anders's smile faded and he was listening carefully now.

"The House of Laurent will continue to control Perpetua and its oil revenue, no matter what the Driedish Parliament does. Any act of aggression on the territory will be dealt with swiftly by the EU and NATO. I'm sure that the United Kingdom, France, and Norway will not approve of Driedish forces taking oil fields by force. You know that never ends well in history. We could bicker and go to international court over this, but in the meantime, Queen Aurelia will renegotiate contracts with the oil companies, ones with extremely beneficial terms. Geopolitics being what they are, the United States government won't much like any tampering with those contracts, either. So yes, you'll leave my grandmother without a crown, but you'll also leave Drieden without forty percent of its revenue."

"You would hold your own people hostage? For a crown? A title?" Anders's voice was dramatic and deep, but I could see he was taking me very seriously. I wondered what Nick was thinking, but I had to keep my focus on Anders.

"Pierre, I already told you I was tempted to give you the Perpetua documents. I agree that the course of history is plain. We are now living in a democratic age."

"What do you want?" Once again, I saw his craftiness. He had made many deals and compromises over the years, and even though I respected him and his service to our country—even if he was a traitor to the Crown—I would not underestimate him.

"You will postpone the vote for a period of five years, and promise to keep private any papers that purport to show your allegations of corruption. In exchange for a portion of Perpetua's oil revenues."

"A portion?" Anders scoffed. "Your own bodyguard told me that your grandmother has stolen billions from her people and you want to give us a crumb from your table. Your offer is unconscionable."

"You haven't heard my offer."

He paused before asking, "What is it?"

I had him. For the right number, I could get him to agree to sell his principles and secure the future of my family.

There was just one problem.

"I have to talk to Aurelia."

Anders threw up his hands. Dramatics, part of the bargaining process. We both knew he had a losing hand. I couldn't be distracted by his faux frustration.

"It won't be a crumb," I promised. "But we won't give you carte blanche, either."

"So there will be strings."

"Feel free to refuse at any time. You can walk away right now with nothing. Or you can work with me and receive considerably more."

He set his jaw stubbornly. He wouldn't walk away from a good deal, but I couldn't push him too far, either.

Anders took his leave and I was filled with a potent urgency, as if I were an arrow on a bow and the string had just been pulled back as far as it could go. I swung around to share my jubilation with Nick, only to find him . . .

Gone.

forty-one

BEFORE I COULD NEGOTIATE WITH ANYBODY ELSE, I had to get the full rundown on what had happened while I'd been tied up in the deadliest pink room ever designed. Since Nick had so rudely run off, I ordered Max to take me to the next person who could educate me.

In a nondescript apartment building, my former security officer was being held behind several fortified steel doors and multiple layers of bulletproof glass.

I should have felt vindicated. In control. But what I thought was that Tamar looked tired. Rightfully so, perhaps, as she had been leading a double life for over a year.

She also looked beaten. Humiliated. Betrayed. I could sympathize with all of those emotions.

"You set me up," she said with a curled lip.

I pulled up a chair and talked to her through a vent in the bulletproof glass. "I'm afraid so."

Tamar started pacing, her eyes blazing. "Christian just left me here to rot, didn't he?"

"Christian is an asshole," I said, because that seemed to sum it up nicely. And then, because I was dying to know: "Did you ever knock him around a little? Maybe punch him in the face, just to show him you were in charge?"

Her shoulders slumped. "Of course not. We loved each other. When Anders made his offer, we dreamt of a beautiful future together. And then . . ."

"You killed too many people?" I suggested.

"I suppose it all went wrong when I stopped him from marrying you." She frowned. "I should have let him."

"We'll agree to disagree on that one," I said drily.

"What happens now?" she asked, her voice resigned.

I explained what I knew: She was being held on charges of murder and kidnapping. She would also be charged with plotting to overthrow the government and her assault on poor Hugh, who had been found in his apartment completely spaced out, the victim of drugs that Tamar had been slipping into his chicken soup—presumably to keep him away from me and Nick while she followed our trail at the palace.

Before I left, I asked her one more time if anyone else knew about the connection between Magdalena Energy, the Queen, and Drieden. She shook her head sadly. "Only me and Christian and Anders. The rest are all dead."

It was so horrific that my next steps became much easier.

HERE, IN THE PALACE LIBRARY, I LAID IT ALL OUT FOR THE Queen. Once again, it seemed appropriate that we meet here, in the set of rooms where Prince Wilhelm had negotiated the 1709 commercial treaties between the Layzerne province and the capital district. If Sybil were here, maybe she could identify the feng shui energy that made this particular corner of the palace so conducive to compromise.

At least, I hoped there would be a compromise. Gran had not agreed to any part of my plan. Yet.

There was nothing in writing. No papers or contracts between the parties would be signed. The success of my scheme would depend on the honor of the persons involved.

On the one hand, there was Pierre Anders, a dedicated Driedish political leader for the past thirty years.

On the other hand, there was my grandmother, the Queen. A monarch who had reigned over a thousand-year dynasty for the better part of a century.

And then there was me, awkwardly balancing on the treacherous tightrope between duty to family and duty to justice.

Wiser people than me would probably argue that I was coming down on the wrong side—of history, ethics, patriotism—take your pick. Some would probably delightedly point out my selfishness in this whole plot. How it conveniently gave me security, safety, and stability.

Well. No one ever said I was stupid.

Neither did my grandmother, after she heard my offer.

"You want to be queen," she summarized, a mix of challenge and pride in her eyes.

I nodded. It would be redundant to point out that it was literally what I was born to do.

"Do you think you're prepared for it?" she asked, surely looking for an angle to approach the negotiations.

But there would not be negotiations. Not on this, not today.

"No, I am not prepared for it," I said brusquely. "That is why we'll set the date for your abdication to coincide with your Jubilee. Next summer, we'll celebrate your forty years and my coronation two weeks after. We'll leave all the flags and bunting up. It's a good use of public funds to not have to redecorate the streets."

Gran's nose wrinkled delicately. "Will I toss you the scepter like a baton in a race?"

"Not in those shoes." I indicated the three-inch heels she still enjoyed.

She only lifted an eyebrow. "You're trying to placate the Liberals by getting rid of me, but that strategy will never work. Anders and his ilk don't just hate me—they hate everything we represent. They will never give up tearing this family apart and burning everything we've built to the ground."

I could have pointed out that perhaps it wasn't the princes and queens of Drieden who had worked to build everything, that perhaps common Driedeners had played an essential role in the development of this country, but I had learned a lot about political manipulation at the hands of a master.

"If we don't placate Anders," I said, "he will expose your deeds with Magdalena Energy and the House of Laurent will truly be over."

There was only one way the House of Laurent would survive. "You will announce your intention to abdicate and name me as the heir, as is your right under Driedish law."

"And you think that will keep the Liberals in line."

"Anders wants to see you punished. He also wants a share of Magdalena's profits. I intend to funnel some of that back into the country. It's only right."

Gran thought about what I had said before replying, "Your father will be pleased, at least. *He* never wanted to be king."

"No, he didn't," I agreed. My father's participation in this scheme was the least problematic portion. "And I am ready to take my place and do what needs to be done."

Gran stood there, silently assessing me for another moment. If she fought me, the death warrant on the Driedish monarchy would be signed—by its own queen.

"For the record, everything I did was for this family, and none of it was illegal," she finally said. "Perpetua belongs to the House of Laurent by law."

What she said was true. From my research, Perpetua was a relic of another time, where monarchs could and did rule absolutely and own lands outright. The fact that she had failed to clarify these legalities to Driedish officials during the negotiation of drilling and pipeline contracts wasn't illegal. The fact that the multinational oil companies hadn't objected to doing business with a presumed Driedish holding and had sent payments to Magdalena Energy wasn't improper under the laws, either.

"Just because it was legal doesn't mean it was right," I pointed out.

Gran smiled slightly and waved a hand at the gilded ceilings and walls. "Once upon a time, women just like us decided what was legal and what was right. We are true queens, Theodora. Born to lead."

A chill went down my spine at my grandmother's words, words of the last queen I would ever bow to.

"Yes, we are."

ONE WEEK LATER, I WAS BACK IN THE LIBRARY, REVIEWING which books I might need to study in my preparations to become queen. A shadow moved. I whirled around and there was the second Fraser-Campbell brother who had abandoned me this year.

Nick, handsome as a devil in his black security guard suit.

Nick, who hadn't bothered to contact me since he'd disappeared from the garden while I spoke with Pierre Anders.

Nick, whom I had tried very hard not think about.

"How did you get in here?" I demanded, all princess again.

"I'm still on staff. Technically."

He stepped out of the shadow, into the light of the small brass lamp that graced my desk.

"I read in the newspapers that Anders withdrew the vote regarding the monarchy. Did you make your deal, then?" The harshness in his voice set me on edge. I hadn't heard that hostility since I first escaped with him down the Comtesse River. When he hadn't wanted me around.

I nodded. "The monarchy is safe."

I had informed Anders that I would be replacing Queen Aurelia on the Driedish throne. He wasn't thrilled by any replacement, but when I had agreed to generously fund the Princess Theodora Trust, which would automatically distribute money to Anders's pet projects, as Pierre Anders was its principal trustee, he suddenly believed that it was in the best interests of the nation that he keep both the existence of Magdalena Energy and the technicalities of who owned Perpetua under wraps, too.

Anders got his money. Millions of euros would be spent on poor and disadvantaged Driedeners, on science and culture and education. And it would all be in my name.

It wasn't my ego. It was insurance. It was both a guarantee that Anders wouldn't renege and a buffer for the royal legacy.

I could have explained it all to Nick, but at this moment he was looking at me with a distant edge, and I was still angry that he had left without a word.

"Why did you leave me at the park?"

His green eyes were guarded. "You were taken care of."

"That's not what I asked." *I wanted you there.*

A flash of something crossed his face—sympathy? I couldn't bear it. And I certainly couldn't tell him the truth.

I needed you there.

"I thought we were partners." Now my ego was talking. It couldn't be helped. I was a woman and a princess. Some things were too ingrained to argue with.

"I left you in that park because I saw a princess taking care of herself, fighting for her country. One who didn't need a man like me to be her partner."

A man like him. He was being ridiculous. "You're a duke."

"I'm not."

"You could claim the title if you wanted it."

He dismissed that with a lazy shrug.

I continued to lay out my case. "You're a highly trained special forces officer."

"And?"

"You're a fucking spy, Nick. I'm sure you could figure out a way to be here." *With me.* "If you wanted to."

"I'm not Christian."

"What's that supposed to mean?"

"I won't be anyone's boy toy."

My laugh was brittle and loud. As if anyone could keep Nick Fraser-Campbell as her plaything.

"I'm not meant for the spotlight. Or for cages," he said, gesturing at the centuries-old painted ceiling above us. "No matter how pretty." He stepped in front of me and pulled me to him. "Neither are you."

"You don't know me."

"I know you'll run. You always do." Nick's eyes glinted. "You aren't meant for cages, either," he said, a dark promise in his words.

I trailed my fingers along the leather spines of the history books I'd been studying. "One man's cage is another woman's duty."

"One and the same, Princess."

I could see where he was coming from. Still. My fingers stopped on a biography of an ancestor of mine. "Queen Elsa-Marie."

Nick sighed and ran his thumb along his eyebrow, waiting for me to explain myself.

"Her husband, King Leopold the Fourth, was never a strong man. He was ill for most of his life. Historians say it could have been something like cystic fibrosis, or a neurological disease, or possibly a mental illness, but whatever it was, he was bedridden and locked away from the public eye by the time he was thirty-five."

"I don't know if I'd fight for this gene pool, Princess."

I waved that off, not wanting to get into the fact that the family tree had been spliced and transplanted several times over since that particular Leopold had fallen off the throne.

"Elsa-Marie was left to lead the country in his place. Her most devoted advisor was the Earl of Brant."

"As fascinating as Driedish history is . . ."

"He was her lover."

That got Nick's attention. As I knew it would.

"Historians say Brant was indispensable to the security of the kingdom, running her military and intelligence networks."

A muscle in Nick's jaw worked. "A kept man."

"Her partner."

"Her boy toy."

I rolled my eyes. "Her consort."

Nick held my gaze for a long minute before giving his head a shake. "I have a job to do."

"I have a job for you."

His lifted brow suggested what kind of job he was willing to do. Maybe if I had taken him up on that unspoken offer, I could have kept him in Drieden, by my side. But I had my duty.

"I want to catch Christian." *I want revenge.*

He laughed. It was a sound without joy. "Not if I catch him first."

"Let's do it together."

He lifted a hand and ran the back of his fingers down my cheek. "Too late, Princess. He's already gone. I'm going to have to start the search all over again, and I'd rather not have you getting shot at any more than you already have these past few weeks."

"What about keeping me safe here, in Drieden? You were so worried about me coming back to the palace and now you're just going to leave me here?"

"From the reports I've received, the person who was responsible for several murders has been securely locked away in a Driedish prison."

He was talking about Tamar. "And what about Christian? He's still on the run and knows everything."

"He had his chance to harm you in that apartment and he didn't. If I know my brother, he's running as fast as he can right now." Nick cocked his head. "Besides, I heard that your security detail was preparing to escort you to Perpetua." He smiled faintly. "The place where they send the uncontrollable women."

"You're leaving." It was a question phrased as a statement.

He dipped his head slightly. "My mission to find out what happened to Christian is finished. Now I have orders to leave the country."

I turned my head toward the shelves of dust-covered, leather-bound books. This princess would not let him see what that did to her. She would not ask him to resign his position and to serve her instead.

I could tell him why I was returning to Perpetua. Tell him that before I took my place on the throne I needed time to study, to learn, and to practice, away from the noise of the palace and the glare of the media spotlight. I could take him by the arm and suggest that he teach me the things he knew about war, peace, and the space in between. I could share the dreams I had—for my country and for us—and pray I could convince him to stand by my side.

But I fully realized then that Nick Fraser-Campbell was a man who needed a thrill, needed the danger. He wasn't a man who would lock himself in a castle and stay home for a princess, uncontrollable or otherwise.

And I wasn't a woman who would beg him to stay.

Still he came to me, as if he heard what I wasn't saying. He answered by cupping my face and kissing me, softly and thoroughly. It was a bittersweet good-bye, full of regrets and containing no promises.

When he pulled away and walked toward the door, there were a thousand things I could have said. He would have stopped. He always stopped for me.

But it wouldn't have changed anything. Nick was going to close this door and follow his destiny. Just as I had to follow mine.

forty-two

ONE MONTH LATER . . .

THE WINDOWS OF MY BEDROOM OPENED ONTO A wide balcony overlooking the North Sea. There was no good reason for this balcony to be here. It's not like we had balmy days on Perpetua, where one could take one's breakfast al fresco.

One day I would uncover the letters ordering its construction, or an architectural plan that revealed why some imprudent fifteenth-century Mother Superior desired a ten-foot-long stone balustrade from which she could watch a ship's landing on Perpetua's tiny, rickety dock.

Maybe that was the reason, simple as it might be. That long-ago nun, that holy Bride of Christ, wished to have a full view of everyone who came to and left this tiny island.

I understood the territorial impulse, now that it was *my* tiny island. As soon as Big Gran had signed the paperwork, granting me guardianship of the island in anticipation of my coronation, I'd started the renovations.

The convent-turned-castle itself was strong and met all of my small household needs. Incremental updates throughout the twentieth century meant we had plumbing, electricity, and satellite dishes.

But the renovations I was ordering had nothing to do with creature comforts.

I tapped the plans on my desk, showing Lucy and Hugh what I was talking about. "Here. This door to the armory. Are you sure this is secure?"

Hugh drew a line across the paper. "There are two different independent systems that operate the armory security and the cell doors." He drew a second line between two other points. "Two more networks control the guardhouse and gate and the safe rooms." He looked at me and nodded. "This is a better system than any I've seen before."

"Good." Lucy nodded to me. "You'll sleep better with a strong security system. Last time you were here you tossed and turned every night."

"I've already been sleeping very well," I told Hugh and Lucy truthfully. Something about the blistering wind and the blasting waves on the rocks lulled me into the deepest of dreams.

It also probably had to do with the self-defense training I was receiving. And the shooting lessons.

The intelligence briefings were mentally taxing, as well.

For the last month, I had turned Perpetua into my own training school, bringing in all the experts I needed to prepare me to lead Drieden for the next forty years. I intended to be the most educated, most capable, most badass queen Drieden had ever known.

My right-hand woman jotted her notes as efficiently as ever in her calendar. I had been so pleased when Lucy agreed to come with me to Perpetua for the next few months. We were a team, and I needed her now more than ever as I prepared for the next steps in my life.

"There was another passenger on the transport," Hugh said.

"Sybil," Lucy said, with an edge in her voice that indicated she knew something of Sybil's reputation as the unofficial court psychic.

"The IT department," I said, with an edge in my voice to remind her that Sybil was an ally now and deserving of our respect. Tea leaves aside.

Lucy sniffed. "Hmph."

On the corner of my desk, tucked under a piece of sea glass I'd collected on my walk around the island during my first day back, was the letter Sybil had given me to open on my thirtieth birthday.

I'd forgotten all about it at the bottom of the backpack that I had carried on my caper with Nick until I set up my Perpetua office, when I took a deep breath and called the final person I wanted to recruit for my team.

Sybil answered on the first ring. "I knew it was you."

"You have caller ID," I pointed out, even though I was pretty sure my satellite number should have been blocked.

"How can I help you?" she asked, deftly skipping my name and my title.

"I want to offer you a job." I described what I needed; Sybil would be my eyes and ears in Drieden. "You'll only work for me," I told her. "No selling information to any other country."

"I've always fancied the sea."

It took me a moment to understand. "You want to live here? On Perpetua?"

"Part-time, I think. Or at least until your coronation."

"How did you know?" The palace would not be announcing my ascension until a month before the Jubilee.

"Your chart."

I didn't believe her. "Did you hack into something?" I made a mental note to speak to someone about the security of the palace computer system.

"Thea, you'll need to believe if we are going to work together."

I rolled my eyes but told myself not to get too annoyed. Sybil would be an asset to my enterprise. Not only was she one of the best hackers I knew, but she was also one of the most well-connected spies in Drieden.

"Do you accept my offer or not?"

"Did you open that letter?" she asked. "The one I gave you for your thirtieth birthday?"

I paused, confused. Where had that letter gone?

"Open it and you'll have my answer."

Then Sybil hung up on me.

I finally found the envelope.

Ripping it open was the quick part. Reading it cost me fifteen min-utes as I stood and tried to make sense of it.

One word: *Yes.* On the paper was taped a tarot card with a depiction of the Queen of Swords. She stood on a rock overlooking the sea, a sword in one hand, a bouquet of violets in the other.

To say I was disconcerted was putting it mildly.

How had she known that I was going to become queen?

It reinforced why I had called Sybil. If there was a chance that she was, indeed, a psychic hacker, I wanted her on my team. Hearing that she'd come to join me on Perpetua was good news.

"Has she seen the tech lab?" I asked Lucy.

"Bright and early this morning."

"Good. I'll find her later, then."

Lucy left after covering a few more points with me and Hugh stayed in the room. My new chief of security had so far done an exceptional job of anticipating my needs and rolling with my sometimes impetuous punches, and from the all-business look on his rugged face, I could see he had something to discuss.

"The files you wanted from the palace."

"Yes," I prompted.

He hesitated. "They were erased, ma'am."

"Erased?" I echoed. "Why?"

"I don't know. But we did a thorough search and could find no re-cord of Nicholas Cameron registering with palace security."

"But he was my bodyguard for two weeks. He had a badge; he filled out paperwork."

"It's all gone."

"Is that usual?" It seemed like that would indicate a severe security problem at the palace.

"Certainly not. Records are kept of everyone granted access to the palace security system."

I thought about it. "The retina scan. I saw him do that. What about those files?"

Hugh hesitated again. "There was one . . . abnormality."

"What abnormality?"

"It popped up in the transfer of files to the Perpetua system. I was going through them, to ensure that everyone who has access to the system here was vetted."

"Tell me."

With a frown, he did. "As I said, all records of Nicholas Cameron or Fraser-Campbell were erased. But we did have one retina scan file of someone who had no other mention in the system. The retina file was named Cornelius."

"Max Cornelius?"

Hugh hesitated a split second. "Yes."

My stomach dropped at hearing the confirmation from Hugh's lips. What it meant, I did not know, and neither did Hugh, but to his credit, when I told him to keep the Cornelius file active in our security system, he did so without argument.

"There was one more thing," Hugh started.

"Yes?"

"I'm requesting that time off we discussed before." Our eyes locked. "It's time to find Christian Fraser-Campbell," he said.

I felt my adrenaline rise at the thought.

"Has there been any sign of him?" One of the first upgrades to the island was a secure line where we could monitor INTERPOL reports that might mention my ex-fiancé.

Hugh shook his head regretfully. "But that's why I need to go. He'll need to be tracked down. Like an animal."

When I had asked Hugh to accompany me to Perpetua, to help me learn weapons and security, he had balked and threatened to quit. He had a personal vendetta against Christian and Tamar not only for their treason, but for drugging him and essentially holding him hostage in his own apartment—a humiliation the lifelong loyal officer could not bear.

Hugh continued. "You agreed that I could go, once you learned how to shoot and fight." He ruefully rubbed his right shoulder, which I had kicked during a sparring session earlier in the week. "And I think you've got the basics down."

I sympathized with Hugh's desire to find Christian and wreak vengeance. Once upon a time, I would have gone with him, but now, I had other duties.

"Go get the bastard, Hugh. Then bring him back here so I can deal with him."

A rare smile broke across my bodyguard's face. Bloodthirsty bonding at its best.

The rest of my day was busy. After briefing Sybil, I toured the armory with my sergeant at arms and attended my daily marksmanship lesson on the range he'd set up on the grassy northern slope.

I returned to my suite of rooms, exhausted and ready to dive into bed and not stir until morning. I showered, changed, brushed my teeth—minimum standards of princess-hood must be kept, even if one was staying on a frigid hunk of rock in the middle of the North Sea.

Speaking of frigid, when I left the steamy comfort of my bathroom, an arctic blast of wind nearly turned my bare feet into ice.

Strange. The doors that opened onto the wide stone balcony were wide open. The ice-blue linen curtains billowed dramatically. Perhaps the doors hadn't been latched securely. After all, the brass fixtures were probably nearly two hundred years old.

It wasn't until I reached the ornate handles to close the doors that I saw it.

A sprig of heather.

It stood in a small glass of water on my desk, which was situated in front of the balcony, in order for me to fully enjoy the views of the sea as I worked there.

My fingers lightly brushed the purple bloom on the desk. No heather grew on Perpetua that I was aware of, but maybe I was wrong. Maybe a maid plucked some in the gardens and thought I would enjoy a bit of nature. Maybe she had opened the balcony doors to air out a musty smell.

Maybe . . .

The last time I'd seen a piece of heather like this had been in a hotel room in Scotland, that morning that Nick had finally opened up to me. Told me who he really was.

I picked up the glass, thinking about taking it to my bedside so that it would be the last thing I saw when I turned out the light. The first thing when the sun rose, shy and pale, in the morning.

I put the glass back down.

No, I thought, closing the doors to the balcony. Decisions had been made. I was moving on. So, I supposed, was Nick. Somewhere.

My bedroom was warmer, thankfully, and nearly pitch black as I made my way to the table by the bed to turn on a light.

Out of the corner of my eye, I saw a shift in the shadows. I reached into the space between the bed and table, pulled a nine-millimeter from the holster there, and swung around, releasing the safety simultaneously.

"Don't move," I warned the figure that was almost invisible in the dark.

There was a movement. I braced my hands and prepared to shoot like Hugh had taught me.

The figure seemed to put up his hands.

"Hello, Princess."

A Scottish accent.

In my bedroom.

In my castle.

On my island.

In the middle of the bloody North Sea.

Nick.

I pulled the trigger halfway back.

"Careful now," he said.

"I know what I'm doing," I said between gritted teeth.

He took another careful step toward me. "It's poor form to greet a guest this way, isn't it?" His mouth slid to one side. "Especially one that's come such a long way."

Etiquette? He was arguing etiquette? With me? "Guests don't break in and lurk in dark corners!"

"Is that it, Thea? Are you mad that I didn't knock?" The gentle tone of his voice came out of nowhere, the way it usually did. And it made my lungs hurt, the way it usually did.

"I'm mad about a lot of things."

"I can see that." He licked his lips and gestured toward my handgun. "Do you think you could put that down? It's distracting me from what I came here to say."

I carefully released the trigger and lowered my weapon. "I'm listening."

"I'm sorry I scared you." His gaze softened as he searched my face. "I didn't think about anything but getting back to you."

The pain in my chest sharpened. "Why?"

He shuffled a step back and his head dropped. "I'd heard there was a job opening. Here. With your . . . organization."

It took me a long moment to realize what he was talking about, and I very nearly wanted to cry when I had to say, "The position for boy toy has been closed."

Nick's dark gaze lifted and was almost frightening in its intensity. "Has it been filled?" he asked evenly.

My head shook, almost involuntarily. "No. Closed. I decided I didn't need one after all. I wanted someone who wouldn't take without giving. Someone who would stay with me for a long-term assignment."

"Really." He swallowed. "Is there anything else available?" He took a step closer. "Maybe something in security? I have some body-guard experience."

I shook my head again. He moved toward me.

"Security is filled," I responded quietly. "And I already have an ex-cellent spy on staff."

He was close enough to touch. "Thea . . ." My name was a rough, throaty sound.

"Why are you here?"

He seemed to put together his words deliberately, to make sure he got it right. "I went back to my old job, and it wasn't the right fit for me anymore."

"It wasn't?" I sounded as breathless as a schoolgirl meeting her pop-star crush.

His knuckles brushed lightly over the top of my arm. "I decided I needed a new challenge. A job I give a damn about. With an uncontrol-lable woman I give a damn about."

My silly, aching heart missed a beat at those oh-so-romantic words, but the pain wouldn't stop until I said what it was demanding. "Now that I think about it, I could use a partner. A . . . a consort."

I dropped my head because I couldn't bear to look at his expression, at the pity or rejection I might find there as I pathetically tried again to keep him by my side, especially once I dropped the big news. "My grandmother is abdicating next summer. I'll be taking her job."

Nick curled two fingers under my chin and brought my face up.

I thought he was going to kiss me. He had that kissing gleam in his eyes, but instead he whispered, "Consort to the queen, eh? What does that benefits package look like?"

I groaned. "You are the rudest, most infuriating, most ill-mannered—" I was cut off mid-rant by his lips ravaging mine, like a sailor who'd been at sea for months, like a soldier who'd been at war. Electricity snapped through my hair, my skin, my veins, empowering me, making me come alive. I already knew I could rule a country by myself. But I could rule the planet with Nick.

His hands were rough on my face and neck and I didn't hold back as I yanked him to me, needing to feel his solid, powerful heat against me. I pushed his coat off his shoulders and my fingers went to the bottom of his thick, sodden sweater. "What did you do? Swim here?"

"Only the last bit. After I jumped off the boat," he rumbled.

"You need a shower," I gasped as his mouth trailed down behind my ear, nibbled across my collarbone.

"Yes, ma'am."

"I like the sound of that."

He chuckled against my throat, a sound that made my toes curl. "You would."

"Nick." Something made him stop, pull away, and look at me. Take me seriously.

I wasn't sure what I wanted to say, but somehow the right words tumbled out of my mouth. "Are you sure? About taking all this on?" The prospects of my future were intimidating for me, and I had grown up in a royal family. I wasn't sure how Nick was going to handle the changes that were coming.

His expression was solemn. "I'm a man of my word, Princess. I won't leave you until we've finished the job."

It was as good as any oath of loyalty on his knees.

He grinned at me and for the first time in months, maybe years, the pressure in my chest lifted. "I'd tell you where the shower is, but I have a feeling you already know."

"Aye." He did a mock bow. "At your service." A minute later, I heard the water come on, and I knew we'd need a good rest after we were done tonight.

After all, tomorrow we had a kingdom to run.

acknowledgments

For a story that came to me in a dream, the process of producing this book has been a dream as well.

A million thank-yous go out to the following:

To my agent, Louise Fury (and her trusty compatriots at The Bent Agency, including Kristin, Victoria, and Sam!!) for sharing her superpowers and superteam with me.

To the team at Simon & Schuster and Gallery Books, Lauren McKenna and Jen Bergstrom and my wonder twin editors, Marla Daniels and Molly Gregory. To Sarah Wright and Lisa Wolff for learning Driedish history like the pros they are, and Ploy Siripant for nailing the cover.

To the fabulous Kate Byrne and everyone at Headline Eternal. To Lucy Stille at APA and Shari Smiley and Ellen Goldsmith-Vein at Gotham, for loving Thea and Nick so much (they love you right back!).

To all the people who watch my computer at Starbucks/Panera/the library when I have to go to the ladies' room. Thank you for enabling me get out of the house to work.

To my HBICs, Mary Chris Escobar, Laura von Holt, Alexis Anne, Alexandra Haughton, and Julia Kelly, who inspire me to keep going, keep writing, and keep being a badass. (And a shout-out to Julia, who told me spy stories were her favorite when I wasn't quite sure what the heck this book was going to be.) To Tamsen, who assured me that it was absolutely okay to write a book out of order (and now my editors know who to blame). To B, who told me to refill my well and write something just for me.

To my readers: in case you haven't realized it, you're the smartest, most good-looking, most interesting people in the world. I'm privileged to write stories for you. If you subscribe to my newsletter (www.lindsayemory.com/newsletter) you'll keep hearing how amazing you are. I'm just saying.

Finally, words can never be enough to show my appreciation and love for my family: J, E, and M. I write because you believe in me. And honestly, I'm a better mom and wife because I do this. No, really. Trust me on this.